D1487630

THE ORCHARD

JEFFREY STEPAKOFF

THORNDIKE PRESS
A part of Gale, Cengage Learning

L P
(1)

GALE
CENGAGE Learning™

Detroit • New York • San Francisco • New Haven, Conn • Waterville, Maine • London

GALE
CENGAGE Learning™

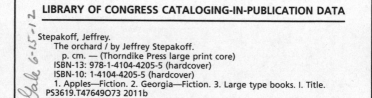

LIBRARY OF CONGRESS CATALOGING-IN-PUBLICATION DATA

Stepakoff, Jeffrey.
    The orchard / by Jeffrey Stepakoff.
        p. cm. — (Thorndike Press large print core)
    ISBN-13: 978-1-4104-4205-5 (hardcover)
    ISBN-10: 1-4104-4205-5 (hardcover)
    1. Apples—Fiction. 2. Georgia—Fiction. 3. Large type books. I. Title.
PS3619.T476490O73 2011b
813'.6—dc22   2011031066

Published in 2011 by arrangement with St. Martin's Press, LLC.

Printed in the United States of America
1 2 3 4 5 6 7 15 14 13 12 11

*For Sophie,
Charlotte,
and Eli
May you all find love everlasting*

When we try to pick out anything by itself, we find it hitched to everything else in the Universe.

— John Muir, naturalist

I love nothing more than being pregnant: it's something beautiful, you feel like a tree that has lots of fruits on it.

— Daniela Andrier,
renowned Givaudan perfumer

FLAVOR & FRAGRANCE

New Guinea

The rain came down in steaming waves, pattering on the fat lush leaves like a tribal drumbeat, but by this point, the six trekkers and their guide were oblivious of it. Night would be here soon, and despite the exhaustion they all felt from hiking since daybreak, they picked up their pace, the trekkers following the guide deeper into the tropical rain forest.

Grace Lyndon, mid-twenties, lithe and tanned in her ripped hiking shorts and tank top, walked directly behind the guide. Grace was the only woman in the bunch, and the only one whose English didn't have a French accent.

"It's getting too late," said one of the men, adjusting his heavy pack. "We should turn around, come back in the morning."

"The winds are picking up," said Grace. "It might not *be* there in the morning."

9

Peeling some wet hair off her cheek and tightening the straps of her pack against her glistening shoulders, Grace looked around, inhaling deeply, struck by the natural beauty of this place. Damp and roasting, the jungle smelled of vanilla beans and wet leopardwood. *This is what it's all about,* she thought. *Everything we come up with in the lab is just theory. This is the beating heart of the business, the reason I got in it.*

"I think I've seen that tree before," one of the men said, and then swatted at an insect. "Are we sure we're not walking in circles?"

"It's just up ahead," the bare-chested Papuan guide said.

"C'est dingue! Ce type ne sait absolument pas où nous allons," another man said in very pointed French.

"Les aborigènes vont finir par nous manger!" replied another.

"I cannot lead you if I cannot understand you," said the guide, understanding enough French to know they were complaining about him.

"They said they're excited because we are so near," said Grace, glaring over her shoulder at the two men.

The guide stopped suddenly and pointed to the top of a massive tree. "There!"

Everyone halted and looked up, seeing

10

high in the huge expanse of branches, at the very top of the thick jungle canopy, a large exotic orchid.

"The orchid will close as soon as the light is gone," said one of the men. "We'll have to hurry. Get the ropes."

They all dropped their soaked packs to the ground with a *thud*.

Grace walked up right under the huge tree. It was nearly seventy-five feet tall, with a thick trunk and without any lower branches.

She looked straight up at the magnificent *Angraecum granulosa* flower, a rare species whose seeds took flight on tropical breezes, setting root only in the hidden treetops, deep in this singular undisturbed part of the planet. Even from the ground, she could see how beautiful it was, just like the antique drawing she'd studied at her company's perfumery school outside Paris. It *was* late, she noticed. They really would have to hurry or this might be as close as they ever got — close enough to admire it, but not close enough to tell the world what it smelled like.

While several of the men pulled ropes and cables of various weights out of their packs, Grace carefully unwrapped a rubberized laptop and an openmouthed Plexiglas globe, about the size of a large fishbowl. She powered up the computer, running thin USB cables from it to the inside of the globe. Then she carefully wrapped it all up and placed the equipment back in her pack, which she zipped and readied. Finally, she slipped a climbing harness around her hips and thighs, snapping it at her waist and pulling the straps tight, so when the rope and pulleys were tossed over the high branches, she could be hoisted up to the orchid along with her equipment.

However, things weren't going very well with the ropes. After tying a fist-sized lead-filled sack to a long lightweight throw line, the men tried repeatedly to toss the sack and line up and over a high limb, but they kept missing, the sack and line falling short. The branches were simply higher than they could throw.

"The ropes are too heavy," someone said, wiping wet dirt off his face.

"It's just too far up," someone else said.

"We need to come back tomorrow with better equipment."

The rain and the wind picked up as the sun began to go down.

One of the men marched forward, picked up the sack, and swung it around forcefully by the throw line over his head in a wide circle. Determination apparent on his face, he quickly let out line as he swung, causing several of the trekkers to duck down to avoid being hit by the lead-filled sack. Letting out even more line, swinging the sack as hard as he could, finally, with all his might, the man released his grip on the line, throwing the sack and trailing line hard, up into the canopy — right at the orchid.

"Careful! You're going to smash the flower!" another shouted, fatigue and desperation perceptible in his voice.

But again, the sack and line missed the branches and fell straight back down, splashing in the mud. This wasn't going well at all. As the men stood in the pouring rain, arguing about their options in French and English, the shadows growing longer, one of them looked up and saw something, and then did a double take as he realized what he was looking at. "Grace!" he yelled out.

All the men looked up to see Grace, pack on her back, a length of rope dangling from a carabiner on her harness, climbing the tree.

They dashed to the base of the tree, and she was already a good twenty-five feet over their heads. The guide yelled up to her, very concerned, "Lady, it's too dangerous to free-climb, please, come down. Come down!"

But the other men simply smiled, some more worried than others, and stood by to help if they were needed. They'd all worked with this young woman long enough to know that when she got something in her head, there was no talking her out of it, or in this case, no talking her down. Her colleagues — most of them, anyway — admired Grace. They also thought, all of them, that she was a bit nuts.

The tree trunk was sopping and slick, but Grace climbed it with virtually every sinew of her body. Pack carefully balanced on her back, she dug her boots into the tree, hugged it tightly with her thighs, shoved her fingers into the deep ridges of the furrowed bark, pulling and shimmying upward with her hands and forearms and knees. Staying focused on the flower above, forcing herself not to look down, she moved surprising quickly and smoothly.

This is crazy! she thought. *I know this is crazy, but I've heard about this flower like some mythical fable for years, studied what little is known about it obsessively for months, finally located one out here in the middle of a jungle, and here it is, just a few meters away, and if this is what it takes to get my chance to*

14

smell it, this is what I'll do.

At the top, Grace unhooked one end of the rope from the carabiner on her harness, threw it around a thick bough just over the orchid, pulled it back, knotted it, and attached it back to the carabiner, securing herself in the treetop canopy.

Then she dropped the remaining rope to the ground and, self-belaying in midair, lowered herself to the orchid. With the men watching fixedly below her, she ever so carefully unzipped her pack and removed the Plexiglas globe, the wires taped to the inside of the globe running to the computer in the pack on her back.

Globe in hand, Grace slowly approached the big orchid, white and fragile and absolutely gorgeous. She very carefully slid the globe over it, and as she was doing so, she put her face into the center of the open flower, smiling as the breathtaking fragrance washed over her — luscious and nectared, candied apricots, airy notes of strange spice. Nothing she had smelled even in the lab back in Paris, nothing in the tens of thousands of little vials, synthetic or natural, was quite like this novel scent. It was thrilling, this discovery. She felt as though she were the first to set foot on a new planet, see a new land. Dangling in the air, looking out above the jungle canopy, the sun setting behind the high mountains off in the distance, she thought about Hillary, the first person to glimpse the world from the top of Mount Everest.

She slipped the globe the rest of the way over the orchid, and she could feel and hear the computer in her backpack buzzing and vibrating as the equipment absorbed, digitized, and recorded the exact chemical makeup of the scent, providing data that could later be used to re-create the fragrance precisely in the lab, all without ever harming the precious orchid.

After a moment, the computer gave one final shake and click as the hard drive finished recording the data, and a moment later, the sunlight waning, the orchid began to close itself up for the night.

As Grace watched the flower rolling itself up, its sepals and petals folding inward and enclosing its delicate inner parts, she put her face close and inhaled one more scent of it. Looking out once again at the clouds above the jungle treetops, feeling strangely connected to them, as though thin cables were now running from *her* to the clouds above and beyond, she committed the fragrance to memory.

"Grace! What does it smell like?" yelled

one of the men at the top of his lungs from below.

What does it smell like? she thought to herself, struggling as those in her field so often did with the imperfect task of using language to characterize scent.

Her body swaying in the breeze, she smiled and yelled down, "It smells like heaven!"

Paris, eighteen months later
There is nothing on earth more elegant, thought Grace as she sipped vintage Veuve Clicquot and surveyed the ballroom, *than a launch party for a new perfume.* Looking stunning in her treasured backless Dior evening gown, Grace stood before a huge poster for her client's new fragrance: Heavenly.

The ad, which featured an up-and-coming Czech supermodel smelling a stylized white orchid, would soon be in magazines and newspapers, and on billboards and bus stop benches, all across the world, but mostly in Latin America, where the vast majority of women regularly wore fine fragrances and much of the focus group testing for Heavenly was conducted.

A waiter approached Grace with an open bottle of champagne. *"Plus de champagne, madame?"*

"Oui. Merci," said Grace, extending her crystal tulip glass by its stem.

While he poured, Grace took in the room. As much as she loved the far-off corners of the world where novel flavors and fragrances waited to be discovered, she felt equally at home among the opulence here in the Hôtel de Crillon. Grace sipped her thirty-five-year-old champagne, reveling in the bubbly buttered toast flavors, enjoying the seventeenth- and eighteenth-century tapestries, gilded furnishings, and works of art all around her. The German high command occupied this very salon during World War II, and today it was filled by the denizens of fashion. In their tuxedos and evening gowns, they meandered and mingled, these rich and powerful people who decided how the world would dress and, now, what it would smell like.

And Grace, too, looked every bit the part — the black dress and black shoes contrasted only by the red flash of her Louboutin soles. She balanced on their four-inch heels with precision, taking in the luxurious scene in front of her. There was a time in her life when she wasn't even aware one could spend fourteen hundred dollars on a pair of shoes, but this was a guilty pleasure

18

she allowed herself on occasion now, one that was delightfully pleasurable to fulfill in Paris, particularly for a young woman who was too busy working to spend money on anything else besides bistro food and table wine.

As Grace absorbed the soiree, a very stylish woman approached, lifted Grace's arm, and smelled the underside of her wrist, where Grace, of course, was wearing Heavenly.

"*Très chic,* darling. You wear it well," the woman purred, and then released Grace's arm.

"Thank you, Madame Brugière," Grace said respectfully to the company's head perfumer. She was in her mid-forties, very pregnant, and looking absolutely stunning in her shamelessly low-cut haute couture gown and diamonds. She looked like what she essentially was: a woman who had the best of everything.

"The UBS analysts raised their rating on Coty this afternoon," Brugière said. "And a little bird has just whispered to me that Credit Suisse will follow suit tomorrow. They are expecting double-digit growth this year for our client's entire business, based solely on the new fragrance. Congratulations, darling, your orchid has moved a market."

"Thank you, Madame Brugière, but it was what you did with the orchid."

"Well, you are an *outstanding* assistant perfumer, *chérie.*" Brugière accepted Grace's compliment a little too readily, Grace thought, unsure if *chérie* was meant intimately or condescendingly. Then Madame smiled at Grace in a way that unsettled her. Grace *was* an outstanding perfumer. She knew that. More than outstanding! This was her life, this company, this job, and she had done more than conceive the idea for the fragrance and go pluck the base element out of the jungle; she had stood by her boss's side day and night for a year and a half while the woman took credit for her work. Grace understood that this was the time-honored European apprenticeship process, and she was deeply grateful to have the opportunity to study under someone so talented and respected and powerful — this was, after all, the woman who was responsible for creating nearly half the world's best-selling fragrances — but Grace was doing more than studying lately, she was creating, too, and she was champing at the bit not just to do more, but to get the recognition for it as well. In Grace's mind, there had been an implicit understanding that this would come, but now there was something in the way Brugière was smiling at her, something patronizing, and Grace did not like it.

Holding up a large camera with flash, a photographer for *Vogue* approached. *"Puis-je?"* he asked.

A natural and regular with the media, Madame Brugière found a glamorous smile, not pursed or ostentatious, but perfectly tempered, and pressed her cheek to Grace's. The photographer shot them a couple times, Grace's smile stunted by pain as one of Brugière's multi-carat diamond studs seared into Grace's face. Then the photographer motioned for Grace to step away, which she did, and the photographer began shooting Madame Brugière alone.

As Grace stood watching — and as other more prominent people, an Academy Award–winning actress and a princess, soon joined Brugière — an easygoing middle-aged American man walked up to Grace.

"She's quite the rock star, your boss," the man said.

"Yes, she is." Grace smiled at the simple truth of that.

"I like your fragrance."

"Thank you. Madame Brugière worked

very hard on it," Grace said politely.

"I'm sure she did. Though I bet she didn't free-climb a wet merbau tree to get its base constituent."

Grace stared at the man. "I'm sorry, do I know you?"

The man extended his hand. "Bill Rice. I run a flavor and fragrance shop back in the States. Maybe you've heard of us. Southern Compounds?"

"Rings a bell. You all did the new honey scents in Burt's Bees body care?" Grace posited hesitantly.

"As you know, I can't discuss our work," he said. Which Grace did know, just as she knew his response was an acknowledgment that they *did* do the work.

"I thought your ideas on that account were terrific. You did the new flavors for them, too, in the lip care products." Grace remembered reading about this company's out-of-the-box work in one of the trades.

Bill smiled. His was a warm, affable one, and something about it was trusting. "We do both flavor and fragrance for a lot of our clients."

"I detect a Southern accent," Grace ventured, but she knew the answer to that, too. It was an accent she knew very well.

"That is because you are observant."

Again, he offered her that easygoing smile. She liked this guy.

"You're from Georgia."

"Indeed. Born and raised, just like Southern Compounds."

"What are you doing in Paris?"

"All the best things. Eating. Drinking. Recruiting talent. What are *you* doing in Paris?"

"Working for the best company in my field."

"Not a bad gig to land for a girl right out of a small Georgia college."

That stopped the conversation. Grace eyed him warily. This guy seemed to know *a lot* about her.

"It's information any decent headhunter can get, Grace." He spoke lightly, trying to put her at ease. "I understand after Agnes Scott you kicked around Burgundy, working in the vineyards for a good while. You must have developed a pretty decent palate before you started your professional training."

She couldn't deny any of that, but wondered exactly just how much he knew about her past. So far he'd gotten everything right, from leaving Agnes Scott after graduation, honing her skills amid the lush grapes of the Côte de Nuits — and finally receiving admission into Givaudan's fabled Perfumery School in Paris. The largest and arguably most influential company in the industry, Givaudan did not advertise or recruit for its elite school, and still the program attracted hundreds of applicants from around the world for the prized two or three places available each year. Graduates were practically guaranteed their pick of choice positions at prestigious companies, though most, like Grace, stayed with Givaudan. Because when it came to perfume, Paris was the center of the universe, and Givaudan was the center of Paris.

They were standing side by side, sipping the toasty old Veuve, as he continued to talk. "You have a great job working here for Givaudan, no doubt. But what if I told you I could offer you even more at this juncture in your career."

"With all due respect, Mr. Rice, I very much doubt you could offer me anything I can't get at Givaudan."

"Really? You see a big promotion coming? Because that would be quite a thing, for an American to move up to a meaningful position in one of the oldest French flavor and fragrance houses."

Grace knew he was right, and she hated it. Still, she'd always felt that she could do anything, even if there was little precedent.

"Technically speaking," he said, "I'm looking for a flavorist."

"I'm a perfumer."

"Yes, and as I'm sure you know, flavor is ninety percent scent. The other ten percent you can pick up on the job. That's part of the opportunity I can offer you. I like my senior managers to have a working knowledge of both parts of the field. We're not a huge shop like Givaudan, so I want the people who present new business to be able to speak to all aspects of it."

Grace took a sip of champagne, trying to hide her interest — which was difficult to do. The chance to expand her knowledge base was appealing on its own, but the idea of actually getting to pitch new business — now, that was intriguing.

A salesman at his core, Bill went on. "You know, part of what I'm talking about here is the opportunity to come back to the States with something to show for yourself."

"My parents are gone," Grace said. "I have no connections to Georgia. Paris is my home." It tumbled out more defensively then she intended, and that was not lost on him.

"Grace, whether we like it or not, we all come from someplace." His tone was gentler, caring, like that of a mentor. "And at some point in our lives, we have to make our peace with that place."

Perhaps it was his manner, perhaps his words, but something about that resonated with her. He seemed to know so much about her, seemed to have prepared for this conversation. And she thought about all of this as she watched Madame Brugière patting her baby bump, posing for more photographers, and waving to someone who looked very much like one of the Spice Girls.

"She may get the credit for the new fragrance design, but did she have the real vision for it?" Bill leaned into Grace as he spoke. "Because if someone works for me, I always make sure that she is both rewarded and recognized when she does good. That's just smart business, something I know a thing or two about, old Southern boy that I am."

Grace considered him, and then asked, "What kind of opportunity are we talking about?"

Bill's smile broadened.

GIRL IN THE GLASS ELEVATOR

Atlanta, Georgia, one year later, spring
Although it was completed in the mid-seventies, the cylindrical Peachtree Plaza Hotel was still one of the most distinctive landmarks in downtown Atlanta. Particularly on a beautiful early spring day like today, when tourists from all over the country — all over the world, really — came to the city to see the dogwoods and azaleas, John Portman's famous hotel in downtown Atlanta was filled with people.

Dylan Jackson sat alone at a linen-covered table in the revolving restaurant on the seventy-third floor of the hotel. The room bustled with cheerful diners. Tall and well built, wearing a soft spring-weight flannel shirt and the work boots that he always wore at the farm, Dylan seemed even more conspicuously alone sitting by himself. Though he was just in his early thirties, sitting here today in this restaurant where he'd

27

always come with his wife whenever they were in Atlanta, Dylan felt much older.

The table cleared, Dylan pulled a medium-sized gift box from a Macy's bag at his feet and placed it on the table. He pulled back the gold elastic cord and opened the box, and was immediately hit with the faint but still powerful scent of the department store: factory-fresh fabrics, shoe leather, and all manner of perfumes and colognes and cosmetics. Dylan carefully peeled back the tissue paper, revealing a girl's sweater folded neatly inside the box. It was an exquisitely hand-knit white cardigan with eggshell blue flowers embroidered on the pockets. He ran his big hand along the small sweater and then picked up a gift card that had been placed inside the box.

Dylan took the pen from the tray with his bill, uncapped it, thought for a moment, and then wrote: *Happy Birthday. Love, Dad.*

Studying the card, Dylan wondered if he should say more. He'd thought about getting a proper card, and had popped into a Hallmark store at the mall and read through many, but none of the sentiments really conveyed how he felt. So the idea of paying four dollars and fifty cents for someone else's words felt hollow and insincere.

Love, Dad. What else was there really to

say? What else could he say? *Every night since your mother died last year, I've stood over you in your room, watching you, minutes pouring into minutes, hours pouring into hours, watching you in the shadows of the moon until you looked just like her. I don't know what to get you for your birthday, what to say on a card. She always knew those kinds of things. All I know is that the promise of you that I saw in her eyes as we stood at the altar is the one true thing now. I'm so lost, but I love you so much, my darling daughter. That I know. That I know better than any card can ever say, any bought words can ever express.*

Dylan placed the tissue paper back over the little sweater, closed the box, put the card into its small envelope, and tucked it under the gold cord. Then he placed the pen back on top of his paid bill, put the box back in the bag, and rose.

Dylan filed into the glass elevator, moving to the very back, where he turned and set the Macy's bag down on the floor against the glass. A throng of happy tourists marched in behind him, pushing him firmly against the back rail.

As the crowd was buzzing loudly, excited with anticipation, the elevator hung motionless, perched on the exterior of the high-rise hotel like a great glass ball in Times Square moments before New Year's Eve.

Though the elevator was filled well to capacity, the attendant waved in an elderly couple, and just as he was about to clip back the velvet rope, a striking woman slipped in. And with a shrill chime — *bing!* — the doors closed.

Dylan Jackson looked across the crowded glass elevator at her, and even though he could only make out glimpses, his heart leapt. *I know her. Don't I?*

Packed into the back, he moved his head, raising it, peering around and over the chattering, jostling tourists with their bags and cameras and outerwear, but he could catch only brief impressions of her. A fine-boned hand pulling hair away from a smallish ear. A smooth high cheek. A long neck, fluid and graceful. And as the collage of her grew more specific and vivid, his pulse began to race and adrenaline coursed. All of a sudden, his body prepared him for some kind of critical response, but crammed into this tight elevator with nowhere to go and no way to get to her, all he could do was stand there and try to keep from going mad — because Dylan Jackson had felt this way about only one woman in his entire life. And she was gone. *Or is she? What's going on here? Am I going crazy? Am I finally just losing it? Or is this real?*

As Dylan looked across the crowd at her, suddenly, finally, the elevator lurched and dropped. "Going down," a pleasant and upbeat recorded voice announced. There were a few light gasps and laughs, and Dylan felt his stomach rise to his throat as, twenty-four feet a second, low-lying clouds and the entire dizzying skyline of Atlanta all around them, they descended.

She turned her head to look at the view, and Dylan could see a little more of her, and for a brief moment, he was certain that she was smiling at him. It was a smile that sent a warm shiver into his soul. He knew that smile, didn't he? Dylan peered around a baby who was held up and against his mother's chest, the infant's plump face following and staring at Dylan with earnest curiosity, but before Dylan could make out any more of her, she looked away, her face further blocked by a soft red scarf that rode up from around her neck. He leaned forward. A carry-on size Coach leather cabin bag sat next to her feet on the floor. Was it hers?

Dylan leaned forward even more, trying to move toward her, but a large British man and his even larger spouse shuffled in front to get a better view of Stone Mountain off to the east. Pushing aside their World of Coca-Cola shopping bags, stepping over their plush Georgia Aquarium whale sharks, Dylan tried to scoot around them, but he was met with an impenetrable wall of jacket-clad backs. Though many had come to Atlanta to see the dogwoods in full bloom, it was April, a decidedly fickle month in the Deep South. April in Georgia could mean eighty-degree weather and clouds of fresh pine pollen, or a sudden subfreezing cold snap that could keep the azaleas in check and bring back out the jackets and scarves.

The elevator dropped through the roof of the hotel's lower-level atrium, emerging inside this large open ten-floor space. Many in the crowd yawned hard to pop their ears. The baby cried and his mother soothed him. Passing the conference and shopping levels, the elevator finally came to rest on the lobby floor, and with that — *bing!* — the doors opened. "Hotel lobby," the pleas-ant voice announced.

The crowd poured out and Dylan did everything he could to keep his eye on the woman. It was hard to see her across all the scurrying people. He tried to push ahead, but the displeasure on the round red faces of the British couple made it very clear that this tactic was not going to accomplish anything beneficial.

Waiting to get off the elevator, Dylan lost sight of her entirely. He scanned the crowd ahead and saw many people heading for the revolving doors to Peachtree Street and others moving toward the concierge desk and others toward an escalator, and just when he was sure he'd lost her for good, he caught a glimpse of her in the lobby. Seeing an opening in the throng, he quickly tried to dart out of the elevator, but the woman with the infant stepped in front of him and instantaneously he stopped in his tracks — just as he was about to slam into the woman and knock the baby out of her arms.

Dylan took a deep breath, let the mother and child pass, and then quickly followed them off. But right as he stepped out of the elevator, something caught his eye. A red scarf. On the floor of the elevator, kicked to the side against the glass by the departing crowd, was a red scarf, deep red, the color of a Macoun on the branch in the middle of summer. *Her* scarf.

Dylan turned, walked back in, bent down, and picked it up. The scarf *was* soft, nearly startlingly so. A scent, rich and heady, a perfect essence of the person whose skin the scarf kept warm, rose from the crimson cashmere drawn into Dylan's nose and triggered a sudden rush of memories and sensations across a broad spectrum of conscious and unconscious experiences in his life. The scarf smelled like a woman.

Dylan turned to dash off the elevator, but he was half a second too late. *Bing!* The doors closed. Called by the attendant on the seventy-third floor to bring more of the lunch-rush tourists back down, the elevator started to ascend.

"Wait!" Dylan Jackson turned to the buttons to try to get off at the earliest possible floor, but there were no buttons to push. This was an express elevator.

Dylan just stood there and looked up. He could hardly believe this.

Then he whipped around and turned to the glass and looked out, scanning the lobby and the people scurrying across it, all growing smaller and smaller as he was rapidly pulled up and away. Fifth floor, sixth floor, seventh floor, twenty-four feet a second, and just as he passed the eighth floor, he saw her.

Hands down and open, in her long fitted coat, she stood alone in the center of the lobby, looking up, watching the elevator, looking directly at Dylan, the cabin bag at her feet.

He stood alone in the elevator looking directly down at her.

The scarf dangling from his hand, he reached up to the glass as though reaching out to her, and just when he thought she was raising her hand back to him — the elevator shot through the roof of the atrium, disappearing into darkness and then rocketing out into the light.

Dylan spun around, cursing the bright sun, as the elevator dragged him along the side of the building, heavenward.

A flat-panel screen near the door flashing a silent stream of information about the current local temperature and commodity prices and happy hour mojitos, Dylan was suddenly aware of the scents of the crowd, which remained all around him. It was a concentrate of human things, garlic on warm breath and cedared sweaters and Mustela baby shampoo — all smells he knew well, but the strange brew of them swirling like spirits in this shooting glass cage only told him just how alone he truly was.

He pulled the scarf to his face and breathed her in.

Finally, the elevator reached the top floor, came to an abrupt stop, and the doors opened.

"Welcome to the Sun Dial," the attendant said, motioning for Dylan to get off. But he didn't move. The crowd behind the attendant stared at Dylan.

"I'm going back down."

The attendant shrugged, unclasped the rope, and a new mob of tourists poured into the elevator. This time, Dylan made a point to stand at the very front.

Moments later, they were on their way back down, everyone in the elevator facing out and taking in the view, everyone except Dylan. He stood directly in front of the double doors, head back, staring high up at the floor numbers above the doors, watching impatiently as the numbers fell and the glass compound was lowered back to earth.

They dropped through the roof of the atrium and Dylan took a few deep breaths and — *bing!* — he was out of there before the doors had fully opened.

He turned and bolted out the elevator corridor and jogged into the center of the lobby floor where she had been standing. But she wasn't there.

Dylan walked to a far end of the lobby, scanning the entire open space for her. He didn't see her anywhere.

Constantly moving his head, he walked

back over to where she had been and continued looking, tourists and businesspeople marching mindlessly past him.

Visibly upset, Dylan stood up on a coffee table and turned in a circle, the scarf dangling out of his hand, looking everywhere for her. Heart pounding, stomach sinking, he was about to call out her name. About to scream it at the top of his lungs. But it was clear to him. She was gone.

A hotel manager who had been watching Dylan walked up to him. "Sir, are you all right?"

Dylan turned and looked at the young woman. Then he got down from the table but didn't move, staring off in the distance, pale and dazed.

"Sir?" she continued.

"Yes. Yes, I'm fine."

"Maybe you should sit down. You look like you've just seen a ghost."

A Poet's Nose

Buckhead District, Atlanta, eighteen months later, fall

The alarm clock went off at 4:55 A.M., and Grace Lyndon's hand popped out of the covers and snapped it off. Grace certainly could find five extra minutes in her day so that she could awaken at a time that did not have a four in its hour, but she liked getting up earlier than she had to. She liked seeing that four. It gave her an edge, she believed.

In the elegant but Zen-sparse bedroom of her small condo, Grace sat up, threw back the Frette linens she had become accustomed to in Paris, and then jumped out of her high bed.

This was a big day, a very big day, and first things first. She stepped into her orderly walk-in closet, flipped on the light, and surveyed her shoes, dozens of them, all neatly arranged. She picked out a pair of open-toe pumps and considered them for a

38

moment as they dangled from her fingers. She knew these shoes were terrible for her feet, but she couldn't resist. Little hand-made works of fine art, she thought them. And admittedly, they cost nearly as much as a gallery purchase. Grace tossed the painfully high pumps into a gym bag, picked out her trusted running shoes with their custom-made orthotic insoles, and tossed them in, too.

An hour later

Moms determined to steal time for themselves, professional models and athletes getting in a predawn workout, executives young and old readying body and mind for the day ahead: Most of the people at the Buckhead Sports Club this time of morning had an axe to grind or a point to prove or a steadfast resolve to fight aging or ill health or — like Grace Lyndon, pedaling intensely on a recumbent bike — a determination in their very core to succeed. You could see it in her eyes as she pedaled with fury, her shoes pushing into the toe cages, pumping through the resistance offered up by the bike. You could hear it in her voice as she spoke into the Bluetooth affixed to her ear.

"Good morning, Emma. How's the world's greatest assistant today? . . . Outstanding. Listen, when you get into the office, first thing, I'd like you to make sure everything is prepped and set for the presentation."

Late twenties now, slender, and in great shape, Grace met any challenge the bike dished out. From her golden brown hair pulled back in a perfect tight ponytail, thick beads of sweat ran down her forehead, down her flushed cheeks, a few falling onto the documents she read before her on the rack between the handlebars. The documents were filled with chemical equations, the sort a scientist would read.

"Great. And please make sure they get the ethyl maltol ratio just right in the sample. You know too much of that molecule gives the composite an alcoholic top note. I'm a flavorist, not a bartender, and we've designed a new soft drink, not a cocktail. Cocktails are for later — when we get the contract. See you soon." Grace tried for an air of confidence as she ended the call. It sounded so natural and authentic that she was almost able to convince herself that she wasn't nervous. Well, almost.

Grace felt the bike pedals tightening as the computer simulated the final and steepest hill of the workout. Never slowing down, she pedaled harder, focusing on the presentation she was getting ready to make, thinking about all the work she had done to get to this point, to get this opportunity. But other memories surfaced, memories of years running from a past filled with voices that said she couldn't do these kinds of things, would never amount to much of anything, voices that could still seem to find her when she was feeling nervous or vulnerable.

She'd left Georgia almost a decade ago now, at the first chance she got to leave behind a childhood that she was determined to forget. A mother who died. A father who was gone. A rheumatic aunt. A double-wide not far from I-20, with a small vegetable garden that Grace tended and loved and which had provided a cherished supplement to employee-discounted breakfasts brought home from Stuckey's after the late-night shift. No, Grace did not want to think about any of that, certainly did not want to talk about it, and she'd discovered that the more successful she was, the further and less relevant it seemed. So much so that she felt soon it would be gone for good.

Dusty old children's furniture left behind after a move, outgrown and discarded. A closetful of hand-me-downs and thrift store purchases. And finally, the little matter about not actually having attended the college she found herself writing on a job application in the Côte de Nuits a decade ago. She'd understood very little French, and the man in charge of hiring pickers for the harvest spoke very little English. He just wanted to see all the boxes filled out, right? So what did it matter? At least that's what she'd told herself, watching the others her age who were being chosen, college students, filling in all the boxes. But somehow what she wrote in that box, *Agnes Scott,* seemed to follow her all the way to Paris, and onto the human resources records that Bill Rice's headhunter got hold of.

As if Agnes Scott would have admitted someone with a background like mine!

She'd always meant to set the record straight, but the record kept following her. And really, what did that matter now? The thing was, she rationalized to herself, no one ever checked, because no one really cared. It just wasn't that important, none of it. Because at the end of the day, her employers weren't truly interested in where a person came from. They cared about where you were going, and what you could do for them. And Grace liked that, because it was more than a clarity; it was a clean playing ground. This was precisely what Grace loved so much about work. It had given her the chance to not only reinvent herself through success, but also make the past so irrelevant, it simply disappeared.

Interesting that after all these years, the biggest opportunity in her life ended up being in the place she had most wanted to escape. Maybe there was an aspect of destiny in that, she thought. And if destiny had a sense of humor, it must be tickled with what it had done with her.

Bill was right: It had felt good to come back with something to show for herself. He had been smart to appeal to her in that way. Not that he knew about her past beyond what the headhunter had given him. That was as far back as the records went, and she was careful and determined to make it stay that way.

Gripping the foam-covered rails of the bike, sweat now pouring from her face, running down her neck, legs pumping, she rode into the resistance, conquering it, pedaling away from the past, until all she felt was her body in perfect control and all she heard was her own steady breath.

Everything in a person's life came down to a few red-letter days, Grace often thought. This was one of them.

Recyclable brown container in hand, Grace moved quickly and intently through the salad bar, gathering her lunch for later in the day. In a classic deep blue designer suit — pencil skirt, matching tailored jacket over a pearl white silk blouse — her impeccably cut hair blown dry, Grace was beautiful. She perpetually carried a businesslike expression on her face, a curious counterpoint to her fresh and vibrant complexion. Indeed, even among the morning rush of indomitable young professional women sorting through the salad bar here at the West Paces Ferry Whole Foods Market in Buckhead, Grace Lyndon stood out.

On top of a goodly helping of baby lettuce, Grace placed a neat rectangle of grilled salmon, and then precisely five cherry tomatoes, five broccoli florets, five baby carrots, five cucumber slices, and five slices of green bell pepper. She liked the balance and symmetry of the meal she had made. Still, she liked almonds more, and daring to disrupt the balance of the universe, she threw in a spoonful of an unknown number.

Grace quickly and neatly closed the container, popping it into the little basket she carried as she strode to the front of the store. Moving rapidly along, she looked at the various lines at checkout, assessing the size of the carts and baskets of those in the line, her brain homing in on the ideal line in which to stand. An odd quirk, perhaps, but it was something she did quite a lot, almost like a game — and it gave her gratification to check out as expeditiously as possible — anything under five minutes in Buckhead was a success.

After a few short moments, and a few brief glances at *Yoga Journal* and *Delicious Living,* Grace swiped her credit card while the woman at the register put the boxed salad and a bottle of Honest Tea into a brown sack.

"Good morning, Grace," said a handsome professional man in his late twenties who walked up beside her.

"Good morning —"

"Patrick," he said, reminding her. "Patrick Hanson."

"Right," said Grace brightly, remembering him. "With Greenberg Traurig. You guys are doing the legal for our rollout on the new nachos for Chili's."

"Good memory. You must eat a lot of superfoods," he said with a playful smile.

The woman working the register raised an eyebrow as she handed Grace her bag.

Swinging the little Whole Foods sack by the twined handles, Grace started walking out of the store. Patrick followed alongside her.

"How's the IFF account going?" Grace asked.

"Now, Grace, you know I can't talk about your competitor's business."

"A moral lawyer, no wonder Bill hired you," she quipped.

"I'll take that as a compliment." He smiled and kept pace with her. "You all set for the Herb Weiss pitch? That's gonna be a massive piece of business."

"Now, Patrick, you know I can't talk about accounts you-all aren't on."

He smiled some more, and then asked, "Listen, you want to have lunch?"

"Bill's the one you want to have lunch with. He's the only one who makes the decisions about assigning out our legal business."

"I know. I'm talking about lunch as in, you know, *not* talking about business."

Collegial repartee broken, Grace slowed for a moment to find her footing, and being slowed always annoyed her. As she started walking again, Patrick grabbed a long-stemmed pale red rose from a bucket at the flower stand right beside them, and then

46

jogged a few steps up to her.

"You know, *lunch,*" he said, holding out the rose to her.

Grace stopped, the bag dangling from her hand. She was having a very hard time maintaining her annoyance. The soft pinkish rose in her face, Grace couldn't help but take in its lovely fragrance. Caught off guard, she found herself accepting it, and then slowly pulling it closer to her face so she could smell it even better. Grace Lyndon generally did everything she possibly could to avoid this sort of thing, fought it tooth and nail, but truth be told, she was a sucker for a good rose.

The unshaven old flower vendor stood there in his soil-smudged apron, watching the scene unfold.

"You do eat lunch, don't you, Grace?" Patrick asked.

"I'm sorry," she finally said, shaking off unwanted feelings and forcing herself back down to earth. "Not unless it's business. But thank you for the offer, truly."

Grace handed the rose back to the old vendor; then she turned and started to walk away.

After a few steps, unable to resist the fragrance still in her mind, she stopped and came back. "Hungarian, right?" she asked the vendor as she pointed to the bucket of pinkish roses, spying Patrick's curiosity.

"They're roses, lady," he said.

Grace bent over and stuck her face right into the heads of the entire bucketful of sweet-scented pinkish flowers. "*Rosa gallica officinalis,* definitely," she said mostly to herself. "I'm betting from east of the Danube, probably in the plains around Szabolcs-Szatmár-Bereg," Grace pronounced with a pretty good East European accent. She smelled them again, pulled herself away, and again mumbled to herself aloud. "Great depth. Would make a killer base note in a spicy summer parfum." She looked again at Patrick and pointed to the pinkish flowers in the bucket, and quickly walking away, she stated with a professional tone: "Those are nice."

Undoubtedly, Patrick noted, this was a woman much more interested in roses than in the men who presented them.

As Grace walked off, the vendor turned to the rather perplexed-looking young lawyer and said, "I been doing this a long time, pal. Can I tell you something? Find a girl who eats lunch."

Marietta, Georgia, one hour later
Grace marched down the well-lit hallway,

her heels clicking steadily along the chic pale limestone tile. In her white lab coat, clipboard under her arm, she looked very much like an attending surgeon making rounds, but her confidently worn Manolo Blahniks suggested a more style-conscious line of work.

Turning a corner, Grace came upon a woman, hair in a ponytail, wearing a tight short-sleeve black Lycra top, her arms fully extended from her body, with two fashionably groomed men holding and meticulously sniffing the full length of them, from the backs of her hands up to her biceps. All three looked intensely serious.

As Grace marched by, one of the men looked up and called out to her. "Grace, what do you think?"

She did not stop, but slowed a bit, leaning in toward them and smelling the air around them carefully. "I think the top note is too astringent," she said, and continued on her way.

"Told ya," said the woman being smelled as she smirked.

Grace called out over her shoulder, "I'd go with some cinnamon. Try half a gram of the absolute."

The men and the woman nodded. Cinnamon: a bit audacious, but a pretty good idea.

"Thanks, Grace!" one of the men called back.

As she turned another corridor, Grace's pace quickened as she headed for the imposing double doors of a conference room.

Her college-aged assistant, bright and confident in her off-the-rack J. Crew attire, intercepted Grace and handed her a folder. "Good luck, Ms. Lyndon," she said.

"Thank you, Emma."

The assistant smiled, eyes moving up and down, unable to fully contain her high regard for this young woman, and for her shoes. Although Grace wasn't even ten years older than Emma, the assistant afforded her the kind of admiration reserved for a mentor.

Grace eyed the doors before her and took a deep breath, steadying herself, and for a brief hiccupping half a second thought, *I'm about to do this. I can't believe I'm actually about to do this.* Then with a well-honed twitch of her head, which both moved all her rich hair behind her and shoved her panicky self-awareness back from where it had come, she pressed through the doors, poised, powerful, exuding just the kind of alluring glow that came from attaining a certain mastery in one's field.

"Grace! Come in," said a very cheerful Bill Rice, standing as he waved her in.

"Thanks, Bill," Grace said to her boss as she entered, the doors closing behind her.

Two men and a woman rolled their plush leather chairs back from the sleek conference table and rose.

"Grace, say hello to Herb Weiss, Mike Koziol, and Melissa Hornbach."

"Herb. Mike. Melissa." Grace grasped a hand of each executive warmly and firmly. "It's such a pleasure to meet you all."

"The pleasure is ours," said Herb.

"I'm such an admirer of your products," said Grace.

Bill stepped next to her. "Everyone here at Southern has been very excited about this opportunity," he said.

Herb studied Grace, then declared, "This new beverage line is going to be a multibillion-dollar international rollout — biggest product launch since I took over, and there was no way I was just gonna go back to our usual flavor suppliers without taking pitches from the new players, and everywhere we go, Southern Compounds' name keeps coming up."

"We must be doing something right," Bill said with a laugh. "And Grace is the very best flavorist we have here at Southern. We stole her back from the French, where she was a star at Givaudan. Even though she's come up through the Flavor Unit here, she's also one of our best *noses*. Fragrance has been known to pull her in on a few briefs now and then."

"Hard to do your training in France and not learn a thing or two about scent," Grace said — trying to sound confident and casual.

Grace and Bill exchanged an easygoing smile. *But what he's not saying,* Grace thought, *is that this is the opportunity he's been dreaming about every day and night since he mortgaged his house and started this company twenty-five years ago. What he's not saying is that I am the one person he picked out of the entire company to make it happen, and if I don't, the entire industry will know that I was the one who blew it and that will pretty much be as far as I go in my career, which — let's face it — is my life. So don't stress out, it's only* my entire life *that's on the line here.* Grace's big toes shifted in her open-toe shoes, the only indication of her inner dialogue.

"Yes, we've heard quite a lot about you, too, Grace," said Herb. In his tailored big-and-tall suit, entire face and head cleanly shaven, it was hard to imagine Herb Weiss doing anything but running a Fortune 100 company.

"Well, don't believe everything Bill says," Grace said playfully.

"Oh, we don't," Herb said not so playfully.

"We understand you were instrumental in developing the chai flavoring for the tea of a certain international coffeehouse chain," Mike Koziol said, his tone somewhere between inquiring and stating.

Grace just smiled politely. "I can't comment on that."

Melissa jumped into the conversation. "And my seven-year-old, I have to say, is a huge fan of the new healthier reformulation of a certain fast-food chain's 'special sauce,' " Melissa said with a raised eyebrow. "Not that she cares that it's healthier, but I do."

Again, Grace just smiled.

"I think your work on the Green World deodorant scent is outstanding," Herb declared loudly. "Hell, I'm wearing Green World right now. The brand's up twelve percent this quarter, and I think I smell pretty damn good." Herb took a sniff of the air around him, and everyone laughed.

"Thank you," said Grace. "But you know we can't comment on work that we may or may not have done."

"All our projects are strictly confidential," Bill added quickly. "Consumers don't need to know that the tastes and scents of their most cherished brands are developed in a lab in a nondescript industrial park north of Atlanta, and not by the actual companies they love."

"Of course," said Herb with a sly smile that conveyed what everyone in the room knew. Yes, flavor and fragrance was a discreet industry, a kind of secret society — there were only a few hundred flavorists in the entire world, and they almost never spoke of their work — but Herb Weiss had the kind of influence and resources that could get him any kind of information he wanted, and before he was even going to consider putting his neck on the line by hiring a new supplier, he was going to use his influence and resources to make damn well sure it was worth his time to get on a plane in New York and fly down to Georgia to hear a pitch.

"So, what do you have for us?" Herb said.

Everyone sat as Grace moved to the front of the room, speaking avidly and assertively, as though she were born to talk about the meeting of commerce and flavor, the business of taste. "You all have given us a very ambitious product to develop. A new beverage line that fits comfortably into your classic — even iconic — brand, but steps out a bit, a tea and juice drink that's healthy but hip, speaking to young moms and millennials without alienating your loyal boomers. We think of it as Snapple meets Tazo. Cool but comfortable. And at once fragrant and refreshing."

The executives from the beverage company all nodded, very much appreciating her take on their new product.

Bill beamed as Grace continued. "Over the last few years, soft drink sales in fountain and can alike have been — well, as we all know — soft. But of course, other segments of the beverage industry have found and built entirely new consumer bases, particularly the herbal bottled tea segment. Why?"

Grace opened the folder she'd taken into the room and read some figures. "In our recent focus group testing on market-leader Honest Tea, consumers responded favorably to a variety of factors: organics, health benefits, environmental sustainability. But the only factor receiving consistent top-quintile response across all demographics was taste." She closed the folder and slid it across the table. "So with all due respect to packaging and marketing and environmental sustainability, the question here is, How do we give them something that tastes good? So good, they can't stop thinking about it?"

"That is precisely what we took a two-hour flight to find out," said Herb, generating a few nervous chuckles.

"Well, good, because I am going to show you."

Everyone sat in complete silence, leaning forward, captivated by Grace as she stepped to the credenza behind her and retrieved a brown glass bottle and a palm-sized glassine envelope. She placed the bottle on the conference table and removed the dark cap. Carefully opening the near-transparent envelope, she slid out a white booklet, flipped it open, and tore out three six-inch-long paddle-shaped paper strips, fragrance blotters, cut from chemically pure paper.

Then she expertly dipped the three test strips into the bottle and fanned them out in her hand like a magician performing with a pack of cards.

"Taste buds actually offer very little information about flavor, beyond sweet or salty, bitter or sour," Grace said, waving the strips in the air. "The true taste of something is really put together by signals sent to our brains by our olfactory systems, which can interpret tens of thousands of aromas. When we chew food, or suck in a beverage, we're releasing aromatic gases that are picked up by receptors in our nostrils and the backs of our throats. So before you *taste* what we've developed for your new beverage, I want you to do something much more important."

Grace reached her hand forward, offering the blotters. "Smell," she said.

Each executive removed a blotter from Grace's fingers and held it before his or her nose, inhaling.

Bill watched attentively, looking from person to person, scanning for some kind of reaction.

A variety of expressions crossed the faces of Herb, Mike, and Melissa as they repeatedly waved the blotter strips before their noses. Unlike the scent straight from the bottle, composed mostly of just the top notes — the spirituous and sharp first part of a smell — the scent on the blotter when exposed to air released a fuller spectrum: the top, as well as the rich substantial middle notes, and even many of the long-lasting deep base notes, a lush, dynamic, all-embracing sensation of the entire aromatic composition.

The executives continued to wave the blotters and inhale the ever-changing scent, the subtle lines in their faces hinting at their reactions.

Still, the room remained silent, very silent, as everyone waited for Herb. The CEO sniffed away, and sniffed away some more, quietly musing, thinking, oblivious of everyone and everything else. It was the kind of high-stakes, potentially life-changing silence that made men like the nervously grinning Bill Rice certain that their pounding hearts could be heard.

But Grace just stood, hands held together behind her, looking entirely sure of her work. Nevertheless, her big toes were anxiously fidgeting in her open-toe shoes.

Notwithstanding the pressure in the room, this was always an emotional moment for Grace Lyndon, when someone was experiencing a scent she had created. When Grace was a little girl, her mother became very sick and lost her ability to hold down food, and in her final days lost her sight. But her sense of smell remained, strong as ever, and young Grace would bring to her mother's bedside fresh cut flowers, lilac and iris and tea rose, the sweet scents infusing the room with light and earth and memories long forgotten, and Grace brought in special foods to smell, like warm orange-ginger rolls, glazed and fragrant as winter holiday mornings, and cotton linens, laundered in lavender water and line-dried so you could smell the sun in them, and slices of ripe apples, a scent so perfect that in the end, it made her mother cry bittersweetly.

Finally, Herb looked up from his blotter. "I like it," he said.

Grace imagined a barometer in the room breaking at the sudden drop in pressure.

"Me, too!" Melissa chimed in.

"Yes, terrific!" Mike added.

"Excellent!" Bill exclaimed, clasping his hands.

Melissa breathed in the fragrance deeply from her blotter. "Uhm, it's warm and comforting, but also . . ."

"Satisfying," said Mike.

"Exactly," said Melissa.

Grace opened a small refrigerator built into the credenza and produced another dark glass bottle, this one larger, while Bill placed three small white paper cups on the table. Grace removed the dark cap from the bottle and poured a tawny-toned liquid into them.

"Now, taste," Grace said.

The three executives each picked up a cup and drank. They all looked pleased.

"Fabulous," said Melissa.

"Delicious," said Mike.

Grace smiled and explained her work. "It's a composite of ethyl maltol, the molecule you taste when you eat cotton candy, cloned tonka bean absolute, sencha green tea essence, and a pinch of my favorite extract, beef tallow."

"You'll never see all that on the label, of course," Bill added. "Just 'filtered water, green tea, and *natural flavoring*.' "

"And a fruit juice base, which we'll work on," Grace continued, "but this is the core of the proprietary flavoring. It evokes deep-seated hardwired emotions — cotton candy, McDonald's french fries — and combines them with contemporary aromas associated with healthfulness, for an overall taste sensation of comfort, satisfaction, and well-being."

"Yes, I like it," said Herb.

"Great!" said Bill.

"So, what else do you have?" asked Herb. The pressure could be felt again.

"What else?" Bill repeated.

"I mean, what else are you going to present to us today?"

"This is our pitch," said Grace steadily.

Again the room went silent. Mike and Melissa shuffled uncomfortably in their seats.

"You don't have anything else to present?"

asked Mike.

"This is our pitch," Grace said assuredly.

"Wow," Melissa said with surprise. "International Flavors and Fragrances presented a couple dozen concepts."

"Elan Chemical had us tasting all afternoon," said Mike.

"As did Flavor Dynamics," said Melissa. "Both times, before and after we gave them our notes."

"Those are all fine companies, and they do fine work . . . ," said Grace, trailing off before she finished her thought.

"I detect a 'but,' " said Herb.

"Okay. But simply put, our work is better."

"That's quite a statement."

"And this is quite a flavor."

Unaccustomed to being spoken to in this way, Herb looked more than a little taken aback.

Grace continued. "Look, Herb, I could keep you all here all afternoon, sniffin' and slurpin' pink Peruvian peppercorns and criollo cacao, and cinnamon and cascarilla and coriander, and caraway and carrot seed and so much climbing ylang-ylang you couldn't tell a cup of tea from a cup of turpentine. The development has been done. Expertly done. And respectfully, that is precisely why you want to hire us. Because we've done the work."

"What if I want you to present us some other ideas, so I can *participate* in the development process of *my* product?"

"I'd talk you out of it."

"What if you can't?"

"I'd try."

"You'd try."

"Yes, because it's the right thing to do. For your company, your brand, your goals, this product. This is the right flavor."

No one dared speak. Mulling this over, Herb Weiss very slowly turned the rotating bezel ring on his big fancy diver's watch. *Click, click, click.* "Bill?"

Bill swallowed hard. He could easily march half a dozen outstanding flavorists in here right now. He had a choice to make. And he made it. "She's right, Herb."

"Have we been clear about what this business is worth? Particularly to a midsized firm down in Georgia?"

"Herb, I go out of my way to hire the best people on the planet and then leave them alone. I'd be a fool not to stand by them."

Grace smiled at her boss, deeply impressed, and at that moment it was clear she had made the right decision to leave Paris and come to work for him. Everything he had said to her was true. He was giving her a shot and standing by her. And now it was her turn to deliver on that trust. The stakes couldn't have been higher, Grace thought.

Herb turned back to Grace and stared at her like a gunfighter in a saloon. "So basically, what you're saying is, 'Trust me.' "

Grace stared back. "Trust my nose. Trust my palate."

"Trust you with a $975 million contract."

"Yes, Herb. Trust me."

"Because you plunk down a bottle of funky-scented chemicals."

"Because I put my heart and my soul in that bottle."

Herb stared again, deeply considering her, deeply considering the heart and the soul of this young woman before him in the white lab coat and the designer high heels with the steadfast jaw and unwavering eyes. *Is this woman's sense of taste — whatever it is in the core of this woman — worth risking nearly a billion dollars?*

And again, Grace stared right back. The room remained silent and still for a very long time. Herb looked her up and down, eyes stopped at her feet, where her big toes were still and resolute, just like the rest of her.

Finally, Herb spoke. "Thank you for your time."

Grace took a deep breath. "Thank *you*." Without knowing her fate, but knowing that she was being dismissed, Grace held up her head and walked out of the room.

An Order to Things

"So? How'd it go?" asked Dr. Monic Jain, looking up from a beaker filled with dazzling yellow liquid and brightening as her friend walked into her lab, a large room filled with an assortment of sophisticated high-tech equipment and rows and rows of dark glass bottles. Complex chemical names were typed neatly on their white labels, containing a multitude of fragrances, some newly made in the lab, some dug out of deserts and rain forests.

"It went," Grace said.

"You didn't get it?"

"I just stood in front of the man *Fortune* magazine called America's Most Hands-On CEO and told him 'my way or the highway.' "

"That's what you do, honey. We wouldn't expect anything less of you."

"You'd think for a billion dollars, maybe I could be just a little accommodating."

"Hey, cheer up — you did your best and you're still standing."

Grace slumped into a chair. "Maybe I should've brought him a bunch of samples like Bill wanted," Grace said.

Monic rolled her eyes, accustomed to this kind of rant from Grace.

"Maybe I should've let him sniff himself into a frenzy, taste himself into a self-congratulatory haze, pat him on the back and tell him he was a *genius* for picking out some vapid malodorous tar to flavor his 'brand-defining' tea."

"Maybe . . ." Monic fed the word to her friend, knowing where it would lead.

"But that would be just downright stupid! The flavor is right! Spot-on, smack-dab, correct, and right! And if Herb Weiss and his suits are too stupid to understand that, let 'em go back and buy from one of those suck-up sycophant suppliers on the Jersey Turnpike!"

"That's right!"

"And I'll just go and develop the next groundbreaking toilet bowl cleaner fragrance." Grace plopped her head on her hands. "If I'm lucky."

"You're gonna be okay, Grace. You're too good not to be." Monic smiled and then turned her attention back to her present work on the center lab bench, where five lemons sat under glass domes. Wires ran from the lemons, up through the glass, into a toaster oven–sized machine covered in dials and meters, a gas chromatograph, which separated, measured, analyzed, and mapped the precise molecular-level aromatic compounds present in the lemons.

Grace was instinctively pulled to the compelling fragrance emanating from the beaker with the yellow liquid, lemon juice concentrate, which sat next to the chromatograph. She leaned over and took a whiff. "Smells good. Yours?"

"Nope. That's nature," Monic said. Then she reached for a plastic nose cup attached to a clear tube that ran to another machine; along its face were several rows of dials and correlating meters, a VOS, or Virtual Olfactive Synthesizer.

Grace took the nose cup and put it to her face and breathed in while Monic watched attentively. With her jet-black hair and dark eyes, her petite, even delicate frame, Monic had a searing curiosity that belied her easygoing laissez-faire attitude.

"Nice," Grace said, reflecting on the lemony scent. "Sharp and bright, interesting, like juiced lightning bugs."

"This one's mine. It's the new molecule.

All the best smells of a lemon, but it'll hold up much better than anything natural. It'll be a slam dunk in everything from lemon-infused vodka to floor wax. The guys in marketing are calling it Lemohydronol."

"Smells like a winner."

"Yeah, think this one's ready for the patent office."

Grace tossed down the plastic nose cup. "Does it ever cross your mind, what an odd thing it is that we do for a living? I mean, you have a Ph.D. in Chemical Engineering from Carnegie Mellon. You could work in any research lab in the world, but you're sitting around in here, playing with fruit."

"Hey, beats working with rats."

"I dunno, some of our prospective clients just might fit that bill."

Monic looked up from her lemons. "Grace, you know what your problem is?"

"Oh, boy, here it comes."

"Yes, here it comes." Monic moved away from the equipment, sitting next to Grace. "Here it comes because you are one of my dearest friends, and it's one thing to love your work, but it's another to be defined by it to the point where a bad pitch clouds every aspect of your world because there's nothing else to it."

Grace studied her friend, recognizing

68

something in her eyes. "Oh, no. I know that look. I know where this is going."

"He's great."

"I am not going on a blind date."

"He's a friend of Simon's. I've met him —"

"No."

"— And we told him all about you, and he's available for a drink any night this week after work."

"No. My life is just the way I want it right now."

Monic raised an eyebrow.

"Well, I can mess it up on my own just fine, thank you," Grace said.

"Seventy-two percent of all happily married couples were introduced by friends."

"Really?"

"Well . . . okay, I made that up, but I'm sure the actual number is something like that. My sister met her fiancé that way. Mutual friends gave her his number. She called him up one afternoon, and they talked until midnight. Pretty much fell in love over the phone."

Grace looked skeptical. "Over the phone?"

"It can happen." Monic reached out her hands, gesturing with them emphatically. "I'm telling you, mutual friends. It's how Simon and I met. I was so close to not going that night to that silly Steamhouse Lounge in Buckhead, but finally, at the last minute —"

"— You and Simon would have found each other, no matter what. You two were born to be together."

"You're right about the second part, but if we weren't looking for each other, when the universe finally brought us together, we wouldn't have known — we wouldn't have known to seize the moment. Einstein was very clear about this."

"Huh, I must've missed his paper on the principles of dating."

"Particles attract not because of gravity, but because time and space bend around them, pulling them near."

"You're such a geek."

Monic ignored the playful dig and looked seriously at her. "You keep running, Grace, and you won't be there when your particle is pulled near. And this guy could very well be your particle."

"Or a guy with no job and bad shoes."

"He's a sports reporter with CNN. He's accomplished and cute. I can't speak to his taste in footwear — which, by the way, I think you can be a little obsessive about — but a quick text message, and you can see for yourself tonight." Monic reached for her cell phone, but Grace stopped her.

"Thank you. I really do appreciate how much you care about me, but especially after this presentation, I'm spent. Maybe some other time, when I've had a better day. Okay?"

Turning away, Grace broke eye contact with Monic. The worst part of not being in a relationship, Grace felt, was not the loneliness that inevitably crept in — that was sort of okay — it was trying to explain to people *in* relationships that you actually preferred being alone.

Grace never really dated — in high school, the boys finally just stopped asking — but in France, there was a man, and an engagement ring, though that didn't last very long, and in the end, it only reinforced her beliefs that relationships were difficult and to be avoided. There were times when she couldn't help thinking about him, or more to the point, about the way it felt to be with another. But Grace found that if she stayed busy enough, if she kept herself in a state of near perpetual motion, these thoughts couldn't find their way in.

The truth was — though she was sophisticated and worldly and expert in the ways of the senses, her knowledge of sensuality was, by and large, academic. Indeed, real inti-

71

macy was a part of life that Grace Lyndon endeavored to avoid. But every once in a while, when her work had left her mind for a moment, she found herself toying with the idea of letting her guard down. Could there be someone out there for her? She did not dwell on the notion, but it was there, like the subtlest of aromas. It was there.

Refusing to take no for an answer, Monic bolted up, moved to her computer, and began to navigate to a particular Web site. "I want you to listen to something." Monic read from the screen: *To the woman in the white knit sweater sitting next to me on the subway this morning.*"

Grace just shook her head. "You have an IQ of a hundred and seventy, and this is what you're reading?"

"Listen," Monic said, and continued reading from "Missed Connections" on Craigslist: " *'Letting you get off at Tenth Street without talking to you I know now is the biggest mistake of my life. I have so many things to say to you. Please respond.'* "

"Do you honestly think anything ever comes of these posts?"

"My college roommate in Pittsburgh saw a man like twenty rows away at a Pirates game. They started exchanging smiles during the last inning, but neither ever approached the other. In the morning, she saw a post for 'girl with the great ninth-inning smile,' met him for lattes in the afternoon, and I was her maid of honor a year later."

"Well, why are *you* reading this?"

"I read it every day, because it helps me find my bearings." Monic took a deep breath and then confessed. "Look, I know it might sound silly, but even after spending the better part of my waking adult life studying the most fundamental laws of the physical universe, I still can't figure out why the vast majority of things happen, and reading this makes me feel that despite the increasingly terrifying evidence that Chaos Theory might, in fact, be more than a theory — there *is* a natural order to things. I don't know exactly how it works. I don't know the coding or who wrote the damn thing, but to hear the voices of longing, and love, is to feel connected to all that is human and purposeful. It's to know that what I have in my house with Simon, and sweet Emily, isn't random, some lucky discovery, but in fact the way It's Supposed to Be, and I'd like to believe . . . No, I do believe, that most of those people that missed their connection — *because of fear,* or whatever — and are *taking the chance to reach out* do find each other. There's an order to this. I know it. If you listen closely, I swear, you can hear it in their voices." With the passion of a scientist talking about a great hypothesis that is more than faith but still beyond verifiable, she pointed to the computer screen.

Then Monic leaned in to her friend, her voice even but quiet now. "There's someone out there looking for you, Grace."

Grace did not speak. She held Monic's gaze, realizing just how much it upset Monic's view of the universe that Grace chose to be alone. After a long moment punctuated only by the clicking of the chromatograph as it decoded and analyzed the natural DNA structure of the lemons, Bill entered the lab.

Grace and Monic spun around to watch him walk in. He was quiet, solemn looking. Clearly, he had just finished a very intense conversation.

He walked right up to them and broke out in a smile. "We got it."

Grace lit up. "That's fantastic! What happened?"

"Well, they loved your work, of course, and there was a lot of debate about how much to let you run with it, and in the end, well, it was the damnedest thing."

"What?"

"He said he liked your shoes."

"What does that mean?"

"Hell if I know. But we got the contract." Monic shot Grace a huge smile.

Bill continued, "Congratulations, Grace. This is going to be by far the largest client we've ever had. You'll need a team under you. I'll be talking to the board about making you Vice President of Development. Congratulations. Go celebrate." Bill patted Grace on the back, and with a gleeful nod to both women, he walked out of the lab.

"Way to go, Ms. Veep!" Monic got in Grace's face. "You heard the man — you need to celebrate. This is the universe giving you a sign."

"I don't believe in signs."

"Well, I do, and I'm thinking drinks, after work, the Four Seasons. I'm texting." Monic reached for her cell phone.

"Okay, okay, set it up." Grace was giddy, nothing short of it.

An Apple

Several hours later

In her office, Grace packed her things into her sleek shoulder bag, hastily getting ready to leave for the night.

Like her home, like her meals, her office was a picture of order. A neat well-upholstered sofa, classic Aeron office chair, a few business-related pictures framed in a blond wood that matched her immaculate desk perfectly. Exactly five manila folders, tightly arranged in order of importance, sat on the matching wood credenza behind the desk. Everything was in its place, just like her life.

"Emma, have you seen the briefs for the Procter and Gamble pitch?" Grace called out her open door.

"Top drawer, credenza, Ms. Lyndon," Emma said without missing a beat.

Grace went to the credenza, popped open the drawer, grabbed the file folder she needed, and shoved it into her bag.

Grace closed the credenza drawer, calling out over her shoulder, "Can you fax the sourcing data to —"

"Already done."

Grace shrugged, impressed with her assistant's intuitiveness.

"You need to send Herb Weiss's assistant the flavor profile for the MiniVOS before —"

"Working on it now," Emma said from her desk outside Grace's office. "Jonah will have it before I leave tonight."

Bag on her shoulder, about to leave, Grace realized she was forgetting something and began to search her office anxiously. Looking around, she turned to find Emma, smiling, standing calmly in the doorway, holding Grace's long tailored fall jacket.

"Have fun on your big date, Ms. Lyndon," Emma said.

"Drinks. It's just drinks, Emma." Grace walked by Emma, grabbing her jacket and exiting her office. "Thank you."

"Whatever," Emma said quietly, and then followed.

"Probably even just *drink*."

"Congrats again on the account, Ms. Lyndon. How exciting!"

Just as she was about to take a step, Grace

noticed a bowl on Emma's desk with a single apple in it. She paused.

"Last one . . . ," said Emma. "You should take it. They're *really* good. People have been flipping out over them."

The apple was deep red with golden amber streaks and interesting russeting, the tiny rough folds on the skin that you didn't see very often on modern mass-marketed cultivars.

Grace found herself reaching out over several packs of multicolored Post-it notes and an iPhone and a photograph in a simple Pottery Barn frame of a handsome young man in a military uniform, and she picked up the apple from the bowl.

She liked the way it felt in her hand, as though it had been cut specifically for her, and she instinctively brought it to her nose. "Uhmm. Smells wonderful." Grace inhaled again. It really did have a lovely bouquet. She plopped the apple into her open bag. "Thank you, Emma."

Emma looked Grace in the eye, pleased that she was able to offer her something that she genuinely seemed to like, and even more pleased that this woman whom she liked and admired so much was off to do something that she felt would bring Grace happiness. "You're welcome."

And with that twitch of her head, throwing her hair back, Grace marched down the hall, legs long and gracile in her pencil skirt, Blahniks clicking along the tile.

Emma thought about suggesting that Grace try to hold back on the head-twitch thing a bit tonight, something that gave Grace a look of control and confidence, but which Emma had noticed picked up when Grace was under pressure.

Emma watched her boss go, deciding to keep her mouth shut and praying that Grace had a good night.

West Peachtree Battle area, Atlanta, a little later that night

Grace drove down I-75 in her leather-upholstered European sports sedan. As it was well into October, the sun had already set. The in-dash GPS displayed a three-dimensional image of the interstate on its touch screen. Although she certainly didn't need a satellite to guide her along this regularly traveled route, Grace left the device on, sound off, finding comfort in the reassuring rhythms of the digital freeway moving along in tandem to the real road around her. She sort of liked the idea that something above was looking out for her.

It did occur to her that since the lease was

up in two months, maybe, just maybe, she would let herself consider getting the convertible she'd always wanted. In so many ways, it was entirely impractical — but didn't vice presidents drive whatever they wanted? *Vice president.* A sudden smile broke out on Grace's face.

It was a stunningly unappreciated truth, Grace frequently mused, that the vast majority of what the entire human race smells in its day-to-day existence and nearly all of what its food tastes like are created by a small elite group of quiet individuals working for fewer than a dozen companies worldwide. Grace was one of those people, and on her way to being one of the more powerful and influential among them.

A bit dreamily, she tapped her fingers happily on the steering wheel. The lights of Buckhead hot spots and Midtown high-rises sparkled all around her, holding their own to the stars in the vastness overhead. There was something about driving into the city at night that was pure magic. People could call her a workaholic or a control freak, Grace thought, but she was quite pleased. Life felt pretty darn good right now. Yes, more or less, everything was going according to plan.

Feeling a little dizzy, Grace rolled down her window just a little and let the cold night air refresh her. She threw her head back and breathed in deeply. Realizing that she had been too busy and too jittery to eat lunch, Grace was hit with sudden hunger. *An empty stomach, great,* she thought, *just the thing for drinks with some guy.*

Then she remembered. The apple. Reaching over to her bag on the passenger seat with her right hand, left hand on the wheel, Grace grasped the apple like a baseball and brought it to her face. Again, she held it under her nose and took in its scent. Wow. Even with the wind blowing around her, the fragrance was full and lush and sweet — though not overtly, like so many of today's commercially bred grocery store apples, but deep, dark, sugared as the night in a Caribbean cane field.

She took a bite.

A little stream of juice and saliva ran from the corner of her mouth down her chin, down her neck and throat, where she swiped it up with her middle and forefinger while holding the apple with the other two fingers and her thumb. She licked her fingers. *What is this?*

She removed a piece of apple skin from her lower lip with her tongue and savored it. Putting her nose into the open flesh of the apple, she inhaled. *This is incredible.*

Grace took another bite, thinking as she chewed, wiping at the stickiness on her skin where the juice had been. Then, before she had even finished swallowing, she hit a speed-dial button on her cell phone.

"Grace Lyndon's office," said Emma, her voice clear over the vehicle's wireless speakerphone.

"Emma, where did you get the apple?"

"The last apple you took, Ms. Lyndon?"

"Yes. Where did it come from?"

"My sister and I picked up a bushel in Ellijay over the weekend. You know, it's apple season up there now."

Grace had a vague memory that the small town in North Georgia was known throughout the region for its apples. "Do you remember where you got them? Which orchard?"

"Culpepper Farms."

Grace listened, considering the apple.

"It was a small place," Emma continued. "*Way* off the beaten track. In fact, we would never have come across it if we hadn't gotten lost. Mercier and Hillcrest were so full of tourists, you couldn't get in there, and the traffic all along Highway 52 was so jam-packed that we got off the main road, drove north, and —"

"Listen, I want you to track them down

and call them."

"Okay."

"And I want you to ask them if they would let us set up some equipment on-site for a few days. Nothing complicated."

"TDS samplers on a few trees?"

"Yes. Not a big deal. We won't disturb anything. Yeah, just a few thermal desorption systems, maybe some Micro Traps. You know how to explain it. Just want to map aroma profiles from the fruit at a gas level, see if we have any novel scent and flavor molecules here." Again, Grace considered the half-eaten apple in her hand. "Offer them twenty-five hundred dollars for their trouble."

"Right. From what I saw, I think they'll be thrilled with that." Emma was taking notes. "I'm almost finished with the flavor profile for Herb Weiss, and as soon as I send it —"

"I want you to do this first, Emma. Do it right away."

"Okay, Ms. Lyndon. Okay. Culpepper Farms. You got it."

Grace hit the end button, disconnecting the call. Then she dropped her focus to the apple again. With her eye back on the road, she slowly brought the apple to her mouth, feeling the weight of it in her hand, taking in its scent and biting into it, focusing on the sound of her incisors puncturing the crisp skin, the blast of flavor across her tongue, and the mouthfeel of the fruit's flesh, the changing aroma and even the crunch as she chewed.

Grace experienced the apple in the fullest way she knew, the fullest way possible, using all senses. *How remarkable,* she thought. *This product of earth and rain and sun. Is there more to it than that? Is this someone's work, or nature let be?* She had to know more about this apple.

A Family of Two

Against the Chattahoochee National Forest, just north of Ellijay, Georgia, a little later that night

The old Victorian house sat right in the middle of the mountain orchard. As the night breezes blew up from the valley below, the sea of moonlit trees, weighted with their ripe apples, cast spidery shadows across the wide wraparound front porch.

Inside, in the cozy living room, Dylan Jackson sat on a deep sofa, big feet in socks up on the worn ottoman, studying a report on wholesale fruit pricing. Across from him, his preteen daughter reclined on a love seat, immersed in a book propped up on the chenille blanket that covered her skinny legs. The dishwasher hummed in the dark clean kitchen behind them. It was a soothing slumberous sound that both of them liked.

Dylan looked up from his report, glanced

at the rooster-shaped wall clock, realizing it was getting late. "Time for bed, Carter."

"Just let me finish the chapter, Dad." Carter didn't even look up from the dog-eared novel in her hands.

"That's what you said half an hour ago." He was nothing short of amazed at how much she loved to read. The kid never went anywhere without a book, and on weekends, she took one to bed so she wouldn't have to get up to start reading. But as much as he loved her company, he knew he was being irresponsible by letting her stay up so late. The bus came very early in the morning, and she was supposed to get a certain amount of sleep. He could never quite keep up with exactly how much, but he knew it was more than she was probably getting.

"Well, I'm in the middle of another chapter now, and I have to finish it," she said, trying to read even faster.

"It's bedtime, Carter." He used the tone that meant he was digging in. It was the tone that meant he was finally serious.

She knew the tone well and sighed, closing the book. Anyway, she consoled herself, she'd gotten an extra half hour out of the guy. "Okay, Dad." She sat up.

"Let me know when you're all set, and I'll come tuck you in."

"Dad, when can I shave my legs?"

"When can you shave your legs?" That took him by surprise.

"Yes. When?" She just sat there, blankly looking at him.

"When you're thirty."

"Dad."

"Carter, it's bedtime."

"Dad, I need to know."

Dylan dropped his report and studied her, seeing that this was not a ploy, but something she genuinely wanted to talk about. "Why are you even thinking about this? C'mon, you're ten years old."

"I'm almost eleven."

"Okay, way too young."

"Not for basically *every* girl in my class."

"Every girl?" He was doubtful.

"Every girl in my entire grade! Except for maybe Judy, but her mother doesn't even shave under her arms."

"Uh . . . TMI." He envisioned Judy's mother.

The topic finally breached, it started pouring out of Carter. "Sarah's been shaving for a year now."

He recalled his daughter's friend, forcing himself to face the matter. "Well, Sarah's older than you."

"Right, by a year. She started when she

was my age, and she can show me how. She said so. Her mom took her to Walmart and bought her lots of the pink razors. So she could give me one."

Dylan took a very deep breath, suddenly aware of just how profoundly unprepared he was for this. He had anticipated he had at least a couple more years before matters of this nature were to appear. He knew very well that she could've gone over to Sarah's and done whatever she'd wanted to her legs and he wouldn't have ever noticed. The real truth, he realized, was that he hadn't even thought about this and might not have until one day when she was fifteen and had been shaving for years. This wasn't even about shaving. This was about something else, something bigger. It was about permission, but it was also about a child wanting a parent to be involved in her life. *Where's the damn manual on this stuff!* He knew there was none.

No, there was just a bunch of entirely conflicting opinions by a bunch of degreed experts who had never met his daughter and had no idea how things operated in their particular family, which at the end of the day actually operated pretty well. Parenting, he and his wife finally agreed — and tossed out all the books on how and where and when the baby should sleep, and how and where and when the baby should eat — was about choosing, and mainly that meant going with your gut. Yes, he was making it up as he went along, and for the most part, he really thought he'd still been getting it right. One look at this bright beautiful child before him confirmed that. Only, she wasn't entirely a child anymore.

"Carter, here's the thing," he stated, putting his big hands on his knees and leaning forward. "You've got the rest of your life to shave your legs."

"I know and when I start, I'll have to keep doing it like every day."

"Well, I was going to say every week at first. But why put that into your life right now? Because other girls are doing it?"

"Yeah," she said, never breaking eye contact with him.

There was something so simple and honest about the way she said that. And now, somehow, his canned speech about peer pressure and all the other kids jumping off bridges seemed amazingly stupid. This was a smart kid, and she deserved better than that.

"Okay, listen, I will think about this. The good news is that swim season is over and this is not a pressing issue right now."

"Uh, it's called gym, Dad."

"Gym?" He forgot about that.

"You know, gym. As in gym shorts."

"Gym shorts," he said evenly.

"You like to repeat things, do you know that?"

"Yes, well —"

"It's okay, Dad. It makes you sound wise, even though I know you just do it because you need the extra few seconds to, you know, formulate a response."

He just stared at her, amazed with her confidence and use of language and really the personality she was developing. She was quite a character, he thought. "Where did you come from?"

"Where did I come from?" she asked, playfully imitating him. "Where did I come from? Hmmm, well, we can save that talk for later, okay, Dad?"

Touché. He laughed, and then focused on the issue at hand. "I'll think about your question, Carter. Okay?" He looked at her seriously. "I'll think about it."

She heard that he'd found that tone again, the one that said he was digging in. But there was enough lightness in it that she felt understood. "I love you, Dad," she said with a wistful smile, and then padded up the stairs. It was not so much an expression of deep sentiment. Rather, there was an amusement in her voice that made him feel as though someone were ruffling his hair.

As he watched her go, trying to process this conversation and, indeed, formulate the right response, the portable phone on the coffee table rang.

He picked it up, turning it over to see the caller ID, which said SOUTHERN COMP CORP. He hit the ANSWER button. "Hello?"

CONNECTIONS MISSED
AND MADE

Midtown Atlanta, a little later that night

The dazzling lights of the downtown skyline before her, Grace veered her car onto the Fourteenth Street exit ramp, took a left, driving back east over the city's major interstate artery, heading into the heart of Midtown.

A few moments later, Grace pulled her car into the elegant driveway of the Four Seasons Atlanta, and before she'd even come to a stop, an attendant rushed to greet her. The young man in uniform opened the door for her, waiting dutifully as she grabbed her bag off the passenger seat and then pulled a few tissues from the storage bin between the seats and wrapped the apple core, put it in her bag, and stepped out of the car.

She took her valet ticket, headed for the front doors, and with that well-honed twitch of her head stepped through them. She moved across the busy and opulent lobby, absorbing the energy of people interacting and enjoying themselves. With the buzz of overlapping conversations and sudden outbursts of laughter, the jangle of jewelry and ice cubes, after the cool dark quiet of the car in the night, the hotel lobby was a sensory onslaught — a pleasant one, but nonetheless jarring.

Grace told herself to relax. She'd been here many times, and she loved this place. She'd nailed the Amato soy drink account at the Park 75 Restaurant here. After her presentation to the entire Colgate-Palmolive senior management team in the Augusta conference room here, they hired her on the spot to reformulate the flavor in their leading Spanish toothpaste brand.

How many days had she started with 6:30 A.M. breakfast meetings here? Yes, she loved this place. It was *her* place. But what she loved was not only all the fine things all around her, but also doing business here, *her* business, where the terms were clear and the goals, with enough work and dedication and all-encompassing commitment, very much attainable. Somehow, drinks for purposes of — what? — getting to know someone was just as disorienting as stepping from the night into this bright bustling place. The rules in business were very clear. In relationships, as far as she could tell, there were no rules.

Grace passed a massive mirror as she moved across the grand lobby and couldn't help peering in it. She straightened her blue jacket, smoothed out her silk blouse. Did she look okay? Or perhaps too okay? She slowed, thinking about maybe doing something with her hair, and then quickly decided against it. Ugh! This was exactly why she hated dates.

Taking in the scents of very high-end colognes and perfumes, a whiff of Joy, a trace of Shalini, equally exquisite whiskeys and wines, a mossy Islay, Lagavulin perhaps, first-growth Bordeaux, Latour definitely, a distant hint of Cohiba, Grace headed toward the bar. A mélange of fascinating and captivating foods, spiced Kobe beef bao buns and Georgia shrimp and grits soufflé and warm Coca-Cola chocolate cake, wafted from a variety of restaurants and open spaces to where Grace stood at the entrance, a cozy intimate living room-like space populated by a very well-dressed, well-heeled, and decidedly young crowd, to which Grace looked as though she belonged.

Approaching the bar area, Grace could see, sitting by himself at the bar, a tanned racketball-fit man with perfect hair in a dark slim-fitting Italian suit who looked very much like the image of the sports reporter that Monic had e-mailed her. He was handsome, very handsome, so much so that from her vantage point, she wondered if he was still in makeup.

She chided herself for being so critical and reminded herself she should enjoy a night out for a change, and just as she was about to approach him, her cell phone rang. Grace looked at him, saw him checking his watch, and then she quickly stepped away from the bar area and answered her phone.

"Culpepper Farms didn't go for it," said Emma.

"What happened?"

"They're just not interested. The owner of the orchard says that the apples are for sale, but not for study."

"Did you offer him the money?"

"Oh yes."

"And?"

"And that's when he hung up."

Grace looked over across the lobby and into the bar, where she could just make out the sports reporter still sitting alone. He looked at his watch again, and then ordered another drink.

"Okay, Emma," said Grace. "Thank you."

Grace hung up. She drummed her fingers on her cell phone, thinking. She knew what she was about to do was rude, terribly rude, and she hated that, but still, her fingers drummed and her legs did not move and her mind raced until, finally, she made a quick decision and hit a speed-dial button on her cell.

"Where are you?" Monic said.

"The Four Seasons."

"And?"

"And what?"

"And what's he like?"

"I — I don't know yet," Grace said, looking down at her toes squirming as though they had a life of their own.

"He's late. I'm gonna kill Simon." Monic groaned.

"He's not late. *I'm* late."

"What?"

"Well, I'm here and I've seen him — I just haven't, well, met him." Grace winced, knowing her friend was not going to like this.

"What's the problem? Is he hideous?"

"No. No, of course not."

Monic knew her friend well enough to hear in her voice exactly what was going on. "Oh, I cannot believe this. You are calling about work. *You are calling about work.*

Aren't you?" Grace remained sheepishly silent. "You are officially a lunatic, you know that? Get off the phone right now and go into that bar. Crazy person."

"Okay, but one very, very quick question."

"I am *not* talking to you about work right now."

"Can we get an accurate full-spectrum TDS profile *in-lab* on peak-season fruit?"

"Not talking," said Monic, digging in her heels.

"Can we?" Grace asked with increasing determination.

"Crazy person!"

"Can we?"

Realizing this wasn't going away, Monic took a deep annoyed breath and finally capitulated. "Yeah, sure, extract from a bushel or two can provide a decent sample."

"How decent?"

"Decent. You know, depends on how long since the fruit was picked, oxidation, sugar degradation, et cetera, but our lab can do a mock-up that would satisfy most clients. Of course, for obsessive perfectionist freaks like you, the only way to reproduce all parameters of an entire natural spectrum wholly and flawlessly is to capture it on-site, on the tree. There's still no substitute for that. Okay?"

"Okay," said Grace, exhaling with relief at getting the information she had to have. "Thank you."

"I'm not even going to ask why you're working on something that sounds new when your hands are already full with the biggest account of your life, but I will tell you to *stop working on it, and go into that bar.* Now."

"I'm going in there."

"Right now," Monic demanded.

"Right now," said Grace.

"Good."

"Okay, bye."

"Go now."

"I'm going. Bye."

"Bye."

Grace hung up and, once again, drummed the phone with her fingers and studied the man at the bar. Several people had gathered around him. She wasn't sure if they were friends or fans, but they were all having a very good time. He really did look like a fascinating man. Obviously quite accomplished, and she was sure he had an interesting life and perspective to offer. Monic was right, of course she was right; he looked like a great guy.

While Grace was watching him, wondering about him, she found herself removing the tissue-wrapped apple core from her bag. Mindlessly, almost hypnotically, she peeled away the tissue and brought it to her nose. As she inhaled the scent of apple, her eyelids fluttered with the simple pleasure.

An affluent graying couple — a gentleman in a tuxedo and his wife in black evening-wear — strolled by, gawking at the sight of this young woman sniffing a ragged, browning, chewed-up apple core in the lobby of the Four Seasons.

Grace didn't even notice them. She absorbed the sensations and, after a moment of deliberation, once again hit the speed dial on her cell.

"Grace Lyndon's office," said Emma.

"I want you to call them back and . . ." Grace thought aloud for a moment.

"Yes?"

"Actually, just dial and patch me in. I'll talk to them."

"Sure thing, Ms. Lyndon."

Grace could hear the eleven rapid-fire touch-tones as Emma dialed the number, and then the ringing signal on the other end of the line.

"It's going through," Emma said.

"Thanks, I've got it."

Emma disconnected herself from the call just as it was answered.

"Ma'am, I am trying to be polite here, so please excuse me, but I have to ask: Are you a little slow?" said Dylan with his low, pondering Southern drawl.

"I beg your pardon," replied Grace, a little taken aback.

"You know, dim-witted. Half-baked. Simple-minded. Ma'am, are you stupid?"

"No, I am not stupid." Grace found herself uncharacteristically searching for words. "Sir, my name is Grace Lyndon, and I work for —"

"Southern Comp Corp," he said, finishing her sentence. "Along with indoor plumbing, we have caller ID up here in Ellijay."

"The woman who called you earlier works for me."

"Then I would imagine that she explained to you that Cully apples are for eating, not studying by the Southern Comp Corp. You do talk to your employees, don't you, ma'am? Now, I'm sure you are a very nice lady with all the best intentions, but respectfully, I have to ask you to stop calling here. I have a daughter upstairs who just went to sleep, and I've got a crop that's approaching harvest. Okay? Are we good?"

"Listen to me," Grace said reflexively, realizing she was about to lose her opportunity. "Never in my life have I tasted an apple like yours. And I have spent the better part of my adult existence scouring the planet for untapped sources of flavor." Grace peered over at the man in the bar, looked at the apple core in her hand, and, unexpectedly, words poured out of her: "I dug wild mushrooms out of a jungle in Gabon, plucked *Vanilla pompona* orchids from Madagascar treetops, tracked down Sichuan hot pot pepper in a seedy back alley in Shanghai. I've sniffed test tubes filled with scents that are not of this earth. But I have never quite been struck the way I have been struck by your apple."

Taken with her bare passion, Dylan stayed on the line, but he didn't say anything. Generally preferring to keep to himself, he wasn't around a lot of people, really, save for his workers and some of the teachers and moms he encountered at school events. He'd somehow agreed to go out for a few fancy coffee drinks with a few women recently, and despite the casual no-big-deal way these fancy-coffee-drink meetings were presented and arranged, they were, of course, dates — and they were strange and unnatural, these rituals of adult courting, where he heard all sorts of things pouring out — but he'd never quite heard the simple heartfelt honesty that he heard from this woman on the telephone right now. It was, to say the least, intriguing.

"I know you're still there," Grace said, pressing the phone tightly to her ear. "I hear you breathing."

"You're a little nutty, aren't you?"

"First you call me stupid, then nutty. I'm a little offended here."

"You don't sound offended."

"Well, honestly, it's the second time tonight someone's questioned my sanity," she admitted, remembering how Monic had laid into her. "I guess I'm getting used to it." She spoke mainly to herself, and he sensed that. Sitting alone in his darkened old home, the dishwasher murmuring, he took in her voice in his ear, sweet but smart, at once feminine and forceful, mesmeric in its warmth, and he realized that there was something she was revealing that he found familiar, that he felt in himself.

"You sound like you're calling from a restaurant. Or a hotel lobby," he said as he rose with the phone in hand, sliding across the worn wood floor in his socks.

"You a farmer or a PI?"

"I'm a father of a preteen girl. I require all my wits to stay afloat."

Grace laughed at that. "Give it a few

102

years, my friend. You'll need more than wits."

"Is that knowing laughter I hear as you envision my fall from reason?"

"No, that is pity. Though something tells me you're going to be okay."

"Really? You get that over the phone?"

She did get that, and it was his self-deprecating nature that told her so, and there was something charming about it, accessible. "Yeah, I get that over the phone." Grace turned away from a group of loud businessmen, shielding the phone with her hand.

He laughed, too, listening to voices in the background and wondering just what she had stepped away from to make this call. "Well, *I* get that you are in someplace pretty fancy," he said. "I hear a piano, right?"

"You're good," she said, peering into the bar at her date and all the well-dressed people sitting near the piano. "Yes, I'm in the lobby of the Four Seasons Atlanta, looking at a grand piano."

"Sounds nice." Not for him, he thought, but it still sounded nice.

"It sounds much quieter where you are."

"I'm in the living room of my old farm-house —" He walked to the window and peeled back the checkered curtains. "—

103

looking out at the moon coming up over the orchard."

"That sounds nice," said Grace, much more longingly than she intended.

"It is," he replied softly, pressing his face closer to the window.

There was a long moment of silence as Grace envisioned him standing there, looking out at the moon, and Dylan envisioned her, standing there, elegant people all around. And Dylan wondered just what was so important that she had to call him in the middle of all that. "So this is a phone call that just couldn't wait until the morning?" Dylan stepped away from the window, walking around in the semi-darkness of his house as he spoke to her.

"No, it couldn't," Grace said, turning away from some German tourists and tossing her hair back behind her head in that determined way of hers.

"You get this impassioned about all your fruit?"

"I'm offering you cash, and you're teasing me."

"I'm sorry." He laughed a little, noticing how strangely easy it was to talk to her. "Look, you're much more interesting than the usual telemarketer — and, in fact, thank you for not asking me if I am happy with my local phone provider — but it's late, I've got work, and you've obviously got . . . something."

Grace realized that the call was about to end if she didn't find another tack. "You're a parent," she said quickly. "I'm betting your year and then some is hanging on the trees all around you. Like most farmers, you're probably pretty well leveraged right about now. And it's late in the season. You're probably juggling a few bills, wringing your hands, watching the weather. Praying a little more than usual." She paused for a moment, assessing. "You've got someone offering you a little peace of mind here, but you reject it. Who exactly is the nutty one here?"

He took in her words, knowing she was right. "Yeah, okay," he said quietly. "I'm a little nutty."

"That's okay," she confessed. "Truth be told, so am I."

They laughed a little, and then there was a charged and lingering silence as they suddenly felt very in sync with each other. And at that moment, it occurred to Grace that there had been no mention, no reference, no indication of a woman in this man's house. Perhaps she'd overlooked it, though she was pretty good at picking up subtext, and what she was getting was that this man was alone, very much so. It was the kind of alone others easily overlooked, and that she knew so well, she could pick up on it. Not that any of that was relevant beyond using it to help her get her apple, she told herself.

"Listen, Mr. Culpepper."

"Mr. Jackson. Dylan Jackson."

"Listen, Mr. Dylan Jackson, I think you have something really special, and I'd just like your permission to attach what are basically a few Plexiglas beakers to some of your trees for a week, capture the gases coming off the fruit, and see what we can learn. For science."

"Science?"

"Yes. And commerce. Look, no one is trying to steal your apples. We just want to understand what makes them so wonderful, and then maybe use some of what we learn to replicate certain parts of the flavor in a variety of consumer products. That's what we do at fragrance and flavor companies, such as the Southern Compound Corporation. Is that really so terrible?" Grace listened intently, trying to gauge his response. "Okay, I'll need to get final approval, but I'm confident that I can offer you twenty-five thousand dollars for a week's on-site study."

Again he was silent, holding the phone,

pacing quietly in the dim pools of light in his kitchen. The dishwasher behind him finished its final cycle and went still.

"I hear you breathing again," she said, holding the phone even tighter to her ear, as if that would shorten the distance between them.

"Ma'am, I appreciate your time and your interest — I really do — and I don't mean to be rude, but the answer is no."

Grace *was* an excellent negotiator, and this kind of conversation went against all her business instincts. But losing what she wanted was never a good outcome. "Are you telling me you need more than that offer?" Once again, he said nothing. She hesitated and then went on. "Because I may have some additional room."

"What I am telling you is *no.* You're not someone who hears that word a lot, are you?"

"I hear that word plenty."

"You just don't listen to it."

"Okay, that's fair."

They shared laughter again, but his ended abruptly. "You sound like a very nice person," he said.

"I am, so let me test your apples."

"But some things are not for sale."

The conversation was really taking a turn

into truly uncharted territory for Grace. She looked increasingly uneasy. "I don't understand."

"I think you do. Anyone who digs up flowers in the jungle and calls this late and keeps a man on the phone who doesn't want to be on the phone understands what it means to hold on to something that is deeply important to you. I think you understand, Grace Lyndon from Southern Comp Corp. I think you understand when something is more important than money."

He paused, listening to her sigh, feeling that he wanted to be as sincere with this woman as he possibly could. "It really was a pleasure talking to you, and I wish you all the very best."

Grace searched for words to keep him on the line, but could no longer find any. She was too caught up in his voice.

"And I think you're going to be okay, too," he said.

Then the line went dead.

Phone in hand, Grace stood there by herself, feeling her aloneness quite profoundly in the loud bustling lobby of the Four Seasons Atlanta, and she imagined him standing there by himself in a quiet farmhouse in a moonlit orchard, and though the connection had been severed, it was somehow still there. Perhaps it was his voice lingering in her mind, perhaps it was the apple remaining upon her senses in so many ways, but there was still a connection.

Grace Lyndon did not like the word *no.* She didn't like it as a little girl, and her disdain for the term grew with her into adulthood. To her, it often sounded more like a challenge than like a statement of fact, and she suspected this man knew that about her. Had those goods on her. That was probably why he didn't mince words. His *no* sounded quite clear and unequivocal, and that didn't sit well with her.

Grace remembered the sportscaster and looked up — just as he was leaving the bar. He walked right toward her, with several others alongside him. Whether they were old friends or new friends, she wasn't sure, but they were all having a good time and he clearly was not going to wait around any longer to have a drink with some friend of a friend's wife.

Grace stood there in the lobby, realizing she still had the apple core in her hand, as he headed her way with his newfound entourage. Should she say something? Should she do something?

He walked right up to her, looked her in the eyes, and smiled a bit. He *was* handsome, and interesting looking, and happy, deeply and truly so. She could see it in his eyes.

Grace returned his look, and just when she was about to say something, he turned his head to a woman walking next to him, exchanged a long laugh with her, and moved right past Grace.

As Grace watched him stroll across the lobby, she noticed that he was wearing the most gorgeous Italian calfskin loafers she'd ever seen — square toed, stacked heel, impeccable topstitching. They matched his suit perfectly.

Watching him walk away from her in his beautiful Ferragamos, she was overcome by a sudden and surprising sense of loss. Basically, she'd just lost what looked like a great guy — over an apple core.

CULLY APPLES

A little later that night

Dylan Jackson was not a man of many words, typically. So the conversation he'd just had with this executive on the telephone was not one he could easily shake. It lingered in his ears as he walked down his front porch stairs, across his over grown yard, zipped up his heavy Windbreaker, and picked up the oversized sack of refined clay. He threw the bag over his shoulder and walked out into the orchard, chilled with the late fall air. Big ripe apples bumped him at every turn. It was dark in the orchard, the moonlight obscured now by the mountain fog clambering in, but Dylan had no trouble making his way. He spent the vast majority of his waking hours in this orchard, and having grown up around these apple trees, Dylan Jackson had a sense of nearly every one of them.

Thinking about it, he hadn't exchanged

that many words with another person that weren't about *Where the Red Fern Grows* or soil amendments in what seemed like years. Oh, sure, he'd *listened* to a lot of people talking, partly because he seemed to be very good at that, at paying attention when something was standing near him, but mainly, he felt, because most people were just good at talking. It amazed him sometimes how much a person could be so naturally disposed to unloading his or her perspectives, as though these deeply personal thoughts and emotions were all endless and disposable, something to be spread upon pasture.

So what got into him tonight? What had possessed him to not only stay on the phone but let his own words unfurl as well? It was the sense that for the first time in quite a while, he had understood and been understood. Plus, he assured himself, it wasn't as though he had poured out his heart to a live person — it was just a voice, just a voice on the phone. Like a ghost, or a woman in an elevator who might be a ghost, a voice seemed more appealing to him than a whole person, certainly any whole and present woman he knew. He'd been thinking about ghosts a lot lately.

Dylan stopped in the orchard, the trees

around him ponderous and shifting like beasts in the night, thinking about the disembodied voice of this woman whose body he now imagined. He let it drift about for a moment, searching for clues in her sounds and words, in her sighs and breath, that might create a fuller image of her, conjure her. And as an image began to form, he found himself suddenly standing alone in the dark with a fifty-pound sack on his back, halted. *What am I doing?*

He shook off these thoughts, relocated the heavy bag on his wide shoulders, and moved on with his labor.

A soaking rain had just stopped, and his boots sank deeply into the nitrogen-rich soil. The entire orchard smelled of wet wood and ripe fruit. It was a strong dizzying scent, and nothing else was quite like it — though his grandfather used to say this smell was identical to the limestone caves of Lower Normandy: cold and dripping, where cask upon cask of Calvados, the great fortified apple brandy of Norman lords, slept away the years.

He reached up and examined an especially plump apple hanging on a densely twiggy branch. He watched as a ladybug landed upon a single aphid, which pleased him. The ladybugs that he bred in the orchard were doing their jobs. Then on closer inspection, he noticed that the apple was shiny and clean, which made Dylan shake his head. A clean apple meant that the organic kaolin clay he'd sprayed all over his fruit last week was now washed away. If he harvested now, like most of his neighbors, he'd have no trouble with moths or blight. But the fruit just wasn't quite there yet. He shoved his nose up against the cold wet apple and inhaled deeply. It was close, very close, but not quite perfect. The couple dozen trees on the western side of the orchard that he'd just harvested had hit their peak, but the majority of the trees needed a few more days of sun to get the sugar levels precisely where Dylan felt they should be.

He let the apple drop, the damp leaves rustling back into place, and continued on into the orchard, realizing that he had a lot of work ahead of him. He'd have to go back and get several more bags like the one he had on his shoulder, and that was just the beginning of tonight's work.

Culpepper Farms was a small operation by most standards. Although Dylan had nearly a hundred acres, only twenty were presently planted with actively tended fruit trees. The land had been in his family for generations, passed along through his mother's side, the Culpeppers. For years, along with an extensive variety of seasonal produce, the farm raised livestock and poultry. Narragansett and Bourbon Red turkeys ran free on the back pasture, and folks from all over Gilmer County came to buy them at the Cully place.

But a world war and a depression changed life for a lot of people throughout the Appalachian foothills, and Dylan's grandfather felt that the land would have to produce more than just immediate sustenance and a little extra if the family was to keep it. So, like many people in Gilmer County, Roswell Culpepper planted apple trees. He planted both Rome Beauty and Golden Delicious as saplings, roots balled and burlapped, careful to place the two cultivars near each other in the orchard, as apple trees are self-incompatible, in that a single type will not pollinate itself, no matter how many bees scatter pollen among its blossoms. It takes at least two trees of different varieties to create a productive orchard, and like most farmers in Gilmer County, Ros Culpepper understood this well. *An apple tree is just like a person,* he was fond of saying. In order to thrive, it needs companionship that's similar to it in some ways, but quite different in others. That was how he would often explain, with a chuckle, his love for his wife, a fiery and opinionated Southern woman who often saw things very differently from Ros.

So like his neighbors, Ros planted the two commonly available cultivars with which he was familiar and which he understood. However, along with these, Ros also planted several ancient varieties from seed, culled from fruit on a tree he came upon in a rambling old orchard in Brittany, brought back in his pocket and stored in the root cellar. *Pips from Charlemagne's orchard,* he'd say with a wink. Most people in the region thought Ros was foolish for mixing a handful of strange seeds in with his tried-and-true modern fruit saplings. Growing apple trees by seed is a hit-or-miss proposition at best, because one never knows what will sprout from seed, if anything. It can take hundreds of plants from seed to find just one with promise worthy of a decade's care and costs.

But those mysteries and associated risks did not deter Ros Culpepper. As the Rome Beauty and Golden Delicious root balls took to the ground and grew, most of those strange little pips he carefully sowed never rose or even produced gangly and withered shoots. But over the years, a select few became large and canopied and productive trees. And over the decades, all these various trees, familiar and foreign, shared the fine North Georgia mountain breezes and swapped pollen, and produced some of the sweetest and most complex fruit anyone in Ellijay had ever tasted.

Some said the loamy mountainside soil was responsible for the wonderful apples; others felt it was Roswell's extensive use of manure and other natural fertilizers and control methods. There was a lot of discussion about his centuries-old farming habits, which ran contrary to the new chemical pesticides and insecticides and fungicides being promoted by the Georgia AgEd men, the Agricultural Education specialists who worked out of the corporate-sponsored labs at the university in Athens. But one thing everyone could agree on was that there was something truly special about Ros Culpepper's apples. On a brisk November morning, folks would come in from as far away as Chattanooga to buy a bushel or two. They'd bring their families, piled into the backs of Chevy pickups in canvas shirts and flannel-lined denims, and Dylan's grandmother would serve them warm apple pie on the front porch with a cold can of soda.

When Dylan was a boy, he loved helping

his parents tend the apples. Small work crews would cycle in to help at various parts of the season, but for the most part, the orchard was a family affair. Blossoms in the spring, fruiting in summer, harvest in fall, pruning in winter — there was a cycle in the orchard that was an integral part of Dylan's life as he grew up.

As time went on, little by little, the farm gave up its livestock and much of its poultry and eventually its vegetable produce. These were simply too time intensive for Dylan's aging parents to maintain to their standards, and with a Piggly Wiggly in town, hard to justify on many accounts. The apple orchard remained productive, and tourists still managed to find the old Cully place. Many of the younger day tourists who would come up from Atlanta during harvest had heard about Cully apples from a grandparent. But by the time Dylan went off to college, the larger, more commercial Ellijay orchards, with their petting zoos and faux-country restaurants and trampled U-pick orchards filled with porta-potties, received glowing coverage in regional travel magazines, while the old Cully place was eventually forgotten, its orchard left wild and untended.

That was until Rebecca Jane, the long-haired natural-faced girl who fell in love with the farm and the orchard, not long after falling for Dylan their freshman year at UGA. She was the most beautiful and captivating girl Dylan Jackson had ever seen, and she stole his heart from the very moment he laid eyes on her — and his soul the first time they spoke.

Dylan brought her home from Athens to meet his parents and see the farm, and on a picnic in the orchard one hazy spring day, apple blossoms in full bloom and air thick with their sweet scent, they held hands and planned their future, which Rebecca Jane knew was to include the orchard. She loved the trees and the seasonal cycle of the fruit and the connection it gave her to all that was living and had been living and was to be living, and at the center of this order for her was Dylan. She saw a man who cared for her with the same force that opened the blossoms and bore to them fruit. And a child was born, and rising with the sun, they worked hard every day, six days a week, pruning, fertilizing, eschewing the clouds of chemical sprays and new pesticide pellets and following the same ageless practices that Roswell Culpepper first set forth in the orchard and about which Rebecca Jane was so deeply, spiritually impassioned. Soon, the trees were again neat and orderly, and life with Rebecca Jane, the wholesome young woman in her ripped jeans, long hair flying around carefree in the mountain breeze, was indeed perfect. Until the accident.

Dylan thought about her constantly, every time he heard the screen door slam, and especially on nights like this, with the orchard so full and expectant, harvest so near. Walking among the trees, by himself in the quiet and shadows, Dylan felt as though she were upstairs right now in her forty-second week, warm and waiting, while he kept watch. And the more he thought about it, let the feelings sink in, and as the mist rose through the orchard, he could smell the little trace of soil that was always on her knees and the scent of apple forever in her hair, the scent in their bedroom, her head on the pillow, hair on the sheets. She was there with him tonight, triggered to life, and he could feel the madness rising once again.

The sack of clay on his back grew heavier as he walked on, but he was so lost in the memories that he hardly noticed. He missed her so badly on nights like this that he felt the hurt in his gut like it was filled with hot lead. It was a pain he'd come to know quite well, and it could bring forth the deepest cries of human anguish, contractions of great sorrow that could double over the strongest of men. But to give in to that did nothing, purged not a drop of grief, just useless tears, so he let the madness rattle around and he carried the lead inside, for there was no solace save work. In that, there was comfort. Work in the orchard kept his mind occupied and his body engaged. It brought him closer to her in a way that he could touch.

She loved the orchard as she had loved him, and keeping it was somehow to keep her. To work the soil by hand and implement was to *do* something, to tie and solder unto a thing he could see and touch as each apple grew, even as the thing spun from season to season to season to season. Memories on the mist could end a man, but keeping the orchard alive was somehow to keep her alive.

Dylan would laugh when Rebecca Jane used words like *destiny* and *soul mates*, and she'd tease him and say that their love was so strong and true that nothing could ever keep them apart. So perhaps he really *had* seen her in the elevator at that hotel in Atlanta, where he'd stood on the table and searched for her. Would she really never leave him? Was their love so true that it really could survive anything — even death?

Or was it, indeed, madness?

It had been just short of three years, and nearly everyone he knew thought it was time to let her go, time to move on. Some would say so in soft therapeutic tones, some with exasperation. Others still silent, he could just see it in their eyes.

And as much as it generally annoyed him, the truth was that lately he'd come to understand and even feel what they all believed, and sometimes, during the day, had started even to consider the terms of letting go. That's why, of course, he'd occasionally go out for those coffee dates. And despite how dreadful those were, the conversation with Grace tonight was nothing of the kind. No, to the contrary, it suggested that he could, in fact, still connect with a living person, albeit the mere voice of one.

But in the orchard, in the night, especially when the breeze would blow through the trees, *she* was still with him. How could he ever let her go? Love was energy, the spokes of the universe, and energy never died.

"Good evening, Mr. Dylan!" a stout man up ahead called out, the syllables deepened with a Spanish inflection.

"Good evening, Pablo," said Dylan.

Dylan approached a clearing in the orchard where Pablo and his eleven-year-old son gathered and tied branches that had fallen. Wearing full-body white jumpsuits, hats, and gloves similar to the sort used by commercial food packers, they put the branches into several wood carts near an old but still sturdy John Deere diesel tractor. It had been painted green at one time. Next to the tractor was a fifty-gallon spray rig.

Dylan dropped the heavy bag of kaolin clay in front of the rig.

"The clay is gone from the apples, Mr. Dylan," said Pablo, shaking his head. The polite black-haired boy just watched Dylan, blinking and silent.

"I know."

"You have to harvest."

"Not yet."

"You have to harvest. The moths are here."

"I'm going to spray."

"I can have the men here in the morning. They are finished in the area. Everyone else has harvested." The seasonal workers, Mexicans and Central Americans, mostly, were eager to move on.

"The fruit isn't ready yet, Pablo."

"You risk too much. A storm could come. The blight."

"I'm going to spray."

"You want me to — ?"

"No thank you, Pablo. I can do it."

"It is a lot of work for one man. It will take you all night."

"I can do it. Go home. Peter needs to get to bed. Go have supper. Kiss Gladys for me."

Pablo couldn't really insist, as Dylan was right. It was late, and the boy did need to get to sleep. Pablo yanked the heavy glove off his right hand and shook Dylan's, and the concern was clear in Pablo's eyes, his concern for the fruit, and for Dylan.

"The men leave for the almonds, Mr. Dylan. For California, any day now. You have to harvest."

"*Buenas noches,* my friend."

Pablo knew there was nothing else he could say to persuade Dylan. And he looked worried. "*Buenas noches,* Mr. Dylan."

"Good night, Peter."

"Good night, Mr. Jackson," the boy said, moved by his father's concern for this situation.

Dylan watched Pablo and his son walk off together. When they reached the edge of the orchard, they removed their hats and gloves, unzipped their dirty jumpsuits, and carried them off.

Then Dylan tore open the bag of clay, hoisted it up, and poured it into the opening atop the spray rig. A cloud of the powdered refined clay rose from the rig and the bottom of the sack and covered Dylan from head to foot.

He grabbed a long heavy hose, turned on the nearby spigot, walked back over to the rig, and began to fill it.

Pablo was right: This was going to be a tremendous amount of work for one man, but tonight Dylan had too many ghosts and memories about him — and the mindless work would be a comfort, indeed.

In the Night

A little later that night

Having returned to her car, Grace found herself driving north again, back toward Marietta. Somehow, her car just didn't seem to want to head to her little condo in Buckhead. As usual, there was very little to do there, besides eat, sleep, bathe, dress, or, mainly, think. She envisioned the collection of white containers presently residing in her cherished Sub-Zero, the half-eaten remnants that had been lovely little meals cooked both on and off the menu by her friends at Antica Posta and Bacchanalia and Rathbun's. She considered consolidating them into a dinner, taken with four ounces, the precise amount to fill the appropriate wineglass by one-third, of a nice Côte de Nuits, while sitting alone at her charming bistro café patio set on her seventeenth-floor terrace, where she had the most amazing view of Midtown.

But Grace was wary of the places her mind often wanted to go, especially at night. She preferred to avoid the hinterlands of the past and fill the dark of the night with something that she could control, like the present.

So like a horse heading back to the barn, Grace drove to work. With most commuters home with their families, I-75 was fairly quiet this time of night, and she soon found herself pulling onto the lot at Southern Compounds, a place where she could not only think but also do. She *did* just nail the biggest account of her life, and she'd wasted enough time already. She needed to think through the next steps for Herb Weiss, who she knew was going to be extremely demanding. This was her big break, and yes, the stakes could not be higher and *everyone* was going to be watching. They already were. She had to get real and focus on work, really focus, and for Grace Lyndon, the middle of the night was often her favorite time to do just that.

From the guardhouse at the main entrance, under an imposing brightly lit sign that read SOCOMPCORP, the night security guard waved her into the industrial park. She drove past the large plant area with its manufacturing facilities and vast storage tanks not far from the CSX railroad tracks, past the loading docks where several tractor-trailers were parked, and pulled up to the front of the executive offices. She got out of her car and, with a *beep-beep,* locked it. A visible cloud of steam rose from a long wide pipe protruding from the roof of a large concrete factory-like building nearby, and the air all around was filled with the intensely savory scent of barbecue potato chips, a flavor presently being manufactured in quantity for one of Southern's vendors.

Grace knew that the barbecue scent came from a massive vat of liquefied compounds, which would be cooled and then poured into hundreds of fifty-five-gallon drums in the morning, carefully sealed, loaded onto tractor-trailers, and shipped out, to be warehoused for as long as two years and then, eventually, utilized in the industrial production of billions of pounds of highly processed potato-based snack foods. She knew what she smelled was a by-product from the manufacture of a highly concentrated chemical.

Nevertheless, the scent evoked picnics in the park, bag lunches in elementary school lunchrooms shared over laughter with her dearest friends, long-buried feelings from childhood that rose from her heart.

Grace walked to the front door of the offices, swiped her key card, and the door unlocked and swung open. Inside the executive offices, making her way down the pale limestone-tiled hallways, even more peaceful under the halogen lighting dimmed at night, Grace headed toward her office.

She plunked down into her high-backed swivel chair and popped the Return key at her computer keyboard, bringing the screen to life. Once she found the intranet file that Emma sent to Herb Weiss's assistant, Grace clicked it open and began reading the details regarding the flavor profile for the new beverage line, global fruit-sourcing charts, as well as the calibration information for the MiniVOS — a portable version of the large Virtual Olfactive Synthesizer in Monic's lab, which she had sent to Herb's team. She'd soon be adding various fruit juices to the core flavoring, and not one for surprises, Grace wanted them in the loop.

This was important work, and for the past few weeks was all she thought about — trying to win this account. But after just a few minutes, her mind wandered, back to that apple. She forced herself to refocus, reminding herself that she'd soon have to present again to Herb, and this time, she wasn't going to be able to blow him away with the wave of a few blotters. A great deal more nuts-and-bolts production design would be required. Actual details that she would need to produce.

Grace worked for a little while, but suddenly found herself lost in thought about the conversation with the owner of the apple orchard. *What am I doing? I have to get apples out of my head!* There's crazy and nutty as in cute and quirky, and then there's neurotic, as in obsessive to the point of ruining one's life.

Reaching down to the base of her chair, Grace snapped up the tilt-lock lever and leaned back. She took a deep breath, determined to focus on work — but still, instead of thinking about fruit juice levels and flavor wheels and MiniVOS calibration settings, her mind was filled with this apple, this damned wonderful apple, and the man who had grown it and said no — said no to *her.*

Where exactly did it come from? she wondered. Had he cloned some rootstock from an illegal cultivar? What was it about this apple that was so . . . what? So special, she couldn't stop thinking about it? *So haunting?* An apple that reminded her of . . . what . . . what was it? What kind of man could grow an apple like this? *Who is he?*

Grace recalled his voice, thinking about

the way he drew out words with his slow and steady drawl. There was something confident in his voice, but something sad, too, a distance that she recognized, and the more she thought about it, the more it drew her in. She closed her eyes, remembering, letting his voice sink deep into her, and envisioned him.

It was well after midnight now, and almost unconsciously, Grace found herself standing up and walking out of her office and over to the bowl on Emma's desk, the bowl that had held the apples earlier in the afternoon.

She picked up the big empty wide-rimmed bowl and placed her face in the center of it and inhaled. It still smelled very much of the apples. She took in the scent rising from the empty bowl, ghostly and incorporeal, focusing intensely with all senses — as she knew she should be doing with the new beverage-line work.

Grace put down the bowl and released it. Then she stood there for a long moment, in the quiet and the solitude of this place that was so much a part of her life. She stood there at her assistant's desk among the faint pools of dim halogen light, alone in the building in the middle of the night, captivated by an empty glass bowl before her, the only sound the clock on Emma's desk counting away the precious seconds like a metronome keeping a beat on the fixed rhythm of her life, and she began to shake her head and laugh at herself because she knew that as stupid as it seemed, as much as Monic would criticize her for this, of all the times in her life to be distracted, lured by her senses, there was something she had to do.

She walked into her office and grabbed her bag.

Grace did know that there were some things more important than money. She knew that quite well. But she also knew that most people wanted something, and everyone needed something. She just had to figure out what Dylan Jackson needed that was more important than money.

ELLIJAY

Blue Ridge foothills, North Georgia, just before sunrise

Still in her business suit from the day before, Grace tapped her hands on the steering wheel in rhythm to the country music on the radio. Now that she had made a decision and was out here on the road, she was feeling better, even enough to cut through the grogginess of being up all night. Grace was back in her element, and this was, after all, work. Not the work at hand, perhaps, but whenever you came across a lead on a new flavor, you *had* to go the extra mile. You had to turn over all the stones, because you just never knew when a scent was going to turn out to be entirely novel, maybe even an international blockbuster, and this *could* be just that.

Still, being a rational person by nature, Grace recognized that more than likely, this was probably just some nice apple from some nice mountain apple tree, some local Red Delicious cross. This would just be a night's lost sleep and a day away from other work and an argument with a farmer who would probably end up producing a shotgun before he let her near his apple trees. And she knew that there were other, simpler ways to go about looking into this and other people who could do it — but the little part of her that wasn't totally rational also knew that something was *pulling* her up here to this orchard.

The GPS navigation system on her dashboard began to flash, indicating that she needed to veer left up ahead. She had entered the address of the orchard into the GPS computer before leaving the office lot. The GPS rapidly plotted the best route and was now guiding her. Following the onscreen directions, Grace pulled onto Route 5, which after a mile or so became South Main Street, which took her right into the center of historic downtown Ellijay, set in the Blue Ridge foothills.

Save for the *Times-Courier* delivery truck, the streets surrounding the town square were deserted. A half-dozen or so traffic lights swayed on their wires in the heavy rolling mist, flashing yellow in continuous synchronous motion, strange beacons to those who would visit this silent tucked-away place.

The mist tore like fine gauze as she drove through it along Ellijay Square. To her right, Grace saw a Civil War–era wooden building. The paint was peeling, and some of the windows looked as though they needed some attention, but the building had been cared for over the years and was still in use, perhaps as some kind of a community meeting hall. She slowed to read something that had been posted with chipped plastic letters on a sign in front of the old building: IF YOU'RE STILL ENOUGH, YOU CAN HEAR HIS WHISPER. She thought about that for a moment, her car idling, and then drove on.

To her left, in the center of the square, was a tall slender granite monument surrounded by nearly a dozen American flags, a memorial to those from the city who had lost their lives at war. Symbols and signs of the season — pumpkins and Indian corn and all manner of gourds, community-made harvest decorations — were also evident throughout the city square. A long farm wagon overflowing with hay, presumably used for hayrides, sat parked and vacant in the square. Several bales were stacked next to it, as were a few piles of hay-laden horse droppings. Grace drove by the North Avenue Carriage House and the Perry House, both quaint bed-and-breakfasts in historic wooden structures. She passed several bike shops and river-rapid outfitters and hiking stores, Shane's Rib Shack and the Pink Pig barbecue, and numerous renovated storefronts that now sold antiques from the area. Grace saw signs for the Apple Country Artist and the Apple General Store and Main Street Apple Growers Association.

What Grace did not see, however, were the apples. Following the directions and the virtual roads on her GPS, she took a right on River Street, which soon became Route 52, which took her east and then north, up into the hills, into the orchards, into the area of the North Georgia mountains called Apple Alley.

Driving along the thin, winding two-lane for quite some time, the Cartecay River snaking along below her to the right, the Chattahoochee National Forest towering to her left, Grace began to worry. She should have been there by now. Ellijay was barely an hour or so north of Marietta, where she worked, and the farm couldn't be too far north of that.

Wondering if she'd missed the turn, she pulled off to the shoulder on the right, and the GPS went mad. RECALCULATING flashed over and over on the touch screen until, finally, she pulled back on the road and continued driving. The green arrow again pointed and flashed up into the hills, where there was no turn to make.

Unable to contain her frustration, Grace banged on the touch screen, which of course did nothing, except perhaps confuse the gadget even more. After spinning and weaving from the heat of her fist like a useless drunk, the green arrow recoiled to its former position, once again blinking and pointing into the woods to her left. Well, it sure seemed determined to tell her there was something up there.

Grace looked up and out, peering fixedly through the fog for a road on which to turn, just as an open-bed truck with half a dozen tool-wielding men in the back popped out of the mist and whizzed right by, barely missing her sports sedan. Startled, she gripped the leather-wrapped steering wheel, focusing hard not to cross the double yellow lines.

Where are the apples? Where are all the orchards? Where is this place?

Chilled and vaporous, the air blew down from the hulking mountain to her left in front of her car and flowed over the relatively warm rushing river to her right, giving rise to an even denser mist over the water, which crept back up the embankment and over the road, mixing with the mountain fog from above, the overall effect being that she couldn't see more than a few feet in front of her. It was as though she were inside a cloud — which basically she was. Grace adjusted and readjusted with her headlights, trying various settings, but the beams just bounced off the white soup and reflected back in her face. She leaned forward, over the steering wheel, gripping it tighter, suddenly very much aware that short tight pencil skirts were not designed to be sat in all day and then all night. Uncomfortable, she tugged on and adjusted the skirt.

Driving very slowly by some handmade signs and a few small billboards, Grace could see text and images referencing the nearby apple orchards and the upcoming apple festival. More signs advertised apple pies and apple fritters and apple cider and apple butter and apple picking and all manner of things apple, but despite driving through what the signs around her indicated must be this famed Apple Alley, she couldn't see a single actual apple.

Out of the corner of her eye, she saw a road to her left, and she slowed and turned onto it. It was small and unmarked, worn but paved, and she could see that it wound straight up into the hills. Trusting her instincts, and really simply left with no foreseeable options, she drove on up, the fog growing thicker.

She rolled down the window and was overcome by the cold and the damp and the smell of manure. She looked around for an orchard or a field or some sign of cultivation by human or beast, but in spite of the smell saw none, so she quickly rolled the window back up and looked at the GPS to see if it was finally content with her choice of direction. The green arrow sat at the bottom of the screen, unresponsive, RECALCULATING flashing over and over. But nothing happened. RECALCULATING. She tapped on the touch screen to no avail.

In frustration, she slammed the GPS off, put her foot to the gas, and just drove. The pavement ended, and with a jarring thud, Grace could hear her wheels engage the mud that covered the dirt road.

She pulled over, stopped for a moment, and turned down the radio. Grace assessed the situation: From what she remembered about the GPS map, there were hundreds of square miles of national forest up here, and for all she knew, she was sitting in the middle of it. The gas gauge indicated that she had less than a quarter tank of gas left. She knew the red light would come on very soon and suspected that AAA would have an extremely hard time finding her up here if she ran out of gas. Not that she'd have any way of contacting them, or anyone, as her cell phone had no bars. She tried it anyway, but it was as dead as the green arrow.

With nothing else to do, Grace threw her head back in what she felt was an act of defiance, though she knew *act of stupidity* wasn't far off, and continued up the hill.

She drove on and up for at least a mile, pushing back the urge to turn around. She'd come this far. She'd lost a guy and much of a day's work. She was gonna see this through. Furthermore, she'd trekked into some pretty desolate places. If she could handle New Guinea, she figured she could handle North Georgia.

With a thump, the road softened further, and her sporty low-profile tires spun and dug to find traction, but she kept going, and soon the ground flattened and the road widened and a fence appeared on either side. It was a low split-rail fence of old wood. Able now to see just beyond the hood of her car, Grace realized that the first hints of daylight were emerging. An alabaster glow began to radiate all around her as the rising sun lit the floating mist blanket.

Grace slowly pulled the car over, off to the side of the road, onto a slight grassy rise next to the split-rail fence. She turned off the ignition and stepped out, immediately struck by the cool and the silence. She walked away from the vehicle into the center of the road and looked around. She raised her arms and stretched her back, taking in a deep invigorating breath of air. The muted fog drifting softly by, she stood in a pocket where she could see maybe ten to fifteen feet in all directions.

The road ran straight ahead, disappearing into the clouds. The soil beneath her smelled rich and wet; the only sound in the absolute silence was her breathing. Grace stood still, as still as she possibly could, and listened to the quiet, to the stillness, absorbing the strange beauty. She became aware of her heart beating, pumping blood throughout her body. As she stood here alone at sunrise on this mountain, it was more than dream-like. Accustomed to a world of limestone-tiled hallways lit by tungsten-filament halogen that smelled of artificial lemon and barbecue chemicals and digitized french fry–flavor molecules, Grace felt that she had stumbled into another world. This high peaceful place, it was heavenlike.

She leaned her head forward, certain she was hearing something, something beyond her, a whispering, or a rustling, something coming from beyond the fence to the other side of the road, and Grace turned slowly and listened hard, going motionless, straining, as the wind murmured by and suddenly —

A loud high-pitched chiming sound rang out from the car. Grace jumped! She whipped around — her cell phone was ringing.

A few steps away from the car, her foot sank down deep into a patch of mud, and as she yanked it upward, trying to free herself from the suction, her shoe popped off — she tripped and stumbled and fell into the open driver's side of the car, grabbed the phone, hit the ANSWER key with her thumb, and brought the device to her ear.

"Grace Lyndon," she panted into the phone.

"Grace! Good morning," said Herb Weiss.

Grace's heart skipped a beat. "Good morning, Herb," she said, trying to put on her best business tone, but with her foot in the mud, her body splayed out across the open vehicle, elbows propped up on the driver's seat, she was glad this was not a videophone conversation.

"I got your fax with the sourcing information . . . ," she heard his gruff voice bark out. "I called your office . . . left a message . . . but I have a presentation to the Research Group today, and I *must* . . . vital data . . ."

"Herb, did you say you need something for the presentation?"

". . . that they have to approve . . . Grace?"

"Herb, can you hear me?"

The connection was cutting out. Grace looked at the phone and saw she had only one bar. She tried moving it around, looking for better coverage.

". . . did you hear me? Where are you, Grace?" Herb sounded frustrated.

"I think we have a bad connection."

". . . call you back . . . Where are you?"

Afraid of losing him for good, Grace backed out of the car, searching for better coverage. "You still there, Herb?" After pushing away from the car to hobble with the phone in her hand, Grace whipped off her other shoe and walked barefoot through the cold mud into the middle of the road and over toward the rise on the other side.

"Herb, can you hear me?"

Herb was gone. The call had dropped.

Grace pulled up his number and dialed anxiously, but there was no ringing tone. She walked around, looking at the phone, trying to find a bar, but there was no coverage to be had.

"What am I doing!" she cried out, putting a hand to her head.

"Biggest account of my life, and I'm standing barefoot knee-deep in mud on a frigging mountaintop! This is insane!"

The word *insane* echoed repeatedly in the mist. Her words thrown back at her, she felt taunted by the mountain, and then even more stupid for standing out here yelling at it. She reached out to the split-rail fence before her, holding on to it for balance as she shook the mud from her feet.

Determined to get out of here as fast as possible, back to civilization — where there was not only decent cell phone coverage but also food! — Grace took a resolute step in the direction of the car when she heard that noise again, like whispers, or stifled laughter, rustling, and then a thump. And as she whipped around toward the noise, right in front of her, out of the mist, down a little grassy hill under the split-rail fence, rolled an apple. It came to a stop and lay on a wet clump of weeds before her feet. A large red russeted apple.

Grace looked at it, mystified. Then she looked up. *What's going on here? Is the mountain listening to me?*

She stuck the cell phone in her pocket and picked up the apple.

Then she stared out again over the fence from where the apple had come. "Is someone there?"

No response. Grace cocked her head, listening, but there was only stillness.

Grace rubbed the apple on her blouse, cleaning it a bit, held it to her open mouth, and she took a bite. Her front teeth ripped into the skin and her tongue slipped up into the flesh and her mouth was filled with an explosion of juice and an overwhelming sweet–tart flavor. She chewed and swallowed, closing her eyes for a moment and tilting her head in full focus on the sensual experience.

It was the same taste as the apple from last night. A hint of wet grass and a pinch of dirt on the palate as well, but it was the same kind of apple, the kind she sought.

Continuing to eat the apple out of hand, Grace jumped over the split-rail fence and bounded barefoot up into the mist.

And just a few steps beyond the fence, mud and damp weeds between her toes, she could make out several large dark objects in neat rows, protruding from the gently rolling hillside. Trees. Apple trees, their limbs and shoots piercing the rolling shroud, weighted and wobbling with fat ripened fruit. Grace looked around at the apple orchard, taken with the dizzying scent of mature fruit on the branch.

Not far from where she stood, there were several twenty-foot-high trees, their canopies growing into each other and overlapping. Along with clusters of gold-streaked red apples, matte with dirt and windblown pieces of wild grass, their branches were covered in supple brown green leaves, the tips just beginning to take on brittle reddish tones. Harvest was near. On further examination, Grace could see that it was very near.

Before her time at Givaudan, when she had first gone to France, along with many other travelers in need of food and shelter, Grace picked grapes in the vineyards in Burgundy, and she learned a thing or two about calculating the right harvest time. The Brix, or sugar-to-water, levels of these apples were amazing, much higher than you'd expect from an apple. The longer fruit stayed on the tree, the riper it got and the higher the Brix levels. But it was getting late in the season. It was getting cold. And if a hard freeze or a storm or some unforeseen act of nature came along before these apples were picked, they'd be finished — good for commercial-quality applesauce maybe, or cheap baby food. Grace looked around at the apples, assessing. Yes, someone was pushing his luck.

Underneath these trees, Grace saw scattered piles of fallen fruit, and focusing, she could smell out a hint of their fermenting scent, ciderlike and candied, as they rotted and decomposed. A field mouse, picking through some worm-eaten fruit below one of the trees, heard Grace, stood up and stared at her, and then ran off into a shrubby coppice of blackhaw. The scurrying sound startled Grace, and she dropped the apple from her hand.

Immediately to the right, at the edge of the small hill, Grace turned to the largest tree in sight. It looked a little different from the others. The branches thicker and higher were wonderfully gnarled, twisted with age. Although similar in wood tone and general varietal type, clearly this sturdy old tree had been planted years before the others. Grace walked over to the tree, moving in under its full broad canopy. She ran her hand down the side of the tree's rough trunk, where she saw a long deep black scar. Quite prominent, set against the backdrop of the rolling white fog, it ran ten feet down the base of the tree all the way into the ground, where its roots took to the soil. Fresh bark had begun to grow over the wound, but there was no mistaking the charred marks all around it. The tree had been hit by lightning, and not too long ago. On close examination, below her feet, Grace could even see the earth in the surrounded area was still darkened.

Still, the gorgeous old tree was filled with clusters of plump fruit, even bigger, it seemed, than the ones on the other trees. She reached up into its high branches for an apple. The large knotted limbs were just beyond her fingers, so she stood on her tiptoes, feeling around in the thick screen of leaves for a big apple, and her hand finally found something, and her fingers slipped around it . . . roundish, fleshy, covered in cloth — and in the instant she realized it was a leg, it yanked upward into the tree!

Grace screamed and recoiled.

Several apples fell to the ground, and then the tree was entirely still.

A few steps back now, her heart beating, she peered cautiously up into the tree. It remained silent and motionless. Too much so.

"Hello?" Grace called up into the tree, her voice cracking more than she wanted it to. "Hello? Who's up there?" Startled, Grace truly didn't know whether or not to run. Was this dangerous or just weird? She was tired and hungry and disoriented, but she was sure she had grabbed a leg, and she was pretty sure that leg was still up there — and it was just the two of them out here in what looked like pretty much the middle of nowhere, an orchard in the clouds.

Grace approached the tree warily, images of enchanted forests from childhood books flashing through her head. As she got back under the tree, she looked up, and she could see a pair of girls' shoes, and in them a pair of legs belonging to a ponytailed girl who was standing up on a big bough in the old tree.

"Hi," said Grace, feeling and thinking half a million things but making sure that her voice reflected only friendliness.

"Hi," said Carter.

"I like your Keds," Grace said, offering an easy smile. "Very cool, and I know what I'm talking about when it comes to shoes."

Grace saw the kid peering down at her, specifically at her bare feet.

"Yeah, I — uh, lost mine in the mud," said Grace, suddenly not feeling like the wise adult here.

"I see," said Carter, smiling at the goofy sight of a lady in a business suit with wet muddy feet. Carter carefully assessed this woman. "So what are you doing out here?"

Grace assessed as well. "I was kinda thinking the same thing about you."

"I'm just sitting," said Carter. "You?"

"I'm just looking for apples. This is apple country, right?"

"Kind of early, aren't you?"

"I suppose I am," said Grace, trying to straighten her suit as she felt herself being interviewed.

"And a little off the beaten track," said Carter.

"You don't get a lot of tourists?"

"On a Tuesday at six A.M.? Not so much."

Grace tried to change the subject. "So that looks like a real good tree for sitting."

"It is," said Carter, and then she sat back down.

"This your tree?"

"I adopted it."

"Spend a lot of time here?"

Carter felt the conversation being changed, and she slowed it down, letting her feet sway while she continued studying Grace. Grace felt herself being examined, a curious and unexpected thing coming from a kid.

"So why were you yelling?" asked Carter.

"Because I thought I was lost."

"Are you?"

That was a tough one to answer. "I . . . I don't think so."

"But you're not sure?"

"You ask a lot of questions for a girl in a tree."

"Asking questions is a sign of intelligence."

"I've heard that. Do your parents know you're out here?"

"You ask a lot questions for a lady who looks like she's been up all night."

"Intelligence," Grace said playfully.

"Barefoot in the mud? I dunno. You don't *look* so smart."

Grace had to smile. This kid *was* smart. A bit of an attitude, but sharp. Enjoying Grace's company, Carter returned the smile and, for the first time, in the light, Grace got a really good look at her. She had auburn hair, close in color and form to Grace's, actually, but it was long overdue for a decent cut. She was thin, bony, moving in the lithesome knobby-kneed way of a girl at the inelegant doorstep of puberty, but that and the ill-fitting tomboyish clothes she wore could do little to diminish the

151

hints of the beautiful young woman she would soon become. You could see it in her when she smiled. Someone had passed on striking features to her, but there was something else that Grace saw, in the girl's big anime eyes, something mature beyond her years that seemed familiar to Grace, and immediately brought to mind the vegetable garden of her youth, where she used to sit and think and spend time alone just like this.

Grace saw that Carter was wearing a spring-weight cotton cardigan with eggshell blue flowers embroidered on the pockets. It was dirty and maybe a little small for her, but it was beautifully made. "I like your sweater."

"Thanks. My dad gave it to me." She tucked her hands into the little pockets.

"He's got good taste."

"Yeah. Especially for a dad."

"Yeah." They shared another smile. "Looks kinda light, though. Aren't you cold in just that?" Grace asked caringly.

"I'm good."

Her feet on the cold wet ground, Grace definitely felt a chill. "You really should have on a jacket."

Carter pulled aside a branch with its mass of leaves, revealing a thick woolen stadium blanket embroidered with a pattern of tiny UGAs, the University of Georgia logo that was as ubiquitous in this region as pinecones. Wrapped around the girl's legs, the blanket was worn soft from who knows how many seasons of tailgate outings.

Grace felt movement right next to her toes, and she looked down to see several large field mice. She jumped, and the mice scampered by her bare feet, running for cover in the tall grass. Grace was unable to contain her discomfort.

Carter laughed a little. "Yeah, they're real cute in the movies when they're singing and frolicking and cooking in French restaurants. But in real life, they're kinda freaky."

"I would agree with that."

"We have snakes, too."

"Nice." Grace scanned the grass worriedly.

"Kidding."

"Good," said Grace, relieved.

"Kind of," Carter said, and then broke out in giggles.

"What is this, scare-off-the-tourists day?"

"I'm sorry. I'm just kidding with you." Carter liked this woman. Her initial assessment was that this lady was okay, also a little weird maybe, but she liked that, too. "I thought your yelling was funny. We do have lots of *rabbits* — for real — cottontails, which are kinda cool. They're super fast and shy, but if you sit up here and you're real still, they come out."

"Now, that does sound cool," said Grace, wondering if this was an invitation to go up in the tree.

Carter observed Grace very carefully. She knew that talking to a stranger like this was frowned upon, something discussed repeatedly in school and at home since she could remember. But there was something about this odd barefoot woman in the rumpled suit. She sounded like the grown-ups who lectured her, and loved her, and barefoot and tired-eyed and a little disheveled, she seemed, like them, somehow vulnerable, and it made Carter feel safe.

"So, you wanna come up?" Carter said, her big eyes blinking.

"Yes. Yes, I would, actually."

"You're not gonna start yelling again, are you?"

"No. No more yelling."

Grace stood on her tiptoes and reached for the branches, but she just wasn't tall enough to grab hold.

"Do you know how to climb a tree?"

Grace straightened her posture. "Yes, I know how to climb a tree."

"Okay," Carter said skeptically.

"When I was your age, I practically lived in trees."

Grace grabbed hold of the trunk and began to hoist herself up. After New Guinea, this was gonna be easy.

"No offense, but you're not exactly my age anymore," said Carter, amused with herself.

Grace squinted at Carter. Then she looked at the wet tree trunk, then up at the girl who was holding her hand to her mouth to stifle the laughter. Grace was more than confident she could just climb up the trunk, but having been messed with, she decided to show the girl a little something.

Standing under the tree, she squatted, and then stood up, and then down and up again, and on the third time, she crouched down as far as she could, and throwing all her weight upward, arms reaching completely outstretched, she jumped as hard and as high as she possibly could, springing from the ground, and with both hands grasped the limb upon which the girl sat.

With amusement and curiosity, the girl looked down at Grace dangling below by her hands, exposed feet swinging in the mist. *What is this lady going to do now?*

Shifting her weight, Grace swung herself

forward and then back, and then forward again farther and back again farther, and forward again even more, and as she swung back, throwing her weight firmly, she simultaneously lifted herself upward and as she rose parallel to the limb pushed down on it forcefully and with a quick twist of her hips — *plop* — set herself down right next to the little girl.

"I *know* how to climb a tree," Grace said.

"Impressive," said the little girl as she raised an eyebrow.

Grace grinned, proud of herself.

"Want an apple?" The little girl sounded like she was conferring a prize.

"How'd you guess?"

The little girl reached for a big fat ripe one hanging near her face, yanked it effortlessly off the branch with a *snap,* and handed it to Grace. A droplet of bright fluid bubbled out of the tip of the apple's long stem.

"Thank you," said Grace, and then she bit right in. And, oh, it was fantastic.

"I'm Carter," the kid said.

"Grace," she replied, and extended a sticky hand.

Carter shook it, sticky and all. "You have a pretty name."

"So do you."

"Not like you. *Grace* is the name of a princess or a movie star or, you know, something from heaven. Grace. The fruit of redemption." Carter said it as though repeating something she'd heard many times, which of course she had.

Grace just chewed, her mouth full of apple.

"At least, that's what they say," Carter continued.

"That's what they say." On the backs of Carter's hands Grace could see a few scrapes, the kind kids get from running around in the woods. Grace remembered when the backs of her hands looked just like that.

"*Carter* means 'driver of a cart.' In Old English or something. But everyone thinks of the ex-president from Georgia."

"Well, I didn't."

Carter stared at Grace, blinking, as though looking for something.

"I think it's a beautiful name," said Grace. "It's full of character."

"It was my mother's last name, before she took my dad's. She gave it to me."

"So does your mother know you're out here in a tree at dawn?"

Carter looked away, smiling. "Yeah. Probably." Her smile grew whimsical.

"Probably?"

"Well, she's dead, so of course, I don't rightly know a hundred percent for sure, but knowing my mother, she knows."

"Yeah," said Grace, quietly, soothingly. "I have no doubt she knows. And given you got a nice blanket to keep you warm, I'll bet she's A-okay with it."

Carter liked that. Grace pulled the blanket tighter around Carter's legs, tucking it in around her. Grace could see that Carter liked that, too.

"Your mother a UGA fan?" Grace asked, pointing to the logos on the blanket.

"Oh yeah. Church on Sunday. Sanford Stadium on Saturday. It's where she met my dad. Freshman year in Athens. They sat next to each other at the Alabama game. The Dawgs lost and my mother needed consoling. And the week after graduation, she became Rebecca Jane Carter *Jackson,* queen of Culpepper Farms, home of the best apple in the South."

Grace was pleased to know she had found the right place, but the quest didn't seem quite so important right now. "I lost my mother, too, Carter."

Carter homed in on that. "Really?"

"Yeah. When I was pretty close to the age you are now."

"What happened?"

"She got sick. There was nothing anybody could do."

"Do you still miss her?"

"Yes, I do." Grace's voice broke just a bit. "Yes, I do. When I was little, people told me it would get easier with time, but it doesn't."

"They tell me that, too."

Grace leaned in close to her. "It gets . . . different. As you grow up, you'll always carry it, but in different ways."

"Like how?" The little girl stared intently at Grace.

Grace ran her hand along the rough bark on a branch while she thought about this. "Like you go on with your life and you do things, you accomplish things that are very important to you, and you know she's with you. You know she's proud of you."

After a moment, Carter looked away, and Grace watched as the little girl processed it.

Then Carter's gaze settled on Grace's bare feet — where the girl noticed a small but pronounced semicircular scar on the bottom of Grace's right foot. Carter pointed to it. "What happened?"

Grace looked at the scar. "See, this is precisely why you shouldn't go barefoot." Remembering, she started to laugh. "One summer when I was very little, younger than you are now, I stepped on a pull tab."

"A pull what?"

Again, Grace laughed, realizing the kid had no more idea about this than she did about vinyl records. "It was a piece of metal you tore off the top of a can to open it. It was very sharp. They stopped making them because, well, for one thing, kids ran around in the summertime and stepped on them." Grace looked off as she spoke, recalling the childhood memory.

Carter nodded, and then, peering at Grace's exposed foot, realized the woman must be cold. "Here," the girl said, peeling off some of the blanket. "You should put your feet in."

Grace simply looked at her for a moment, truly touched by the gesture, and then moved in closer to Carter and slipped her feet in next to the girl.

The mist blowing below them, they sat together in the apple tree as though it were a boat bobbing in the middle of a vast white sea.

Finally, Grace saw something rising on the horizon, over the neat rows of treetops — a small beige cloud — and she broke the quiet. "What is that?" Grace said, lifting her head to see it better.

"*That* is my dad."

Carter reached for a branch above her head, grabbed it, and, steadying herself, stood up. Grace followed her, and the two of them looked out at the little cloud in the distance.

"He's spraying the apples with clay," Carter explained. "He'll be out there for a while. He has to do it every time it rains, which is *a lot.* Everybody else covers the apples with bug spray a couple times in the summer and that's it, but not my dad. Everything has to be 'organic.' " She said the word teasingly while making quotation marks with her fingers, as though she'd heard it quite often. "Most everyone else has pulled their apples already, but not us. He waits for the exact right time. Not too soon. Not too late. Has to be perfect."

Grace nodded, getting it. "Good time to just sit in a tree, huh?"

Feeling understood, Carter nodded and smiled.

They sat back down, together in the quiet, and Carter stared at Grace's bare foot again.

"Funny," said Grace, "I haven't thought about that scar in a very long time." Grace looked off again. "I remember collecting those tabs. Then I'd sit outside of where we lived in an old lawn chair, plastic web over aluminum tube, by myself, and link them together, tab after tab into a long chain."

"Look," whispered Carter, pointing at the ground. Grace looked, and sure enough, a couple dozen long-eared rabbits of all different sizes scurried along under the tree, a moving, hopping gray white carpet of them, nibbling on the high green grass and milkweed.

Carter watched Grace, the two of them sharing this moment just after dawn, and Carter could suddenly see the younger version of Grace sitting alone in an old lawn chair as she had described. Then Carter remembered something, too. "I want to show you something," Carter said. "Come on."

And with that, Carter whipped off the blanket and jumped out of the tree, bending her legs and landing like a kid who knew how to jump out of an apple tree.

The rabbits ran off and Grace followed suit, landing just as nimbly right next to Carter.

Carter headed off into the orchard, motioning for Grace to follow, and the two of them strode off in the clearing mist, apple trees all around, the light of the new day fully upon them.

"So, you're not really out here because you're a tourist, are you?"

"You're a smart girl, Carter. Smart girl."
Grace patted Carter on the back as they continued on.

Carter and Grace tromped way down the sloping hillside, out of the orchard, and headed toward the house. It was a classic white Victorian with a massive wraparound porch that grew larger and larger as Grace and Carter approached it.

"You want to test our apples?" Carter asked.

"I want to find out what makes them taste so special so that we can share that with other people, maybe lots of them." Grace saw Carter's perplexed expression. "You ever had a fruit-flavored soft drink?"

"Like an orange soda?"

"Exactly. Well, somebody found the perfect orange somewhere, studied it carefully, and then made a formula based on its special flavor so that anyone anywhere in the world could taste it."

"In a can of soda."

"Right."

"Very cool."

"Do you like peach ice cream?"

"Yes!"

"Well, a lot of the 'all-natural peach flavoring' that you taste in that ice cream is really Gamma-Aldehyde C-14, a molecule created by Nanjing Yuance Trade Company, which I'm sure is based on a perfect peach they found somewhere."

"So you're like a scientist-cook," Carter said excitedly.

"Something like that." Grace smiled.

"Very cool. Did you have to go to college for that? My dad talks about college *a lot.*"

"College is a very good thing, Carter. I highly recommend it when you're older."

"Did you go to UGA, too?"

"No." Grace paused for a moment as she was once again tripped up by that detail in her past. What was one more little white lie? It was harmless, and promoting the notion of college was nothing but a good cause. "I went to Agnes Scott College, but I did my work training at a company called Givaudan in France."

"Why did you go to France? Is that what you studied at college?"

"Yes," Grace said flatly. There was more to it, of course, but Grace couldn't explain it any better.

From the distance, as they approached along the mud-laden driveway — split-rail fence and rows of apple trees on either side — the home was magnificent, almost fantastical in its bygone-era splendor.

But as they got closer, Grace could see the details: Discolored white paint could be seen peeling like river birch bark in several places along the fine porch millwork and on some trim pieces along the extra-large sash windows. A couple of ornamental brackets under the highly detailed eaves looked as though they'd been through more than a few memorable storms over the years. A few of the slate shingles on the round tower part of the roof could use a straightening, and one of the spindles on the front porch railing was in obvious need of repair.

But despite these blemishes — in fact, because of them — the house had a charm that was true and apparent. Standing near, you could feel it as though the house were a living, breathing thing. This was not a showplace, not some B&B to be featured in *Southern Living* magazine, its enduring craftsmanship and meticulous preservation detailed in rambling prose, product placement for some trendy new vintage paint line. No, with its nicks and bruises, this hundred-year-old house was a home, and just as the families that had lived here weathered the winds of life, so did this structure. Its framing and support beams and internal workings were solid. The important things, they were all there.

Carter and Grace stood together on the rambling overgrown lawn in front of the house, the long gravel driveway winding off into the distance through the apple orchard behind them. Grace looked around, taking in the big rocking chairs along the front porch, their backs worn smooth from years of use. The house sat in the middle of the orchard, and off to the left near the trees she saw a large wooden shed, in front of which sat a sturdy old John Deere diesel tractor and numerous wooden carts. Along with the scent of ripe fruit and the rich damp loam all around them, Grace smelled freshly cut hay and a faint barnyard note. It reminded her very much of the vineyards of Burgundy on harvest morning. A rooster cackled nearby.

The morning chill really getting to her now, Grace couldn't stop from shivering. Carter noticed.

"Just a sec," Carter said.

And while Grace stood there before the house, Carter ran up the front steps, bolted across the front porch, opened the front door, and dashed in. She returned a moment later with a clean, warm pair of women's hiking boots, some thick wool socks, and a small towel.

She handed them to Grace, who smiled and very gratefully took them. "Thank you, Carter."

Grace sat on the front steps, wiped her feet, put on the heavy socks, and slipped on and laced up the full-grain-leather lug sole boots. They fit well — she was a 7 1/2 Narrow and these were a 7 1/2 Regular, but they were close. Didn't do much for her rumpled suit, but who cared? Her feet feeling wonderful, Grace stood, and a warmth radiated up into her entire body. Okay, now *these* were great shoes. They reminded her of the boots she wore in New Guinea, which got her into the jungle and up that tree, and they reminded her how much she missed that kind of fieldwork.

"Come on," said Carter, and with a nod of her head to the right, she began walking toward a massive red wood barn, the apple barn.

Constructed of long hardwood planks and cladding on a classic American barn frame, high multigabled roof, huge open sliding doors on both sides that were big enough to drive a tractor in, the big barn had been painted McIntosh red decades ago. Like all apple orchards with commercial intent, the barn's primary purpose was for storing the fruit. Kept cold, though not frozen, and protected from sunlight and harsh elements, apples could be stored for months in these barns; many hardy thick-skinned varieties would keep well into late spring.

The sun at their backs, they walked through the big open east-facing door, designed to let the rising sunlight into the barn to keep the apples warm through short winter days.

"This is where we keep the apples," said Carter. "And other things!" Carter ran in and Grace followed.

Inside, Grace marveled at the size and spaciousness of the empty barn. Along with the bright sun that poured in from the east door, shafts of light shot through numerous openings between wood planks, purposefully increasing the circulation within. Tiny pieces of dust and dry grass rose from the hay-covered floor and danced up through the streaks of light. The telltale scent of season upon season of apple harvests persisted in the lumber of the old barn, a smell that she suspected was always here, as enduring as the very earth below.

Carter ran through the barn, heading for

a storage area in the far back corner. She looked as comfortable here as any kid in her own backyard. Carter disappeared into the shadows and Grace followed, walking by small piles of Halloween decorations, presumably put back here for storage.

This back part of the barn was filled with an assortment of old items, bric-a-brac, many of them rusty and dusty, some ridden with cobwebs. Several pieces that Grace could see surely looked like junk and gim-crack. Other items she suspected, after a little cleaning and polish, would fetch top dollar in one of the many antique stores in downtown Ellijay. Next to a vintage Coca-Cola vending machine, probably from the 1940s, a rusting wagon wheel, a big section of an old barn roof, cracked and insolated, that had SEE ROCK CITY painted on it, and an oversized wooden chicken, wedged behind a beautiful antique wooden bureau partially covered in a moth-eaten bedsheet, Carter found an old wood barrel. She removed a big box of yellowing newspapers from the top of the barrel and threw it down to the ground.

"What do you have back there?" asked Grace, amused as she approached.

"I've been playing in here my whole life." Carter reached her hand into the top of the open barrel. "And I always wondered what this was."

"What's that?" Grace leaned over the barrel.

"This." And Carter pulled out a long chain of pull tabs, the metal pop-top pieces yanked from countless old soda can tops.

"Is this what you were talking about?" asked Carter.

"I can't believe you have this!" said Grace, laughing. "Yes, this is exactly what I was talking about. I haven't seen one of these in years."

Together, Grace and Carter leaned over the barrel and saw a massive seemingly endless chain, pop-top after pop-top, linked together and filling much of the barrel. They reached their hands in and began pulling it out.

Grace felt like a little kid again as she laughed and tugged at the chain, feeling all the small metal pieces in her hands while she yanked it out of the barrel.

"Let's see how long it is!" Carter squealed.

"Okay!"

Pop-top chain in her hands, Grace jogged backwards, pulling the chain out of the barrel, the metal tabs clinking and jangling like holiday bells as the chain poured out.

"Keep going!" yelled Carter as she leaned

over the barrel, seeing there was still much left. "Keep going!"

And Grace did, awash with memories of those summers spent outside, a little girl alone making these chains, a time so long ago filled now with ghosts that seemed all around her. Passing by a life-size scarecrow, his body bursting with hay and his sewn-on face greeting her, she continued pulling on the chain — *clink, clink, jingle, jingle* — it popped out of the barrel and slithered along the floor. Scooting around a cracked terra-cotta jack-o'-lantern, kicking the ribs of a lanky clay skeleton, out into the middle of the barn Grace went with the chain flowing from her hands — *clink, clink, jingle, jingle.* Skipping clumsily in her tight skirt, oblivious of the hay in her hair, she felt like a kid again — *jingle, jingle,* she tripped and fell, but she didn't care. She got up laughing, her suit jacket dusty and askew, wrapping some of the chain around her neck, it bounced against her silk blouse as she ran faster, giddy with this fun, when out of the corner of her eye she saw something move, moving toward her, and it startled her, and she turned, and through the big east door of the barn, a figure strode in, directly toward her, backlit by the stunningly bright light pouring into the barn behind him.

Grace froze. Clinking pop-top chains swinging from her hands, she just stood there, still, and looked at him.

He was covered, literally covered, from head to foot with light gray clay. His boots, jeans, belt, flannel shirt rolled up at the sleeves, his skin, all thick with dry kaolin like a figure who'd just stepped from the doors of an open kiln. Flecks fell from him as he moved.

As he continued coming toward her, his form tall and steady, cutting precisely into the brilliant light and throwing a long shadow before it, Grace tried to make out his face, but there was nothing to make out. The sun directly behind him, features masked with dry clay, he seemed imagined and unreal, but he kept walking straight at her, slowly, methodically, a pair of black high-heel shoes hanging by their straps from the fingers of his right hand.

Grace stood speechless as he walked right up to her, silt rising between them. She was a woman who had faced off with some of the most powerful men in America and remained unflustered, but this man gave her all kinds of butterflies.

He stopped before her and spoke. "Wow, you weren't kidding. You really don't listen when people say no."

And from his voice, Grace knew immediately it was him, the man on the telephone. "Hello, Dylan Jackson," she said confidently, raising her chin so she could see better into his eyes.

"Hello, Grace from Southern Comp Corp," he replied just as evenly.

Grace had felt more than a little trepidation about just how she would be received, but at that moment, hearing the way he said her name, she knew it was going to be okay.

"You're not gonna turn a shotgun on me now, are you?" she asked with a hint of a grin.

"Haven't decided yet."

She laughed a bit, in that same warm and open way she had last night on the phone.

Perhaps it was her playful, easy nature with him, perhaps the way he got a sense of her last night, but he was much happier to see her than he would have expected. Dylan considered her, examined her, and she let him, holding his glance when he returned to her eyes. Her hair a disaster, rumpled-up designer business dress, a pair of someone else's hiking boots, and a chain of old soda pop-tops wrapped around her neck like play jewelry, none of this could hide the fact that she was lovely — actually, more than that. She was captivating in a way that made his heart speed up involuntarily. *Can she notice?* He hadn't had these kinds of thoughts about a woman, at least a living, breathing one right before him, for some time, and he was suddenly aware of that — and the clump of feelings that came with that. Yes, there was something about her, meeting and holding his gaze, despite her general state of dishevelment — in fact, because of it, and because she didn't seem to care about it — that not only made Dylan notice how naturally beautiful she was, but also made him like her.

"Well, you have a lovely farm," she said.

"Thank you, and it looks like we're both wearing much of it."

Grace pulled some hay out of her hair, noting what a mess *he* was. "Yes, isn't the idea to cover the *fruit* with the clay?"

"This helps me bond with my apples. You know, feel what they feel."

"How's that working out for you?"

"Itchy, actually. Kinda itchy to be an apple."

"You know there are women in Buckhead who pay big money for treatments not unlike that."

"I can hook you up."

"Thanks, but I'm good with the hay and the dirt. And actually already had my share of the mud this morning, too."

"Yes, I've seen. These your shoes?" he asked, holding up her mud-encrusted heels.

"Yes," she said, watching him, and as he leaned a little closer to her with the shoes, she could see deep into his eyes. They stood out like pools of clear water on a desertscape, and they continued to focus intently on her.

"My grandfather used to say you can tell a lot about people by their shoes." Dylan raised them a little more. Her black pumps dangled before her by their straps from two of his long mud-crusted fingers.

"What can you tell about me?"

"That you wore the wrong shoes to come to an apple orchard."

She smiled a little, as he was right, of course. A streak of light playing on his face, he smiled, too.

Without ever looking away from his eyes, she took her shoes from his hand. "Thank you."

Then his gaze traveled down her again, stopping at her feet, at the boots she wore, and she watched him looking at them, watched him take in the sight. She had wondered if the boots had belonged to *her,* and now she was fairly sure, and she had no idea how he was going to respond or what he was going to do right now.

Grace leaned forward, studying him up close, able to make out some of his facial features in the clay mask: strong brow, broad cheekbones, prominent jawline and chin. As a flavorist, she was familiar with kaolin clay, a virtually tasteless edible mineral often used as an anti-caking agent in processed foods, various toothpastes, and originally in kaopectate. But she'd never encountered the raw product out of the lab, and certainly not like this. She leaned closer to him.

He smelled of sediment and mostly sweat, a decidedly masculine note, the precise replication of which one could base an entire career, and then some. Even the most skilled perfumers in the world, experts in the animal secrets of civet and ambergris, couldn't get it just right. It was a human thing. And she'd studied it, androstadienone and most of the known male pheromones, and she knew the effects certain concentrates could have on certain women. She'd written the reports and seen the CT scans of activity in women's brains. Still, knowing about it intellectually and rationally did not in any way lessen what it was doing to her right now, the effect it was having on her senses and her body. *Can he tell?* she wondered.

Lean and broad-shouldered, he had the build of a man who spent his days using his body in labor. She could see it in the way the mud set into the ridged musculature of his forearms, like the russeting across a firm apple. Still, the inner details of him escaped her. His hair was caked with dry clay, and she thought of the figures she'd seen artists craft in their hillside studios in Montmartre, with the Sacré-Coeur church on the summit above and the bawdy Moulin Rouge crowds teeming below. He looked like that, an unglazed unfinished sculpture of a man, but for his eyes, vast and deep, and very much alive, as if he were trapped inside his statued body.

He looked back up and right at her, and what she saw, she was certain of it, was a man on the edge of something, a man who walked carefully and steadily so as not to chip or crack through, as though he were, indeed, made of clay.

"Have you two met before?" Carter asked, both amused and confused by the attention these two seemed to be paying each other.

Both of them immediately turned — hay falling from Grace, clay falling from Dylan — to find Carter standing next to them.

"We spoke on the phone," Grace said.

"Oh," said Carter, processing that.

"Last night," added Dylan.

"Oh," she repeated, wondering if she was missing something here, but liking what she was seeing.

Then Dylan absorbed more of the scene in the barn. "Carter, were you back in the barn? You know you're not supposed to be playing back there."

"I know," she said sheepishly.

"My daughter is extremely willful and doesn't listen to me half the time," he said to Grace, lightly but also reprimanding.

"I'm sorry, Daddy," Carter said.

"She is also very thoughtful." He looked at the boots Grace had on her feet, then back up at her, offering a tacit approval, which Grace was relieved to hear.

"Daddy, Grace wants to study the apples."

Dylan nodded slowly, focusing on a section of the pull tab chain in Carter's hand, too. "Have *you two* met before?"

"A little earlier," said Grace, noticing Carter widening her eyes, trying to tell Grace not to say too much more. "Yes, Carter was showing me the rabbits."

"Were you out in the tree again, Carter?"

Carter shrugged guiltily, for the second time so far that morning.

Dylan let that go as his eye followed the pop-top chain along the floor to Grace, then back to Carter, noticing the chain flowing between them as though they were somehow linked by it, and that thought seemed to soften him. He reached out and touched some of the chain from around Grace's neck.

"I haven't seen this in years," he said. "Some of the pop-tops must be several decades old. People used to come here from all over the country to buy apples, and they'd often get a piece of pie and soft drink, and they'd toss their pop-tops from the can into that barrel. It used to sit out in front of the porch. Carter, when your mother was pregnant with you, she would sit on the front porch while I worked the orchard and make long chains from those pop-tops. For months, belly growing bigger, she'd just sit out there in her rocking chair, by herself, and link those things. I'd forgotten about that."

Smiling and running her hands lightly down the chain, Carter loved hearing about this.

Realizing this would be a good time to focus on her agenda, Grace spoke up. "I was hoping we might be able to revisit our conversation from last night."

"Not that I don't kind of admire your lunacy, but I think I was pretty clear."

"There are shades of clear."

"You're relentless."

Carter knew that word, as it had been used on her more than a few times. This, of course, made her want to help Grace even more.

"So again," Dylan went on, "while it has been an unexpected pleasure to meet you, it's really time —"

"— for breakfast!" Carter blurted out.

"Pardon me?" Dylan said.

"I need breakfast before school, and Grace is actually a real cook."

Now Grace widened her eyes at Carter, who returned the look with a *go with me here* face, none of which was lost on Dylan, who had already picked up on the little friendship between these two.

"Grace trained in France."

"Well, yes, that's true," Grace said, tucking some hair behind her ear.

"And she could totally cook us breakfast."

"I could," Grace stated flatly, though it was really more of a question. "Yes, I could," she said more firmly.

As much as he liked their apparent bond, Dylan wasn't so sure about this. "I have no doubt that would be very nice, but —"

"C'mon, Dad, when was the last time you had a good meal?"

"Carter, Ms. Lyndon really didn't drive all this way to cook for us."

"I'd love to," said Grace.

"And you need to get off to school," said Dylan.

"And what better way than with a full stomach," said Carter.

"Well, there's nothing really to cook," said Dylan.

"Pablo brought some of Myra's sausages yesterday."

"Yes, but —"

"And we have eggs!"

Her energy was hard to fight.

"I can do amazing things with eggs," said Grace confidently.

"You two are wearing me down," he said, shaking his head. Then he turned to Grace. "Eggs, huh?"

"I think I can handle that. You have coffee?"

"Coffee I got."

"Good, coffee I need."

Dylan thought about all this, looking from girl to woman and back again.

"C'mon, Dad," pleaded Carter with a very sweet smile.

He was too tired to fight. "Okay. You run

and go get ready for school."

"Okay!" Carter ran off, and Grace and Dylan walked together out of the barn behind her.

"Bet when you were calling from the Four Seasons last night, you didn't figure you'd be up in the mountains at dawn cooking eggs," Dylan said.

"No, I didn't. But that's okay." Grace smiled to herself. "I'm recalculating."

He wasn't quite sure what that meant, but by the expression she had on her face, he was pretty sure it meant something.

As they stepped out of the barn and into the day, Dylan began walking away from the house.

"Aren't you going to take me to the kitchen?"

Dylan stopped, looked at her, and then broke into a huge grin, so big that a big chunk of clay cracked and fell off his face.

"What?" asked Grace.

A Country Breakfast

Grace stuck her hands into hay next to the rear end of a very large and particularly ornery chicken. The chicken clucked loudly at Grace, annoyed at this intruder who was disturbing the henhouse.

"Sorry," Grace said to the chicken as she picked eggs from the hay and placed them into a basket she carried.

The eggs were brown and spotted and uneven in size, very different from the perfect white ones produced by the millions of commercial fowl in great numbers for her fast-food clients. In fact, looking at these various tan-colored eggs lying in the hay with all their spots and slight imperfections, those millions of perfect white eggs she saw on factory tours seemed to have been pressed out of a machine, as if too perfect to have been made by nature.

In fact, those factory tours had much to do with Grace's penchant for shopping at

Whole Foods and the like. She loved reading the pretty labels above her fruits and vegetables and meats that described from where the food had come and even showed pictures of smiling farmers and their clean happy animals on nearby farms. Yes, she very much believed in the farm-to-table philosophy. But it was very clear to her right now that Whole Foods or the occasional trip to the Piedmont Farmers Market was about as close as she really got to the farm. The farm in fact smelled a bit more . . . lively than the grocery store. There was very little space between farm and table here, and this was more than a philosophy. This was chicken's butt to table.

Keeping her head down so as not to bump it in the low-roofed wood-and-wire structure, Grace moved on to another pile of hay and began gathering eggs and placing them in the basket. Several chickens scrambled over to her feet and started clucking at her. She jumped a few steps back. They stared at her in an accusatory fashion, and she wondered if they somehow knew that she worked for the company that was developing a special sauce for a major chicken franchise.

Her basket full of eggs, she darted out of the chicken house and into the fenced-in grassy area around it that allowed the chickens to roam freely. Careful not to let them out, she opened the wood-and-wire gate and made off with the basket of eggs.

On her way back to the house, taking in the rambling beauty of the mountain farm on this clear damp morning, she noticed a small cleared plot off to her left, set into a loose grove of wild pines, with several old tombstones. Curious, she walked over to it. Basket still in hand, she peered over the peeling low white fence and read the headstones. She saw the hand-chiseled granite stones of Roswell and Sarah Culpepper, who — judging from the dates — were Dylan's grandparents. She saw Dunbar and Martha Culpepper, great-grandparents. There was a very small stone 1911–1918, a Spanish flu victim Grace surmised, and that made her heart sink a bit. And there were a couple that dated back to the Civil War. What there was not was one for *her.*

Grace returned to the meandering dirt path that led to the house, the air around her clean and crisp. Crunching across the wind-tossed piles of dry ruby and gold leaves, swinging the basket of eggs, Grace approached several Narragansett heritage turkeys and their poults as they stood in her way on the path, all fussing at her. Undomesticated, they were small and colorful and feisty. She glared at them, facing off with them — if she could handle Herb Weiss, she thought, she could handle free-range poultry — and after a moment, they moved aside. Feeling rather empowered, Grace ambled on toward the farmhouse, swinging the basket in her hand.

The kitchen smelled amazing. Turkey-apple sausage sizzled in a blackened iron skillet on the sturdy old eight-burner gas range. Thick slices of bread toasted in a shiny vintage Toastmaster. Hair tied back, sleeves rolled up on her blouse, apron around her waist, Grace tossed a handful of pecans into the skillet and let them brown with the sausage while she flipped a cheddar-filled omelet in another pan. The heady aroma of freshly ground black dark-roast coffee filled the kitchen.

"Ugh! Why do I need to know Pre-Algebra?" complained Carter as she sat at the long farmhouse kitchen table, doing her homework and eating an omelet. Over her faded jeans and heavy cotton sweater, she wore a fluorescent orange Junior Safety Patrol belt and shoulder strap.

"Well, aside from the practical reasons, math helps you develop logical thinking," said Grace.

"I *am* thinking logically. There's no logical reason I could need to know this stuff!"

Grace laughed as they heard a voice from the next room. "How about you need to know this stuff because if you don't get a decent grade on your next test, you're losing computer privileges," Dylan said as he walked in.

"Okay, that's a logical reason," said Carter.

Grace looked up from her cooking and couldn't hide her double take. She was surprised by the sight of him. He was barefoot, in dryer-warm jeans and a clean flannel shirt, shower fresh, his damp dark hair neatly combed back, and for the first time she could see what he really looked like. The strong features and bone structure of the vigorous man covered in clay were all there, but she also saw a kindness, a gentleness, in his face, and it was striking.

"You need to get going, honey," he said, walking over to her and kissing her on the head.

Carter glanced up at the old wall rooster clock and realized he was right. "Yes, sir," she said, simultaneously springing out of her seat and taking one final huge bite of her breakfast, then packing her homework into a green backpack.

Dylan ambled over to the stove, standing next to Grace, peeking at what was cooking. "Smells good in here."

Grace peered up at him — even when he was barefoot, she still had to — and really took in his eyes again. In the bright kitchen light, she could that they were deep and brown, and soulful.

"I found some things in your pantry," she said, working the eggs with a spatula. "Hope you don't mind."

"I don't mind." He looked around, soaking up the image of the brown eggs on the rustic granite slab counter before him and the open sack of pecans and a chunk of plated butter and a beautiful woman, standing in the middle of it all.

Grace tried to focus on her cooking, but his presence next to her was distracting. She leaned over for some butter on the counter, just out of her reach.

"Let me help you," he said, going for the butter.

She turned and they bumped into each other, the palm of his hand brushing against her hip.

"Sorry," said Dylan, pulling his hand away.

His clean skin had a sweet earthy scent, like ripe roasted breadfruit, or warm oiled saddle leather. It was an evocative fragrance that rambled through her blood, at once comforting and licentious.

"All you can help me with is sitting yourself down." She motioned with her head to the table, and he saw that it had been set. A jar of peach preserves sat near his plate. He'd forgotten all about that jar and was thrilled to see it.

Dylan smiled, backed away, letting her do her thing. He was nothing short of ravenous. He pulled out one of the worn but well-made ladder-back chairs and sat, watching Grace. He remembered watching his wife cook right there. She would look at him and carry on entire conversations while simultaneously cracking eggs over a hot skillet. That always amazed him how she could do that, crack the eggs without looking. Such a little thing then, but now it actually seemed so big.

Grace knew he was watching her, and while she wondered very much what he was thinking, she continued cooking away, surprised by how entirely comfortable she felt working in this country kitchen. How different it was from the lab kitchens.

Noting the time on the wall clock, Carter popped her math book and another book on the table, *Sarah, Plain and Tall,* into her backpack, zipped it, yanked it up, and shot across the kitchen to Grace. "Thank you *so* much for breakfast, Grace."

"Thank you for showing me around, Carter. It was fun meeting you."

"Hope to see you again soon." She said it to both of them as she bolted for the door.

"Coat," said Dylan.

Carter rolled her eyes and grabbed a coat.

"Kiss," he said, tilting his cheek toward her.

She walked over and gave him a peck.

"Capital of Michigan."

"Lansing."

"Ratio of the circumference of a circle."

"Dad!"

"Ratio of —"

"Pi." She rolled her eyes and he lifted a fist. She raised hers and bumped fists with him.

"Go, little safety patrol."

And she smiled and ran off.

Dylan raised his head and watched her through the window as she ran up the driveway, amazed, as he often was, with her level of energy.

"She's a great kid," said Grace.

"She's her mother."

"I see a lot of someone else in there, too." Grace said it softly, watching him watch his daughter go.

Grace brought the pot of coffee to the table, and he instinctively rose to help her. "Sit," she said.

"You sure? I'm not used to this sort of thing."

"I'm a very successful career woman. I'm very secure serving a man," Grace said as she poured him some coffee. "Especially when I have an agenda."

He couldn't help but laugh.

She poured herself some coffee as well, set the pot down, and began plating their meal. "Those apples sure look ripe, Dylan. The Brix levels must be through the roof right about now."

"They have a ways to go still." He watched her every move as she served the meal.

"You think? Skin has good color. Flesh is firm. What kind of readings are you getting on the refractometer?"

Dylan just stared at her, impressed with her knowledge, as she set a full plate in front of him. "You sure know a lot about fruit farming for a woman who drives a European sports sedan."

"Food is my business. Well, the taste of food. And before I did my formal training, I worked in Burgundy, in the vineyards."

"They don't use refractometers in Burgundy."

"No, they don't," she said, now staring at him, impressed. "They taste."

"As do I. Every day as harvest approaches."

"You sure know a lot about Burgundy for a man who works on a farm in Georgia."

She put a plate of food down for herself and sat, and through the steam coming off the warm eggs, Dylan got another chance to really look at her, and everything he'd heard in her voice last night, the way he'd pictured her, it all made sense. Grace had pulled back her hair and rolled up her sleeves and jumped right into things. She must've thrown some water on her face because her skin was clean and smooth, her entire face, ears, full lips, long neck, the top of her chest, so fresh, her skin seemed to glow. And he remembered what her body felt like in the brief instant that he touched her hip a few moments ago, the rounded top of her hip where it began to curve off and away from her small waist, and how it had sent a charge into him, and though he'd pulled his hand away, the feeling of her body was still there, as was its effect. It had been three years since he had put his hand on a woman like that, accidental or not.

"France," he said, forcing his mind back on topic. "It's all second-hand knowledge, trust me. My grandfather loved France. Spent time there for the government on an agricultural trade mission before the war. The old man loved wine, loved the whole process in the vineyard. He brought a lot of what he saw in France into the orchard."

"No refractometer. Your neighbors must think you're a bit kooky."

"They want a device to tell them when to pick, which I understand. But the laws of science can go only so far. At some point, you have to just taste. You have to close your eyes and smell and taste and, ultimately, you have to just go with that. Sound kooky?"

"Yeah. Sure it does. But I understand."

"Yeah?"

"Hey, remember, you're talking to someone who just drove into the mountains in the middle of the night to see about an apple."

Sitting across from Dylan, Grace realized that he was politely waiting for her to start eating. She could see that he was dying to dig in, and the food smelled *so* good, its aroma filling the entire room.

"I'm sorry," she said. "I'm so used to putting flavors in front of people and waiting for a response."

Then she picked up her fork and knife and began to eat. As hungry as she was, Grace forced herself to cut small pieces of the cheese omelet and eat slowly.

Dylan took a big bite of turkey-apple sausage with a roasted pecan. "This is good," he said with food still in his mouth. He swallowed. "Okay, this is really good." He wiped his lips with the napkin on his lap, reminding himself to use the good table manners he was always trying to teach his daughter. But then he shoveled in several more bites, hunger getting the better of him, eating like a man who'd been doing hard work all night and hadn't had a meal like this in a very long time.

She loved watching him eat, as she always loved watching someone enjoy her flavors. But this was also very different. She could hear him breathing and making involuntarily sounds of enjoyment while he chewed and swallowed. It was primal, and she was intrigued, watching him lose control and give in to that.

He looked up, embarrassed at how quickly and passionately he was eating. "Sorry," he said.

"No, don't be," she said sincerely.

"I'm really hungry, and this is really good," Dylan said, trying to slow down and be a bit more civil.

Grace swallowed a mouthful of sausage and egg and immediately followed it by taking a big tearing bite out of a hunk of buttered toast smeared with peach preserves. "Wow, this *is* really good." Grace was having the same trouble slowing down.

He was thoroughly enjoying the sight of a woman eating with such abandon. "When was the last time *you* ate?" he asked.

"Feels like a century ago."

"I hear you."

Then she made a gut decision and looked right at him. "You know what? Let's just eat, okay?"

"Just eat?"

"Can we just do that? Just eat for enjoyment, like we would if we were alone and not trying to be polite. I mean, I'm really hungry and you are, too."

"Sounds great to me." And he picked up his buttered peach-smeared toast and bit off a huge delicious bite. "If you ask me, politeness is highly overrated," he said with a mouthful of food.

"Yeah, politeness is for tea at the Four Seasons," she said, shoveling in a forkful of eggs.

Dylan cracked up laughing. "Here, you need more preserves."

"Yes, I suppose I do."

He slid the canning jar of peach preserves down the table to her like he was sliding a beer down a bar top, and she caught it in her hand and whipped off the top, scooping out a heaping spoonful of the super-sweet preserves, which she plopped onto her toast.

After sniffing blotters and sipping from test tubes and subsisting off obsessively arranged vegetables at the Whole Foods salad bar, Grace reveled in this hearty, wholesome, fattening meal. She reveled in eating food instead of thinking about it.

And Dylan watched her eat, delighted, fascinated.

After breakfast, Dylan cleared the table.

"Let me help you," Grace said, jumping up from her seat.

"You can help me by sitting," he said, motioning for her to sit. "More coffee?"

"Yes, thank you," she said as she sat back down. "You make mighty fine coffee."

"Well, coming from such a highly renowned taste expert, that's quite a compliment."

She leaned back in her seat, allowing herself to enjoy being served as he poured her more coffee, but also noting again the scent of his clean hair as he leaned over her.

"So you learned to cook in France?" he asked, removing the rest of the dishes and flatware from the table and putting them in the sink.

"Well, I think Carter was stretching things a bit."

"Yeah, she likes to do that."

"I trained at Givaudan, the big flavor and fragrance company in France. I started in the Perfumery School."

"Really?" This was fascinating. "You went to school to learn to make perfume?"

"Well, fine fragrance is just one application for those skills. Someone put a great deal of work into the scent of that Redken product you washed your hair with this morning."

"How did you know — ?"

"That's what I do, Dylan."

He nodded as he absorbed this interesting new knowledge. "How do you get into this kind of school? Is math involved? I could use that with my daughter."

She laughed. "It's not easy. Givaundan really has one of the only formal programs in the world. Only two or three people are admitted every year, and very few of them are Americans."

"But you were admitted."

"The woman who owned the vineyard

where I was working at the time was fanatical about biodynamic viticulture, which I was, too. She took a liking to me and made some calls."

Grace did not say that one of the other reasons she was admitted was because she was highly talented, but Dylan was wise enough to have picked that up already.

"How'd you end up in Marietta?"

"I was offered a position with a lot of responsibility, a chance to work on fragrance *and* flavor, a chance to really do something with my career."

"Like focus on Georgia apples," he said, turning from the sink with laughter in his eyes, but with a questioning tone, too.

And Grace knew it was time to discuss business. "I know I must've come on a bit strong last night. But I meant everything I said."

Dylan sat down, feeling that she deserved some kind of explanation. "A few years ago, the Hendergill Company came through and did some tests on a few of my neighbors' orchards. Based on that data, it developed a new genetically modified sapling suited for North Georgia orchards that was able to survive ActiKill sprayings. ActiKill decimates the curcilio apple weevil *and* it also happens to be made by Hendergill. So not only does the company get paid when it sells farmers hundreds of millions of gallons of its toxic insecticide, but it also gets a 'technology fee' for every one of its genetically engineered trees that produces fruit, which several of my neighbors planted."

Grace nodded, understanding perfectly. "So you might own the land, but you plant a Hendergill sapling, you're working for them."

"Exactly. And it gets worse. One buddy of mine refused to plant the new saplings because he was opposed to paying the fee, but the wind blew some other orchard's Hendergill tree pollen into his trees, and his fruit became ActiKill tolerant, among other odd things, and the real kicker is that now Hendergill is suing him because it says whether the wind blew the pollen or not, he owes them for their work, which is showing up on his apples."

Grace furrowed her eyebrows, and Dylan saw the authentic disgust on her face. "So when some representative from some company calls you and makes you an offer to test your apples, your instinct is to hang up on her."

"Yes, ma'am."

Grace already knew enough about this man to detect from his intonation that there was more to it. "I understand your concern, I really do. But you strike me as someone who's a pretty good judge of character, and I think you know that I'm not the Hendergill Company or one of its evil minions."

Dylan nodded, exhaling deeply. Of course, she was right. "There's more," he admitted, taking a moment to find his thoughts. It was difficult to explain, and he wasn't even sure that he could. But looking at Grace, he truly felt that he wanted to try. "I lost my wife about three years ago."

"Carter told me. I'm sorry," she said with deep sincerity, seeing in his eyes just how painful this was for him.

He nodded. "She loved this orchard, cherished it, so much so that it was a part of her. And still is. And the idea of selling off what's special about the orchard . . . I don't know, it just doesn't sit right with me."

Grace found her most gentle tone. "Because you don't want to let her go."

He closed his eyes for a brief moment as the truth in her words settled. It was one thing to know that truth in his head; it was another to hear it spoken aloud.

She leaned closer to him. "Dylan, you share the apples with the public, right? So you let her go every time you do that. You share her and what she loved so much about

201

this wonderful place every time someone bites into one of your apples. I think there's something beautiful about that."

Again, he nodded. "I know. And it makes me happy because I know it would have made her happy."

"Maybe she would've liked what I do."

Dylan gazed at Grace, really thinking about all of this for quite some time. "Tell me more about what you do," he said.

"We study ideal creations in nature, capture and record their design, and use that as a template to re-create their flavor. Like you said, the laws of science can go only so far. At some point, only nature can create something as perfect as the scent and taste of an apple. So my job is to go out and get that design."

Listening to her talk about her work, Dylan understood even more about Grace Lyndon and what drove her.

Sensing his interest, she went on. "So in your case, we would hang a few instruments, take some measurements, and create a genetic map of your apples. Then we'd use that information as a starting point to develop a variety of new flavors and scents that could end up in yogurt or pastries or shampoo, in any number of wonderful flavors and scents that people all over the world could enjoy."

She leaned forward even more. "I want to use your apples as a sort of mother for a new apple design," she said.

"The Eve of apple flavoring," he said a bit whimsically.

"I think that's a beautiful way to look at it," she said, genuinely feeling this way.

Dylan smiled, and leaned back in his chair. "I think she would've liked that."

"It's a really special apple, Dylan," she said, wanting him to know that she understood him. "A really special orchard."

He looked off, out the window where he could see the early sun warming the fruit trees. "Even after working out there all morning, she would take her lunch back out and eat it in the orchard. It was her favorite place in the world. She had this long thick hair, and she'd spend so much time out there that her hair often had the scent of apple in it."

"That's a good scent," she said softly, knowingly.

"She lived in the orchard, and she died there." He paused for a moment to allow in the memory. "She was out jogging and a storm came in, and on her way back, lightning hit a big apple tree just off the driveway. The current shot through the wet ground."

He paused, processing the memory, and Grace immediately knew which tree he was talking about. She wondered if he knew that his daughter liked to sit in it.

"I think she would've liked the idea of the apples touching so many people," he said with a slight nod. "She believed in the connectedness of things, that everything was somehow tied together. She'd say that there was a reason a Cully apple got into your hands." Dylan grinned a bit at the idea. "What do you think?"

"What do *I* think? Well, quite honestly, I've never been one to believe in things like that, so considering my agenda, I think that's a trick question."

They laughed together, and Grace noticed what a warm and deep smile he had. She imagined him sitting here going over schoolwork with Carter, and laughing with her just like this. This was a really great guy, Grace thought, who'd been through something horrible.

"What do *you* think, Dylan?"

"Well, in truth, I think about this more than I care to admit, and I guess the conclusion I've come to is that I have no idea if there's a reason things happen. I mean, I've never been one to believe that coincidences happen for a reason, never really bought into the whole idea of destiny —"

"— Me neither."

"— But who really knows? Maybe you're here because something unseen pulled you, or maybe because you're just good at your job. I have no idea." He thought for a moment about something he was champing at the bit to share, and figured, *Why not?* It felt right. "You want to hear something that's *really* nutty?"

"Please."

"I haven't told this to anyone."

"I love conversations that start with that," she said with a grin.

She was so easy to talk to, Dylan thought, and then he paused, pulling up the recollection. "Last spring, I was in Atlanta and I had lunch at the Peachtree Plaza Hotel, upstairs, at the Sun Dial."

"Know it well."

Dylan jumped up, still barefoot, and walked to the nearby coat closet while he continued talking. "And in the elevator, on the way down, I think I saw her."

"Who?" she asked nervously.

"I think, I mean, I could swear with certainty that I saw my wife."

Dylan reached up on the high top shelf in the closet and from the far back retrieved the red scarf. He carried it with him back over to the table and sat.

Grace remained quiet and let the man talk.

"She was standing in the front of the elevator, wearing this scarf. I couldn't get a direct look at her, because I was in the back of the elevator and it was packed, but I saw enough."

"You really think it was her?"

"I told you this one was really off the charts."

"So what did you do?"

"Tried to get to her. Tried to reach her. But the elevator was filled with people and all their packages and luggage and I couldn't get near her. It was maddening. When the elevator finally stopped, I ran after her. But before I got to her, I noticed that she'd left her scarf, which I went back to get — just as the damn elevator doors closed. By the time I got back down, she was gone."

"Why didn't you just call out her name?"

"I know! I ask myself that every single day. I kick myself for not doing it when she was right in front of me, just a few feet away, but I guess I wasn't completely sure at the time. And the thing is, I still don't know if I'm completely sure, but I swear to you — I am not sure that it *wasn't* her."

Grace took a deep breath, and then responded softly. "You know, Dylan, a lot of people would say that this was simply a man wanting his wife to be alive so badly that he wished her so."

"I know, I know. And I think that myself half the time. Makes the most sense, of course, right? And this is why I haven't told anyone else."

He leaned across the table, in close to her, and she saw in his eyes that he was not, in fact, a madman and he really believed what he was saying.

"Except there was this moment," he said. "This one moment, when I was in the elevator shooting upward and I looked out the glass into the lobby and she was standing there, looking up, looking straight at me. I saw her and she saw me and . . ." He trailed off.

"And what?"

"And we connected."

For a brief moment, Grace could feel the emotions that he must have had and must still be experiencing, and then she was hit with the sheer craziness of it. "Can you really recognize someone from that distance in a moving elevator?"

"At the time, I thought for sure that I did, but now . . . like I said, I just don't know."

207

He looked up, and Grace plainly saw that this was a man who hadn't spoken to anyone in the way he was now in a very long time. He was a man who needed to reach out.

He looked at Grace intently. "She used to say that what we had would always be there, that it was everlasting. That it was destined."

Listening to him, watching him, Grace saw that this was not just a man who had lost someone dear to him. He had lost someone, but he wasn't sure she was gone. And at that moment, Grace really understood why he held the orchard so close, and she understood his torment, what was haunting him.

"And you think, what? Her ghost came to see you in a hotel elevator?"

"I don't know. What *is* a ghost?"

"You got me."

"The thing is, she didn't look like a ghost," he said, revealing just how reasonable it seemed to him.

"So you think she's out there now? Somewhere out there?" she asked, her voice soft but direct.

"I don't know."

"Reincarnated? Or just walking around, waiting for you to find her?"

"Grace, *I don't know.* Look, you took a bite of an apple and it had an effect on you. I saw a woman in an elevator, and I can't stop thinking about her. I'd like to find out — one way or another — who this person is, or what this is, if anything, but all I have is a scarf. She had a carry-on bag with her, and she was on her way out of the hotel, so I don't even know what city she lives in or, for that matter, what country!" He held up the scarf and pointed to the label. "A red Burberry scarf made of cashmere. Do you know how many stores sell this scarf? Well, I've checked, and it's a lot — a lot more than does me any good."

Grace reached out and took the scarf, feeling it, studying it. "Well, whoever this mystery woman is," Grace said, "she has very good taste." Then Grace held the scarf to her cheek to feel the material, and almost immediately, a smile began to grow on her face. "Did your wife wear perfume, Dylan?"

"Yeah," he said with a slight nod, knowing what she was getting at. "I noticed a very faint perfume on the scarf. She never wore anything like that, but I'm pretty sure she would have loved it. *I* think it's amazing."

"Of course you do," said Grace, holding out the scarf before her with both hands. "This is Clive Christian Number One. It's one of my favorite fragrances, and one of the most exquisite. It's made from entirely

209

pure ingredients, mainly natural aged sandalwood from India and Tahitian vanilla, but a lot of the other ingredients — the ones that produce the fine top notes — they change slightly every year, depending on availability and the perfumers' preference."

Using her skills, she smelled the scarf. "Pineapple, plum, mirabelle, and peach, heart notes of jasmine, ylang ylang, orris, and carnation, I'm betting this is the '08."

"Where are you going with this?" he asked, enjoying her excitement.

"Don't you see? Not only does the formula change every year, but each batch has certain markings based on precisely which ingredients were used and with the proper knowledge and equipment and access all of that can be detected and traced, and there are very few places to get this fragrance. It's costly and rare. I think just their boutiques and Saks." Her mind raced. "I could help you narrow your search, to a city and even a certain retailer, and maybe when it was purchased. That won't give you her phone number, but it could help you fill in some blanks, find another place where she might have been, or . . ."

"Or what?"

"Or where someone else she knows was."

Grace watched Dylan consider that, the

210

idea that someone could have purchased something as intimate as perfume for this ghost-woman he thought was his wife, and Grace was amazed at what an unconsidered idea this seemed to be to him, but he digested the notion. And while he did, something else occurred to Grace, something she realized was very obvious.

"You know, there are Web sites people use to find each other."

"Really?" This didn't surprise Dylan. It was simply out of his regular purview, not something typically employed by the people he knew in Ellijay. "Do they work?"

"Did for my friend's college roommate."

"What're these sites?"

"There's a bunch. Every city has some. 'Missed Connections' I think is the one she used. Actually, we could get the information about the perfume, maybe find out where it was purchased, and then you'd know at least which city or cities to look in. My friend can help you post, too. She pretty much lives for this sort of thing."

"Do you really think this woman would be spending her time regularly reading a particular Web site, looking for some guy she exchanged a glance with in an elevator a year and a half ago?"

"Oh, I'm sorry, are we applying logic here?

Because then we'd have to have a serious conversation about the whole ghost matter."

Dylan laughed a bit.

"I think I can help, Dylan. Whether she's out there or looking, that's another thing."

"Well, it sounds like we both have something the other wants," he said.

"Yes, I suppose we do."

Again, they shared a little laugh. This was certainly not the kind of negotiation Grace was expecting when she drove up here. Nor did she expect to truly enjoy herself this much.

"So what do you say, Grace from Southern Comp Corp, some info on a scarf and twenty-five grand for some info on some apples?"

"You drive a hard bargain, Mr. Dylan Jackson. But okay." She grinned and extended her hand, at right about the same time he was extending his, and she took it. And they shook hands for a long moment, looking into each other's eyes, connecting. Then they let go.

"But we have to do it soon," Grace said. "Because in order to capture these particular flavors, we have to get the fruit while it's still on the tree. And with all due respect to your gut instinct, *my* gut instinct says that you don't have a lot of time left this season."

"Feel free to start as soon as you like."

"Okay." Grace rose, the scarf in her hands.

"C'mon, I'll walk you to your car."

Grace remembered something. "Oh, let me give you back the boots."

"You know what? You hang on to them and bring 'em back next time. You can't be walking around here in those heels, and we certainly can't have you barefoot out there."

"Thank you, Dylan," Grace said quietly, wanting to say more.

He walked with her to the door, which he opened for her, along with the screen door, which he was careful not to let slam as he closed it, and they walked out onto the porch and into the bright clean day.

She'd gotten what she came for. Grace didn't take no for an answer, and she'd won. She'd figured out what it seemed Dylan Jackson wanted, and she was happy about that. Still, as she stood there on the porch looking at him, she seemed very much like a woman who was missing something.

"When I was a kid," he said, "I used to run around this place barefoot, until I stepped on one of those pop-tops. I have a semicircular scar, big one, on my heel."

A hand on the doorframe for support, he lifted up one of his feet and pointed. She stopped, looked, seeing the little scar that was virtually identical to the one on *her* foot.

She stared at him.

"What?" he asked.

Grace didn't respond. She just threw her head back in that way of hers, tossing her hair behind her as the breeze hit her face.

SKYPE AND SODA

Marietta, Georgia, a few hours later
Head up, shoulders back, showered and changed for a new day at work, Grace marched rapidly down the tiled hall. Turning a corner, she encountered the smell of fried chicken. One of the test kitchens had been working on a new product for a fast-food client, developing a proprietary sauce for a new kind of sandwich to compete with one KFC had recently brought to market. It had no bun, but rather two pressed chicken segments deep-fried in a shortening of processed lard and beef fat, wrapped around thick shingled bacon and a slice of provolone, and smothered in this hydrogenated oil-based sauce. The kitchen was in another part of the building and the cooking had ceased hours ago, but this was a smell that lingered.

Grace continued on, increasing her pace as she approached the Product Development office suites.

Emma saw her coming, grabbed the folder she'd prepared, and jumped up from her desk to meet her boss. "They're waiting for you in the conference room," said Emma with an anxious tone.

"Thank you, Emma," Grace replied calmly in her *everything is under control* tone. Grace grabbed the folder without stopping, moved by Emma's desk and into her open office.

"You made the *Atlanta Business Chronicle*."

Grace turned and saw that Emma was holding open the morning copy of the Southern business trade paper, and it featured a very stiff corporate picture of Grace in a dark business suit, taupe blouse, and pearls. Grace leaned in to the picture where she saw herself on the "Movers & Shakers" page, headlining a story about how she'd brought Herb Weiss's billion-dollar beverage business to Atlanta. As rushed as she was, Grace couldn't help but stop for a breath and savor the moment.

"I like that picture," Emma said.

"Liar."

"Well, I love the article. Way to go, Ms. Lyndon. Way to go."

"Thank you, Emma," Grace said, uncharacteristically beaming as she threw her coat and shoulder bag on the sofa and quickly headed out of her office.

As she was walking away, she saw Patrick, the young lawyer, briefcase in hand, coming toward her.

"Hello, Grace," he said with much more reserve than he had yesterday morning.

"Hi, Patrick. Off to a meeting." She nodded at him politely, threw her head back Grace-like as ever, and continued on her way. She didn't want to be rude, but she simply could not be slowed, especially not right now. She had to focus.

Emma watched, wondering why Grace couldn't be a bit more cheerful to such a nice guy.

"Hi," Emma said to him, smiling brightly in her boss's departure.

"Good morning, Emma," Patrick said, returning her smile.

Marching down the hall, Grace opened the folder in her hands, zipped through the information on the sheets inside, and then came across a greeting card envelope. She tore it open, rapidly scanning a card with printed words that said: MY HEART IS IN THE WORK. — ANDREW CARNEGIE. Written on the inside in pen was, *Way to go, Ms. Lyndon! Congrats! Emma*

Grace smiled for a brief instant and then tucked the card away.

Herb Weiss's massive smooth head filled the six-foot-diameter projection screen on the wall in the conference room. It was the first thing Grace saw as she threw open the big doors and walked into the room, suddenly feeling like Dorothy taking audience with the Wizard.

"We don't like it," Herb declared on the screen. "I don't like it."

"What's the problem, Herb?" asked Grace, making a conscious decision to slow and deepen her breathing.

Having been alone in the room with the Wizard for several minutes now, Bill turned to face Grace, very much relieved that she was here.

"If you'd taken my calls this morning, you would know," Herb said, leaning in to the camera, filling the screen with his big balky face.

"I'm sorry we got cut off, and then I was out of range." Grace decided it was more powerful *not* to point out that he was after all calling at 6 A.M. "Anyway, I'm taking your call now. What's the problem?"

Bill witnessed the frustration building in Herb's face, and he jumped in before things got out of hand. "Herb and his team are getting bumped by the flavor profile re-created by the MiniVOS when they mix your formula design with the fruit juice data you sent them to try."

Herb jumped in to clarify. "We're getting *bumped* because this perfect flavor you cre-ated for us was one thing in a little bottle down there in your conference room, and something entirely different up here when we add the juice bases."

"Did you calibrate the MiniVOS?" Grace was composed, speaking patiently, almost as though she were talking to a child.

Herb turned and barked out over his shoulder, "Jonah, did we calibrate the Mini-VOS?"

Grace opened the file that Emma gave her and read some notations. A young man's mumbled voice could be heard off the screen, and then Herb's big face returned.

His tone was much more polite, contrite even, at least by Herb Weiss standards. "We didn't calibrate the MiniVOS."

"The digital settings were all sent to you last night, Herb." Grace went out of her way not to mention the poor assistant by name. The young man to whom Emma had sent the setting information had overlooked the e-mail attachment and was certainly about to have a very bad day.

"We'll call you back," said Herb, and the screen went black.

She had a way of handling this top CEO — this bear of a man who was so well known for being petulant and demanding — that was nothing short of remarkable. It made Bill nervous to see her go toe to toe with Herb Weiss, but it also impressed him. Herb was unaccustomed to anyone standing up to him, and for better or worse, the real truth of it was that he was certainly unaccustomed to a young woman standing up to him. However, the kind of resolve and firmness Grace displayed gave Herb confidence in his suppliers. And Bill knew that this was precisely what a man like Herb Weiss needed more than anything. Herb Weiss might demand deference, but what he really wanted was someone who knew what she was talking about and someone who was self-assured enough in her work to look him in the eye and tell him when he was wrong.

Bill leaned back in the plush leather chair and took a very deep breath. "We missed you this morning, Grace."

"I know." The *I'm sorry* was implied.

"Everything okay?" The *Where the hell were you?* was implied.

220

"Of course. Very much so. I was doing some work, something very interesting and promising that I want to talk to you about."

"Is this a new project?" he asked. *How could she be thinking about another project?*

"It is," she said, working to sound certain of herself.

"Grace, we reassigned everything else you were on so you could focus on the Weiss business. What are you doing?" His voice was purposely even, engaged into control mode.

"This won't in any way interfere with the new beverage flavor, but it's something that I thought you'd want to know about. It's something really special, Bill."

Bill looked worried and confused by this entirely unexpected development. *Really, what is going on?* he wondered.

But before he could find out, the screen came back to life, and there was Herb.

"An error was made by one of my staff, and it has been duly rectified," Herb said, his deep voice loud and measured as it came in over the conference room speakers. "We're calibrating the machine, and we very much look forward to trying your core flavor with the juice flavors later in the day."

"Gee, that sounds like an apology, Herb," said Grace sarcastically.

Poor Bill Rice literally put his head in his hands.

Herb just stared at her. And Grace stared back.

Then Herb turned to Bill, and Grace could see that this gruff CEO was fighting a smile. "I like this one, Rice," Herb said. "You be sure to keep her happy."

"That's my plan," Bill said with relief.

Then Herb turned to Grace. "How's that for an apology, young lady?"

"I like it," she said, returning his smile.

Sensing that everything was now okay, Bill joined in on the smiling.

"Oh, and one more thing, miss. Do you know huckleberry?"

"I know huckleberry," said Grace, playing along with wherever this was going.

"Do you know Cole Thomas?"

"Yeah, I know Cole Thomas." Boy, did she. Grace lit up. "Sous at El Bulli, came up under Keller, and he just opened a new restaurant in Buckhead, which I'm dying to get into."

"Well, Queen Weiss and I are big fans. We eat at his Chicago place whenever we're in town. I am particularly fond of what he does with huckleberry, which I strongly feel we should be investigating for one of our flavors."

"We can talk about that," said Grace, the flavor wheel already spinning in her mind.

"Good, and as I'd like to talk to someone who is informed, I want you to go to his place in Atlanta and see what you make of the huckleberry sorbet. He's obviously mixing other flavors. Rhubarb, maybe? I can't get a straight answer, or any information about his suppliers. So I would very much appreciate your expertise here. I am increasingly certain that if anyone can get to the bottom of this, it's you."

"Well, thank you for the vote of confidence, Herb, and it would be my pleasure to see what he's doing, believe me, but I hear you can't get into that place until next spring. Even if you know people."

"How's tonight?"

"Tonight?" Was he serious?

"I know people who know people," he said with a wink, and clapped his hands once emphatically. "So, good. I'll have a reservation made for a party of two there tonight at seven."

"Well, great!" said Bill, looking from Herb to Grace and back again. "That sounds great."

Before she could respond, Herb went on with something that grabbed Grace's attention. "Bill, I trust you will brief your team on the input we got from Research?"

Grace glared at Bill as he nodded to the screen. "Yes, I'll take care of it."

"What input?" asked Grace, immediately concerned.

"Well, you all have a mighty fine day down there in Dixie," said Herb blithely. And the screen went black.

"What input?" asked Grace as she turned to Bill, jumping on this information.

Bill took a deep breath, readying himself for how this was going to be taken. "They want to sweeten the line with HFCS, Grace."

Grace took a moment to make sure she was hearing this correctly. "What are you talking about?"

"Their Research Group presented some very compelling testing that supports a strong consumer preference in this particular demographic to HFCS-enhanced beverages."

"That's insane. Aside from the fact that the right fruit juice alone can make it sweet enough, people are specifically *avoiding* high-fructose corn syrup drinks. C'mon, Bill, that's the whole point of this new line!"

"The point is to sell soft drinks."

"And people are buying healthier ones."

"They're buying ones that taste good, and

if they think they're healthy, they buy more."

"Well, I say we conduct our own research. This sounds fishy."

"They feel their results are conclusive," he said emphatically.

"Well, it's our job to tell them when they're making a mistake. Right?" She wasn't backing down.

"Grace —"

"HFCS on the label is *contrary* to the image of the brand!"

"People don't read labels, and you know that."

"Well, you know what? I don't think we're giving them enough credit."

"Well, Herb Weiss doesn't care what you think about this."

Grace opened her mouth, about to take major issue with that statement.

"Grace," said Bill, firmly cutting her off. "Why do you think I'm giving you this news and not him? Think about it."

She did, and her face registered her frustration.

"His research says his demo wants a sweeter-tasting drink in healthier-looking packaging," Bill said. "And we're gonna deliver that to our client as requested. It's not a subject for debate, and putting your foot down is career suicide. There's a line.

There's always a line. And this is it. I will stand behind you, you know I will, but you cross this line, Grace, I can't go over it with you."

Finally, having absorbed and accepted this, Grace sighed. "So let them use a little cane sugar."

"They have a strategic relationship with American Corn Refiners, and they can sweeten with HFCS for a tenth of the cost of sugar."

"Right," she said, shaking her head, getting it. "And a fifth of the cost of increasing the fruit juice ratio."

Bill just stared at her.

"*That's* what this is about," she went on. "Money."

"Of course that's what this is about."

Grace swung her chair away from Bill and stared at the wall. She couldn't refute any of what her boss was telling her, and she knew it. "You know what bugs me the most," she said. "HFCS just ruins the taste of something that could be really wonderful."

"People like HFCS, Grace," he said gently.

"What people? A dozen Red Bull–slurping college freshmen paid to sit in a room with a one-way mirror for a couple hours?"

"The people who bought your work. *They*

226

like it. The people who are paying us a billion dollars."

Again, knowing he was right, she was silent.

He measured her, his concern growing. "Grace, this is everything you've worked for. This is why you left France, for this kind of shot, and you took it and you made it. But I need to know that you're up for this. Are you?"

She leaned into the table. He was right, of course. This was why she had come here, for this kind of commercial opportunity. She was getting what she wanted.

"Yes, I'm up for it," she said with her most confident voice. "You bet I'm up for it."

Bill looked relieved, but not entirely. He knew her very well, and he needed to hear more. "Grace, I know flavorists are protective of their work. Hell, I wouldn't trust one who wasn't. But even if they want to sweeten it a little, the client loves what you created for them — *bought it in the room* — and in our business, that is a slam dunk."

"I know."

Bill swiveled in his chair, thinking, assessing, and then smiled. "You know what? It's time for me to tell you a story. I'm the boss, and it's in my purview to tell stories when I think they are warranted. And I think one is warranted."

"I love stories," she said, leaning back in her chair, lightening up a bit. "Does this one have a happy ending?"

"Depends on your perspective," he said, swiveling in his chair a little as he spoke. "Several years ago, I finally agreed to take a much-needed and long overdue vacation with the family. Christmas week, gray freezing weather here in Atlanta, I took the family down to Cozumel."

"Very nice."

"Yes, it was. Great place right on the picture-perfect beach, clear blue Gulf waters, and seven straight days of warm beautiful sunshine. Well, on the first night, I figured we'd get out of the hotel and drive into town and have an authentic meal. So I pile the family in the rental car and we drove into town, and we got a bit lost on the little back alleys, but that was great because we came upon this little restaurant filled with locals. Jimmy's Tacos. It was a hole in the wall, thatched roof, dirt floor. No one spoke a word of English, which was fine with us. It was an adventure. There was no menu, and we just ordered the fish tacos that everyone in the place was eating, and after my wife and I had polished off an iced bucket of Coronitas, the meal came out.

Well, let me tell you, these were the greatest tacos I'd ever had, any of us had ever had. It wasn't just the fresh fish, there was this spice, a cilantro-something mixture that just stayed in your mouth and memory like a thing that you dream about. Which we did. I was a bit of a hero, having found that place. So the next day, while everyone was hanging out on the beach, I drove back into town to get a few bags of Jimmy's Tacos for lunch. But I couldn't find the place. I drove up and down the winding little back alleys for several hours. I asked people in my broken Spanish. But it was like the place never existed. My wife was annoyed I was gone all day and told me to forget about it. But I couldn't. I had been a hero. To my wife, my whole family. I had found this amazing place. And I couldn't stop thinking about those tacos. Well, I hate to tell you how many more times I went back out and tried to find it, how much time I spent asking dumbfounded locals."

"And you never found it?"

"Never found it again, and instead of enjoying my family and enjoying the sunshine, I spent much of my vacation chasing a taco. And the thing is, Grace, it wasn't really about a taco." He stopped his story, waiting for a reaction from her.

But Grace didn't seem impressed. "And you're telling me this story because — ?"

"Because I don't want you to miss the sunshine."

She looked unsure about all this, and he went on.

"What I'm getting at is, I think you should really consider why you went up that tree in the jungle."

"I went up the tree because that's where the flower was."

"You know what I mean."

"Because nobody else was going to do it."

"Risking your life was in your job description?"

"I spent nearly a year researching that orchid. I fell in love with it, and I wasn't going to leave that jungle until I had a chance to smell it."

"So you were motivated by love of the work?"

"Yes."

"And yet when I met you in France, you were frustrated, said you wanted *recognition* for the work, *compensation* for it. So apparently love in and of itself has its bounds."

"Is this the part where you tell me about the nobility of compromise in business?"

"It would seem so, but I think you're more complex than that. Grace, before I met you

230

in Paris, I did a lot of due diligence on you. And there's a lot out there, as you made quite a name for yourself in the industry and even Burgundy in such a short time, which was very impressive and telling. But before college, your life is a black hole. Nothing. Now, normally, I don't expect to find much about the average seventeen-year-old beyond a good report from a manager at the local Dairy Queen. But you're not average."

Grace felt a sense of anxiety creeping over her. Was he asking her a question? What was he getting at?

Her unease registering, Bill moved on. "My point is that I think you are motivated by something beyond love of the work. I have two mortgages, five children, and three hundred and twenty-five employees, and I know a thing or two about what incentivizes people, what drives them. For most, a salary that meets or slightly exceeds their needs is enough. For others, it's something else. Love of work, passion, call it what you will, it's a tricky thing. Some people are drawn to it. Many are just downright frightened by it — they may not say so, but trust me, they are. And for a manager, passion — particularly the unbridled sort — causes a lot of headaches because how do you man-

231

age it, direct it, trust it? Well, what I've learned is that even that kind of relentless zeal comes from somewhere. It's classic Maslow, Marketing 101: Human beings are a composite of their wants and desires, but only *unsatisfied* needs truly influence behavior. So the question, Grace, is what need do you have in your life that is unsatisfied?"

Grace opened her mouth.

"It's a rhetorical question. I'm not your shrink, I'm your boss, and there are certain things that I don't want to know. I'm asking *you* to think about it. I'm asking you to think about why you took this job and what it is that you really want. Why are you the first one here every morning?"

Grace remained silent, absorbing all of this.

Seeing that his words were getting to her, Bill continued, making his point even more precisely. "And I'm here to tell you that virtually everything you seek, from the bottom of the pyramid up, shelter, security, respect, confidence, esteem, is attainable through financial security — even the unsatisfied need that drives passion. I know that sounds crass, and it in no way demeans the wonderful notion of one taking great joy in what one does — that's profoundly important for a variety of reasons — but I mean

232

it. You like nice shoes, nice food, a nice car, sure money's great for that. But more important, it means you don't have to do anything you don't want to do. It means freedom — no matter where you are, *or where you came from.* It means *tangible* success, that recognition that you were talking about in Paris. It's a way of keeping score, proving a point, just like being the person with the guts to climb a tree and get the prize, only at the top of this tree is an instrument negotiable for virtually anything you want. Just think about what you really want, Grace, what your *real* goal is, and I think this will be crystal clear to you. I'm not telling you to compromise. I'm telling you to focus on why you really took this job and how you can use your talent and skills *and love of the work* to do the job to the best of your ability."

Grace thought about everything he'd said. She did have goals, and yes, they came from deep-seated places, and they did get her up very early in the morning. And she certainly didn't want to miss the sunshine. "I know I can be pretty intractable at times," she finally said.

"I think that's one of the things Herb likes about you," Bill said with a grin. "You remind him of himself."

"But I understand what you're saying, and you're right — no, no, of course you're right. This is a business, and if our client wants or needs to sweeten with a more cost-effective product, so be it."

"Good. Very good." Bill felt an immense sense of relief.

Grace thought she'd settled things with herself. Still, there was this one little thing that she just couldn't seem to let go. "But I still would like to be lead on this novel apple investigation."

Bill groaned and leaned back in his seat, knowing that sooner or later, one way or another, she was going to win this battle, too. "Okay. Shoot."

"Ellijay orchard on an isolated high ridge, lot with full western exposure. The trees are at least fifty years old and the farm has always been organic. This fruit is special, really unique, exquisite. . . ."

He saw the passion in her eyes as she spoke about it, and he had decidedly mixed feelings about that.

"Crispness of a Rome and flesh of Golden Delicious, but with a profile that's not quite like anything you've come across in this country. It's interesting, there's almost a European sensibility to the fruit, like a Cort Pendu Plat or a Pomme de l'île or an old

Ananas Reinette from Brittany. Trust me, this is the kind of novel flavor that Givaudan and IFF send teams all over the world to find and bring in."

He knew she was right. He knew she had the skills to identify this kind of novel flavor, and he knew that if it panned out, the licensing rights could be quite valuable. It was true — he didn't have the resources to go out regularly in search of new flavors in the field like the big multinationals. If this was what she said it was, it had fallen into his lap, and he'd be kicking himself if he didn't at least do some testing.

She saw him thinking, getting it. "You need to map these apples, Bill."

"Fine. Get some thermal desorption systems and Micro Traps up there. But put someone on it."

"I will. And I need twenty-five thousand dollars for the farmer."

"Fine. Just put someone on it."

"I will. But I'd like to *oversee* the project."

"Grace —"

"I won't let it distract me."

Bill stared at her, wondering if there was anything else he could or should say realizing that he just wasn't going to keep her happy if he kept her off this project. Story time was over. "I think you're spreading yourself too thin. But, okay."

"Good. I can handle all of it."

Once again swiveling, he gauged her, and then took a deep breath. "Herb really does like you. You are key to this account and the account is key to this company and the board knows that. If it approves your promotion, you will receive a fairly significant amount of Southern Compound stock options as part of your executive compensation package. I don't know if you followed it, but after word of the deal hit the trades this morning, our stock has been up over seventeen percent."

He headed for the door, stopping when he got there.

"Stay on track with the Weiss account, Grace. Don't get distracted, don't slip, and you're going to be financially independent at a very young age. Just make sure this is really an apple you're chasing and not a taco." Having made his point, he turned and opened the door, about to walk out.

"How many times have you told that taco story?" Grace asked.

"A lot. Remember, I have five kids."

Just Friends

Later that afternoon

Covered in grease and hydraulic fluids, shirt off, listening to Randy Travis on the radio, Dylan replaced the spark plugs on the old diesel tractor in the clearing off to the side of the front of the house. The skies above were crystalline blue, the air around him under the dappled shade of the old oak, matte and soft.

Man, it was warm today, he thought, reaching for a cool glass of cider on a nearby cinder block. He knew how much these sunny days increased the sweetness of the fruit still on the limb, but they could take a toll on the workers. He took a long drink, then took off his old John Deere hat and ran his fingers, cold from contact with the glass, into his warm scalp and dusty hair. Tiny streams of sweat ran down his firm stubbly cheeks, leaving streaks along his oil-smudged face, neck, and chest.

He heard the slam of the screen door and instinctively looked up, as he always did, expecting to see *her* there on the porch, dress fluttering, but it was just the breeze.

Then he heard the big tires on gravel in the distance, looked up, and saw the cloud of dust on the horizon, and then the yellow bus as it appeared and snaked its way down the orchard road. Dylan reached up high for the top of the open tractor hood, stretching his entire upper back and shoulders until he finally grasped the heavy steel and, with one determined move, slammed it shut. He picked up the oversized torque wrench he'd been using, tossing it into the open tool kit, which he snapped closed. Then he wiped his hands as best he could on a clean work towel, dragged the towel across his damp chest before tossing it, and threw on and buttoned his lightweight chamois shirt. The school bus stopped, lights flashing, red stop sign extended from the driver's side, and the door opened and Carter came bounding out. Then the stop sign came back in, the door closed, and with a loud release of the brakes, the bus steered into a turnaround in the road and headed back up.

Dylan met Carter in the wide cleared area in front of the house. She looked adorable in her safety patrol belt, he thought. He put his arms out as he always did, holding his hands away so as not to get her dirty, and she hugged him. He'd noticed that she was turning sideways a bit when they hugged lately, and he suspected he knew what that was about, but he refused to stop hugging his daughter as they always had. So he pulled her tight with his big forearms, which, as always, she liked.

"How was school?"

"Good," she said flatly.

"Whaddya do?"

"Nothing."

"Whaddya learn?"

"I dunno."

They walked toward the house. He knew the routine, and he also knew the best way to get her talking. "Did you have dessert at lunch?" he asked energetically, hitting on something from left field that would most likely be of interest to her.

"Yes. Peanut butter balls."

"Peanut butter balls!" he exclaimed, goofing around. "I still don't see how a big wad of peanut butter rolled in powdered sugar qualifies as food."

"Because it's not 'organic'?" she asked, teasing him.

"Because it's the government using school

239

lunch programs to burn off outrageous subsidies to state peanut farmers."

"Dad," she moaned, rolling her eyes. "It's just peanut butter. Anyway, if you don't like it, you can throw it real hard and it sticks to the ceiling in the cafeteria. One of them has been up there since like the 1980s. It's kind of a legend."

"A legend? I wonder if that's the one I threw up there."

"Dad." Again, she rolled her eyes at his stupid joke.

They arrived at the front porch and sat next to a paper plate filled with apple slices and cheese, which they both nibbled on.

"Anything else for lunch?" he asked.

"Chicken-fried steak."

"How was that?"

"Terrible. Just the government taking advantage of helpless children to burn off outrageous subsidies to chicken farmers."

"I see," he said, laughing.

"So what *is* a subsidy, anyway?"

"Something they make much more complicated than it really is. It's basically when you get paid too much for what you grow."

She nodded, "How do *we* get a subsidy?"

"Grow something besides apples."

They both bit into thick juicy apple slices, chewing, staring off into the orchard.

"Dad, you think you'll ever get remarried?"

"What kind of question is that?"

"Uh, a simple one?"

"Do I ever think I'll get remarried?"

"Repeating-the-question alert."

"Sorry," he said, realizing she was right, and deserved an answer. He took a deep breath. "Carter, I don't know. That's the most honest answer I can give you."

"Well, do you want to? I mean, someday."

"I don't know. Really. I don't think a lot about 'someday.' Mainly I think about today."

That made sense to her. "Well, would you tell me if you liked someone?"

"Yes. Yes, of course I would."

"Well, I like Grace."

"Carter —," he said, trying to hold off his exasperation.

"I do. I think she's nice and pretty."

"Okay."

"Do you?"

"I'm not even going to answer that."

"Oh, so you do."

"Stop it. It doesn't even occur to me to think like that," he said convincingly.

"Because you're still in love with Mom? Or because you just don't want to talk about love with a kid?"

"These are really hard questions."

She just stared at him, her eyes piercing, and he knew he had to respond.

"Okay, yes, because I'm still in love with Mom, and yes, I don't want to talk about love with a ten-year-old —"

"— Almost eleven."

"— And yes, while I do think Grace is pretty and nice, it doesn't even occur to me to think about that, because even if I did, it has nothing to do with anything because for starters *she* has no interest in the things you're thinking about."

Even to a ten-year-old, that sounded like a tacit confession. "You don't know that," she said lightly.

"Carter, Grace is interested in our apples. It's business."

"Does she have a boyfriend?"

"I have no idea. Now, stop this. Relationships are very complicated."

"In the olden days, men would just post ads in the newspaper, and women would come and before long, they fell in love."

He thought about that, remembering some of the books he'd seen her reading for school. "Well, maybe things are different now," he said rather patronizingly.

"Maybe you're *making* things more complicated than they really are," she said very plainly.

He put his arm around her and pulled her close. "We do okay, don't we, Carter? You and I? We do okay, right?"

"Yes. We do great." There was so much she wanted to say, but she sensed how hard this entire topic was for him. But there was one thing, above and beyond all else, that she felt he should know. "Dad, if you do want to fall in love again — it's okay."

"Thank you, honey. Seriously. I'm really glad you told me. It's good to know, and you can always talk to me about your feelings."

"I wasn't talking about *my* feelings, Dad. It's okay with me, too, but that's not who I was talking about."

He nodded; then he put a hand to her face and kissed her on the head, his insides swimming with so many feelings that, at least for him, were very complicated.

Carter rose. "Remember, you're taking me to Sarah's later."

"I remember," he said, trying to cover the fact that he'd completely forgotten.

"You're a terrible liar, Dad. That's one of the things I love about you." And she headed into the house.

■ ■ ■ ■

Bag over her shoulder, Grace threw open the door to the lab. Monic looked up from a beaker filled with a citrus-flavored soda on which she was taking effervescence measurements, and the two of them just stared at each other, but quite a lot was being said.

Finally, Monic started to shake her head. "Grace," she said in disbelief. "You stood him up?"

"You have to believe me when I tell you that was not my intent," said Grace, dropping her bag.

"You went there and you saw him and you couldn't bring yourself to talk to him? What are you, like, twelve?"

"I was going to message you from the car."

"But you didn't."

"I started to."

"But you didn't."

"It was hard to explain with my thumbs."

"Okay. If you care to use words, I'm listening." Monic put a thermometer into the beaker and stepped away from it, looking intently at her friend.

Grace sat down at the lab table across from Monic. "I got sidetracked by work,"

Grace said simply. "That's really all there is to it. I went there and I was making a couple quick calls, and before I knew it, he was walking out."

"You didn't want to stop him?"

Grace looked away, not responding.

"You didn't want to grab him and say, 'Hey, I'm the friend of the wife of the friend that sent me here, and even though I hate this sort of thing, you seem like a nice enough fellow, I think, and even if you aren't, I promised my friend I would be here! So how about a quick vodka tonic, we'll toast my sweet gal-pal who is trying to look out for me, and I'll be on my way.' "

"I'm sorry, Monic," Grace said sheepishly. "Simon must be really tweaked."

"It's okay. I gave him a backrub and we stayed up late, saying all kinds of nasty things about you. We both feel better."

Grace looked away, a pensive stare on her face.

Monic was playing around, but she knew her friend well enough to see that Grace was truly preoccupied by something. Monic leaned in closer. "Grace? Really? What were you thinking?"

"I was thinking . . . I was thinking about an apple." She said it to herself as much as to Monic.

"This is the work that sidetracked you?"

"I came across a novel flavor in an apple, and I had to track down its source."

"At eight o'clock at night in the lobby of the Four Seasons?"

Monic knew her well and deserved an honest explanation — but there was so much to tell, and truthfully, Grace wasn't sure she could even rationalize it into words yet. Grace thought about trying to explain that she was on the phone and by the time he walked by with his new friends, looking like he was having such a good time, she felt stupid and froze up, which made her feel even more stupid and then anxious. Then the last thing she wanted to do at that point was stop him and say hi and sound like a complete idiot. And then there was the guy, well, at the time he was just a voice, but he'd gotten into her head in a way that had taken hold of her, and she couldn't quite explain it to herself, so how was she going to explain it to someone else? How could you explain any of this?

"I know it sounds strange," Grace said.

"What? That you chose pomaceous fruit over a sports reporter?"

"There's more to it than that."

"I'm a scientist, honey. I like to boil things down to their essence, and a fifth-grader

246

could see the essence of this."

"And what do you think that is?"

"I think when it comes to work, you're fearless. But when it comes to love, you're a fraidy cat."

"A what? Who's 'like twelve' here?"

"I have other names to call you, if you like. Simon and I were up *late*." Monic gave her a big playful grin.

"Well, let me make it up to you," Grace said, eager to move past this. "How would you like to go to dinner at Cole?"

"The new one? In Buckhead?" Monic wasn't sure if Grace was serious.

Grace nodded, pleased with herself.

"Oh, that'll work. That'll so very work. Wow, I know you're an up-and-coming big shot, but can you really get into that place?"

"I have reservations tonight," Grace said almost teasingly, enjoying the excited expression on her friend's face. "I know people who know people, who know people."

And then, the gleeful expression left Monic's face as she remembered something. "Oh, shoot. Shoot, shoot."

Grace looked concerned. "That doesn't sound like anticipatory joy."

"That is me remembering that Emily is a daisy tonight."

"Dance recital?" Grace asked, unable to hide her sadness.

Monic nodded. "The video camera is charging as we speak."

"She's five. How much dancing does she do?"

"None, really. They all stand there, hopping back and forth and turning around a few times with their arms up, but it's so cute and the daisy outfit with those big petals coming out from her sweet little cheeks is so delicious." Monic lifted her hands up like a dancing flower, reflecting on all the times she'd prepared her daughter for the routine.

"Well, daisy trumps hot restaurant," said Grace, resigned.

"I'm sorry I can't fulfill my regular function as date for you, dear friend, but you see, along with foot-rubber and dishwasher-unloader, this is just one of the many useful tasks for which a man is actually of some use."

"I'll find someone," Grace said.

"Well, the sportscaster is out. As is pretty much all of Simon's contact list for the foreseeable future." Monic furled her brow as she thought further. "What about Patrick the lawyer guy? Have you seen how he looks at you? I have. If we bottled and synthesized that look — Lust: The Fragrance — we'd be quite, quite wealthy."

"Stop it," said Grace, not wanting to confess that Patrick was very sweet and, in fact, had recently asked her out at the Whole Foods, but he just wasn't someone with whom she wanted to sit through a four-hour dinner. "Really, I'll find someone," Grace said confidently. "It's not a problem." Grace wondered what Emma was doing tonight.

Monic raised a finger, having an idea, but Grace cut her off, determined to change this subject.

"Listen, I have a favor to ask you." Grace grabbed her bag, lifted it up, and put it on the lab bench.

"Until I mother the little flower, I'm all yours."

Grace carefully removed the neatly folded scarf from her bag, feeling the soft material as she held it before her. Monic looked at the scarf, intrigued.

"Can you run the fragrance on this material and see what you can find? I'd like to track it down."

Monic nodded, familiar with this sort of assignment. Then she picked it up, taken with how soft and lovely it was as she held it to her face and smelled. "It's nice. Clive Christian?"

"You have a good nose."

"I have expensive taste."

"Is this *another* project in the works?"

"This is about the apple."

"Ah, the date-busting apple. Which is related to the scarf how, exactly?"

"This apple is amazing, Monic. I've never tasted anything like it. The owner of the orchard gave me consent to map it, and I agreed to see if I could help him track down some information about a woman he saw in an elevator at the Peachtree Plaza who he can't stop thinking about. She left her scarf behind."

"Oh, that is so romantic."

"He thinks it's his dead wife."

"And crazy."

"I know it sounds that way, but if you heard him talk about it . . ." Grace remembered Dylan's words and his expressions, and Monic could see how much Grace took that to heart.

"If I could hear him — what?"

"He's actually a really great guy. He's kind and funny. Sensitive. He's got this terrific daughter, Carter."

"Go on." Monic was paying very close attention. She'd never really heard Grace talk about someone this way before.

"And he's wonderful with her."

"What's he look like?"

"He looks like a guy that's had a terrible thing happen to him and he's doing everything he can to hold it together."

"That's not what I asked you."

Grace knew what she was asking. *What does he look like?* Grace envisioned Dylan; he was tall and had strong features, a powerful jaw, and thick dark hair. She recalled his forearms covered in clay, and the way his face was open and gentle when he kissed his daughter on the head standing there barefoot in the kitchen in his dryer-warm jeans and fresh flannel shirt.

"He looks comfortable."

Monic knew exactly what that meant, not from the words, but primarily from the expression on her friend's face as she said it. The tone in Monic's voice softened. "You know, a man who loved deeply once is a man who can love deeply again. It's a law of nature."

Grace was skeptical. "Einstein's Law of Mass–Energy?"

"Ephron's *Sleepless in Seattle*."

Grace laughed. "I don't know, Monic. If laws are meant to be broken, I think this is the guy whose heart breaks them. This guy, Dylan . . . as much as you feel for him, for this unfathomable trial he's undergoing, when you hear him talk about her . . . it's moving, to know someone's capable of loving that way."

"Sounds like some apple," Monic said teasingly.

"Stop."

"You know what, honey? When it comes to love, the universe works in funny ways. And sometimes it takes all your senses to find it."

Monic reached out and grabbed Grace's forearm, giving it a squeeze. And Grace just smiled, enjoying the moment with her friend.

"Hey, I saw your picture in the paper this morning," Monic said, cracking a smile of her own. "Nice pearls."

"Shut up." Grace gave Monic a playful whack on the arm, and the two friends laughed together.

Emma looked up from her extra-wide flat-panel screen to see her boss coming down the hall, bag on her shoulder, heels clicking like a metronome. Grace stopped at her desk.

"The new profiles with the HFCS modifications are in the top files. And you're all set for tomorrow morning, Ms. Lyndon. All the equipment is reserved and ready, and I have a call in to Culpepper Farms to confirm the time."

"Thank you, Emma," Grace said, impressed once again with this young woman's efficiency. "Listen, what are you doing tonight for dinner? I have to do some work at an amazing new restaurant, and I thought you might want to go."

Emma looked elated. "Tonight?"

"Yes," said Grace, wondering what was up.

"That is so nice of you to think about me," said Emma, feeling flattered. "But actually, I have plans tonight. With Patrick Hanson."

"The contract attorney?" asked Grace, more than a little surprised.

Emma nodded, looking quite happy.

"Well, that's great," said Grace, finding an upbeat note. "Wow, I'm just . . . I didn't see that coming."

"Really? I think he's cute."

"I just kind of thought you had a boyfriend," Grace said frankly, pointing to the picture on Emma's desk.

"Oh," said Emma, understanding the confusion. "No. That's my brother." Emma's tone changed. This was hard for her, but she needed to explain. "He died last year, around Christmastime. Before I started here."

"Oh, Emma, I'm sorry. I didn't know."

"It's okay," Emma said kindly, not wanting her boss to feel bad. "He was in Kandahar. Roadside bomb. He was a good guy."

And for a brief flash, Grace saw the pain in her assistant, and even more, a depth to this young woman that she hadn't known was there. It had never really occurred to Grace to ask about the fine details of Emma's life beyond anything that had to do with job qualifications. Grace wanted to leave her own personal affairs out of the office, especially matters from her past, and she just assumed Emma did, too. But looking at Emma now, Grace also had to admit that she had been so involved with work, and with herself, that it didn't even cross her mind that there might be more going on with this person who took such good care of her.

"I'm sorry."

"It really is okay. You know, honestly, everyone said after that, you have to go on, live your life, seize the day, all that sort of thing, which is easy to say. But working for you, and watching you, seeing that you really do live like that, you inspire me more than anyone I've ever known. Honestly, that's probably the main reason I asked him out."

"You asked *him?*"

"Yeah! Can you believe it? For lunch."

"Lunch. Wow."

"Yeah, but he had to work all day — but he asked me out for tonight."

Emma was just thrilled, and before she could say anything else, as Grace was absorbing all this information about her assistant's personal life, and how Emma felt about her, and Patrick, not to mention the new HFCS formulations that just came in, the phone on Emma's desk rang.

Grace felt dizzy. "That's great, Emma. Really great. I hope you have a terrific time. I know you will."

As Emma picked up the phone, Grace went into her office and plopped down on the sofa, her mind reeling.

Looking at the new Weiss account folders that Emma had placed on her neat desktop, Grace's musings were interrupted by Emma's conversation.

On the phone at her desk, Emma spoke as professionally as ever. "Yes, Ms. Lyndon will be at your farm first thing in the morning tomorrow. She'll have some very brief contracts for you to sign."

Listening to her, thinking about Dylan, and everything Emma had said to her about seizing the day and being an inspiration,

Grace found herself jumping up. "Emma," Grace said, popping her head out the open door to her office.

Phone to her ear, Emma just looked at her.

"Put him through to my office," Grace said firmly.

Emma nodded, and before she could even utter an acknowledgment, Grace closed the door.

Grace went to her desk, and as she sat, the phone rang. She smiled to herself, determined, and picked it up. "Hey, I know this is really short notice, but it never hurts to ask." Grace threw her head back. "I need a favor."

ALL SENSES

Early that evening
The big black stretch limousine wound its way down the driveway and through the orchard, the crunching gravel getting louder as it approached. Carter sat on the front steps next to a soft overnight bag, hair ponytailed back with a ribbon, her mouth slowly falling open as the limo came closer. She secretly wished her friends were here so that they could see this.

The limo pulled up to the front of the house and came to a stop. A door opened, and the driver, in a dark suit and tie and hat, hopped out, marched around the long vehicle, and waved to Carter.

Before Carter could speak, she heard the screen door squeak open behind her, and she turned to see her father step out, dressed for the night. In simple timeless Brooks Brothers pretty much from head to toe, charcoal gray gabardine slacks, solid broadcloth shirt, rep tie, and a classic two-button navy blazer, Dylan looked very much like what he was raised to be and, once the clay and grease and oil came off, really was: a Southern gentleman.

"You clean up good, Dad."

"Thank you, honey," he said, a big grin on his freshly shaven face.

"Good evening, Mr. Jackson, Ms. Jackson," the driver called out, polite and professional, standing before the extra-long vehicle. "Are you ready?"

Dylan walked up beside Carter and offered her his arm. She looked up at him, just giddy, loving all of this, and wrapped her little arm around his.

"Yes," said Dylan. "We're ready."

"Very good," said the driver. He opened the door to the limo and stood beside it, as Dylan and Carter walked down the steps together, arms interlocked.

As they approached the limo, Dylan grinned at Carter: *Is this cool or what?* And Carter returned the look with raised eyebrows and a huge smile, then promptly jumped into the open door. Dylan followed his daughter, and the tickled driver closed the door.

Inside the limo, which headed back up the gravel driveway, Carter jumped around, examining the crystal decanters, fiddling with the television, making the screen between the driver and the back go up and down, lying and sitting and bouncing around on all the leather seating surfaces.

"Carter, you've got to take it easy," said Dylan, amused. "You'll be worn out before we even get you to Sarah's, and I'm still not so sure about this sleepover on a school night."

"It'll be fine, Dad," she moaned with her classic impatience.

"Well, I'll be there bright and early tomorrow. Sleepover or not, you've still got farm chores before school just like Sarah."

Suddenly Carter stopped, realizing something very important, and looked straight at Dylan. "Dad, did you get her a corsage?"

"Carter, seriously, this is not a date." He said it with such conviction that he almost believed it.

"Dad! You have to get her a corsage!"

"Carter —" He tried to calm her down, but she'd have none of it.

"A giant carnation with lots of baby's breath she can wear on her wrist during dinner."

"I seriously doubt she wants to wear a giant carnation on her wrist."

"Yes, she does," Carter said urgently.

"Trust me. And pink is best. It'll match basically anything she wears."

"Where do you get this stuff?"

"Girls talk, Dad." *Duh,* her expression said.

Girls also watch a lot of Disney Channel, where school dances seem to be major storylines, he thought. "Oh, okay," he said. "I'll keep this in mind for future reference."

"You have to bring her something."

"I'm not getting her a corsage," he said dismissively.

While Dylan really did see this evening as a business favor — well, mostly — Carter saw it as something else. She slammed her finger on the button that made the privacy screen go down. "Stop the car!" she barked at the driver, who immediately complied.

"Carter! Stop this!" Dylan was about to give her a rather impassioned lecture, but before he had a chance — she opened the door and jumped out and dashed up into the orchard.

The driver, hands still on the wheel, looked back, but Dylan was already out the door, following his daughter.

"Carter! What are you doing!" he called out, following her over to the side of the road, up the little embankment, to a massive apple tree filled to bursting with ripe fruit.

Dylan caught up with her just as she'd laid her hands on one of the most perfect, big, round, blemish-free apples on the tree and yanked it off, leaving a long stem and several lush little green leaves.

"You have to bring her something she likes," said Carter, extending the apple to her father.

The limo motoring behind him, the sun going down on the western ridge to his left, Dylan just stared at his daughter holding an apple before him, and he started to shake his head. Realizing how important this was to her, he took the apple. "Thank you."

They jogged back to the limo together and hopped in.

Inside, Carter took the ribbon out of her hair, grabbed the apple from her dad, and wrapped the ribbon around the apple, tying it in a pretty bow. She handed the ribbon-wrapped apple back to Dylan. "You know," Carter said thoughtfully, looking at her father sitting there, knees together across from her in the back of the limo, holding the apple, "this is probably better than a giant carnation."

"Yeah," said Dylan, ceaselessly amazed by her. "Probably so."

A couple hours later

In stocking feet, though still in her sharp designer suit from earlier in the day, Grace sat on a barstool at her kitchen counter, sipping Pellegrino from the bottle and working attentively on her laptop. Even though the day was almost over, she still had so much to tend to on the Weiss account. Herb worked 24/7, as did Jonah, his lead assistant, and the correspondence and information flow never stopped. This was usually fine with Grace. She loved this kind of high-stakes adrenaline-driven work. But despite what she'd told Bill, Herb's intent to sweeten her project with high-fructose corn syrup annoyed her. Still, Grace was a pro, and she knew how to focus when she had to, so she was trying to do what she could to make the best of it. She studied the chemical designs of several flavor profile templates, wondering if she could make some slight adjustments to account for the HFCS, which did, in fact, impart a noticeable taste differential.

Her cell phone rang, and she reached for it, read the caller ID, and answered. "Hey," said Grace pleasantly.

"Hey," said Dylan. He stood next to the stretch limo, which was parked downstairs on Peachtree Street, right in front of her building. "This is some town car you sent."

"Do you feel like a rock star?"

"I feel like a farmer with a very impressed daughter."

She laughed and asked, "Where are you?"

"In front of your building."

Phone still to her ear, Grace walked to the patio, threw open the sliding glass door, and stepped out. The breeze rippling her skirt, she looked down at the street below, where she saw Dylan in his blazer and tie, standing next to the limo, cell phone to his ear, too. "Well, I think you *look* like a rock star," she said.

Dylan gazed up, scanning the balconies until he finally saw her. "Hi," he said, extending his arm, waving to her.

"Hi," she said, waving back.

"You want to let down your hair and I'll come up? Or you could just buzz me in and I'll take the elevator."

"That's okay, I'll be right down."

A few people walked by, looking at Dylan, wondering if he was, in fact, a celebrity, not such an oddity in this part of Buckhead. Dylan smiled at the onlookers, then waved again up to Grace. "Okay, I'll sign a few autographs while I wait for you."

Grace walked back inside, closing the door. *Cute, definitely cute,* she thought to herself, laughing quietly and suddenly aware that she was looking forward to spending time with him.

She went to her closet and picked out the perfect pair of shoes, popped them on, grabbed a matching handbag, and headed out.

Grace pushed through the big front doors of her condo, looking fashionable and stunning, the doorman tipping his hat to her as she passed.

Standing on the sidewalk in front of the limousine, Dylan didn't take his eyes off her as she approached. In his hands was the apple tied with ribbon.

She walked right up to him and smiled. "Thank you for doing this."

He just smiled back and extended the apple to her. "I don't have a rose garden, but —"

She met his eyes, beaming in a way people who knew Grace had never seen before.

The doorman watched, so pleased with what he saw.

Buckhead, an hour later
The low hum coming from the small group of well-dressed people who sat at the twenty-four tables in the chic little room

was so intense, you could almost feel it. Though this privileged crowd was accustomed to the finest dining, they all felt fortunate to be in this restaurant tonight. Heads turned discreetly, peering around to see who else was here, and indeed there were several recognizable faces.

The restaurant was furnished in dark woods, warm colors, plush upholstering, and a few pieces of familiar art, originals from famous artists. The room was dimly lit in most areas, though strategic pinpoints of light illuminated a circular area just over each table.

Dylan and Grace sat across from each other at one of the black lacquered wood tables. It was entirely empty, no tablecloth, no flatware, no napkins, just their hands across from each other — evoking the image of a bare stage.

Dylan looked around, pretty amazed and tickled with the whole thing. "This is some job you have. Five-star reconnaissance."

"It's important to stay abreast of what's going on in the industry."

"I understand. On Saturday afternoons, I have to go to old Marvin's fruit stand and surreptitiously acquire some of the competition's apples. Gotta stay sharp."

Grace grinned. *In his immaculately tailored*

blazer and tie, hair neatly combed back, what he doesn't realize, Grace thought, *is that he looks like he hangs out with this crowd all the time.* Of course, anyone who saw Grace entirely comfortable at work in the jungle would be equally surprised to see her here.

"Good evening," said the waiter, stepping up to the table, dramatically dressed in all black. "Welcome to Cole. Chef has prepared twenty-eight courses for tonight, and the sommelier has paired a wine with each one."

The waiter handed them menus. Dylan scanned the long thin paper, seeing that there were no appetizers or main courses or desserts, just a long list of strange and unrecognizable dishes. While Dylan was absorbing all of this, the waiter placed a single perfectly folded white linen napkin in front of each of them, and nothing else.

"Your dinner has been paid for this evening. Compliments of Mr. Weiss."

Grace and Dylan exchanged a look. That was nice to hear.

The waiter took a few steps back and was gone.

"Twenty-eight courses?" Dylan mused.

"Get comfortable," Grace said with anticipation.

They came on little spoons, tiny plates, in

small glasses, atop mini-pedestals, even speared and hung, suspended on custom-made wire serving devices like little edible works of art, which was entirely the point: mint-scented lamb lollypops, osetra and oysters on frothed tapioca, beet gazpacho and savory mustard shooters, foie gras porridge with a sweet ginger spritz in an atomizer, ankimo sashimi on house-made pop-rocks, plums in powdered yogurt, goat cheese marshmallows, venison maple syrup mastic, warm black truffle gumdrops with chilled sauternes centers. Foamed and freeze-dried, often accompanied by little spray bottles of fragrance and tiny scent-filled pillows, the food crackled and smoked and hissed and sizzled, appealing to all the senses. Thin slices of blast-frozen Kobe carpaccio were hung on little wire stands to thaw between courses at the table. All sorts of textures and presentations were set forth. Many were entirely novel and unexpected renderings of traditional dishes.

Intrigued and delighted by the sensory spectacle, Dylan and Grace enjoyed the experience immensely, ooohing and ahhing, and mostly laughing. For as strange as each course might be, as curious as the decorative objects that presented them, each one was an adventure of sorts, and without exception, each one was delicious, some to the point of profound. And each one came with an expertly matched extraordinary wine, in the precisely correct Riedel glass.

While leaning forward on the lacquered table — serving pieces and stemware whisked away as soon as they were no longer needed — Grace and Dylan, close to each other, focused mostly on the fun of it all during this first part of the meal. Grace felt several eyes in the room on her, Atlanta big shots, and she knew it was good for her career to be here.

After several courses, Dylan looked at the menu, noting that "Cheeseburger" was next up. "Okay, this is something I recognize," he said with relief.

"Don't get too excited," said Grace knowingly as she sipped the last of a bright and barnyard funky Romanée-Saint-Vivant from a big-bowled burgundy stem.

The waiter stepped out of the shadows and set two servings of the next course on the table simultaneously. Another server placed two very large Bordeaux stems on the table, and then carefully filled each with just one and a half ounces of wine. "This is Chef's cheeseburger," the waiter said. "Paired with the '70 Latour." The waiter and other server then backed away.

Dylan and Grace leaned forward, examining the strange creation. It smelled amazing, though it looked much more like something from a science class than from a Michelin-starred restaurant — a tiny piece of freeze-dried cheese on a teaspoon of bison tartare, lying atop a small lettuce pillow that had been filled with Vidalia onion smoke. It sat on a small warm open-face wheat bun, and the whole thing was presented on a miniature plate on which was a little pool of foamed heirloom tomato, and another of foamed mustard seed. And it was all topped with a few droplets of pureed brined Japanese cucumber.

Dylan just stared at it. "I feel like it belongs in a museum."

"I know. It's almost too beautiful to eat," Grace said.

They were both captivated by the variety of scents coming from the presentation. It did, indeed, smell like an amazing cheeseburger.

"Well, I'm gonna try," said Dylan, putting the little top bun on. Grace watched as he picked it all up with his thumb and forefinger, dapped it in the foamed tomato and mustard, and popped it in his mouth.

Dylan's mouth and nose were filled to bursting with all the expected flavors and scents of a great cheeseburger — bread, meat and cheese, ketchup and mustard, lettuce and pickle. Oh, wow, it was good. And as he chewed, he popped the lettuce pillow, adding just the right touch of sweet onion scent and flavor to the mouthful.

Grace was familiar with this type of cuisine, but had never quite had such a masterful expression of it. She followed suit, popping the "burger" right into her mouth.

Staring and chewing simultaneously, each one appreciating exactly what the other was experiencing — it was both intimate and hilarious, ridiculous that this riff on a cheeseburger would be so explosive. It was like holding hands in the front row of a roller coaster.

As they were washing the course down with the luscious little pours of Latour, a very well-dressed man and his wife, both in their sixties, approached the table. "Grace! How are you!" the man said forcefully, stepping up to them.

"Hello, Carl," Grace replied, turning her head to greet them. Her voice lost the giddiness it had when they were talking about the cheeseburger, a change in tone that was not lost on Dylan. "What brings you to Atlanta?"

"We had some challenges with one of our

vendor contracts at the Georgia Dome. We're in good shape now, though I can't say the same thing for your Falcons' offense this year."

"It's still early in the season. Don't write them off just yet," Dylan said, jumping into their conversation.

Carl turned his head to get a better look at this young broad-shouldered man who disagreed with him. "Matt Ryan can't find a wide receiver to save his life," said Carl like he was laying down the law.

But the man's conviction didn't deter Dylan from speaking up. "This time last year, Ryan might not have been throwing very deep," said Dylan assuredly, "but he ended up finishing the year throwing — what? — at least three thousand yards, and twenty-two TDs."

The older man nodded, amused by Dylan's impassioned take. "You have a point," he laughingly conceded.

Grace watched the interaction carefully. This was a very powerful person Dylan was talking to, and he seemed entirely confident doing so. Grace was impressed, and a bit attracted by his boldness.

"I'm sorry," said Grace, introducing them. "Carl Fisher, Dylan Jackson."

"Good to meet you," said Carl, who

turned to the woman next to him. "This is my wife, Claire, and this is Grace Lyndon, rising star down here in Atlanta."

"Good evening," Claire said in her refined voice, honed for introductions just like these. Then she turned to her husband. "Why isn't she working for you, dear?"

"That is a very good question," he said, turning to Grace. "Why aren't you working for me?"

"Because you can't afford me, Carl," she said good-humoredly.

"Oh, really?" he replied with a smirk. He could very much afford her, and then some.

"Carl, I didn't realize you got directly involved with vendor relations," Grace said, moving things along.

"I get involved where I need to be involved," he stated gruffly.

"Oh, tell the truth, dear," Claire said, turning to Grace. "He also desperately wanted to come here for dinner, and we needed an acceptable excuse to use the corporate jet." She patted her husband's arm. Then she turned to Dylan. "So what do you think of the molecular gastronomy cuisine, Mr. Jackson?" she asked, turning the subject to something with which she was comfortable.

Carl jumped in first. "In fairness, I probably should warn you that my wife is a big Alice Waters devotee, whilst I am partial to Ferran Adrià."

Grace looked a bit nervous, unsure how Dylan was going to respond to references of famous chefs and this borderline obnoxious questioning — not to mention the whole thing was interrupting their meal.

"Well, you know what they say," Grace said, trying to help him out. "Give Alice an apple, and she'll make a wonderful apple cobbler; give Ferran an apple, he'll freeze it and foam it and turn it into something delicious that no longer looks anything like an apple."

Dylan thought about that for a few seconds and said, "Well, as I like to say, give me an apple, and I'll tell you about its orchard."

"Ah, a diplomat!" Carl laughed.

Then Dylan went on. "Quite honestly, this is one of the greatest meals of my life."

"I knew you'd be on my side," said Carl.

"But it's quite something, that this is what eating has come to. . . ." He trailed off, looking at a frozen cube of meat dangling from a wire affixed to a little pedestal sitting on a nearby table.

"Yes?" said Claire, inquiring further. "It's come to what?"

Dylan shrugged. "Well, food theater." He wasn't being critical as much as he was simply giving it his best honest shot. "I think it's delicious, but also, well, it's fascinating to see how far we've gotten away from the farm, so far that our food looks like modern art."

Carl and Claire considered his words, still not entirely sure whose side he was on.

Sensing a rare pause, Grace decided to close the matter. "You're right. He's a diplomat."

"And clearly a smart one!" said Carl.

"What kind of work do you do, Mr. Jackson?" asked Claire.

Dylan just could not refrain from breaking into a grin. "I own an apple orchard. On a family farm."

The couple looked at Grace, and she nodded, and they all broke into laughter.

"Bravo, Mr. Jackson! Bravo!" said Claire.

"Well, my company is always looking for good produce suppliers. Feel free to get in touch." Carl took Claire's arm. "Nice to see you, Grace. Congrats on the new account, and don't let that old coot Herb give you a hard time."

Carl reached into his jacket pocket, produced a business card, and slipped it to Grace. "I've got my eye on you."

Grace nodded demurely, but secretly delighted to be on Carl Fisher's radar — putting the card discreetly into her bag just under her chair.

Dylan watched the couple move on. Then he turned back to Grace. "He's a big shot, isn't he?"

Grace nodded. "He runs a very large and well-known company."

"How well known?"

"Andy Warhol painted their products."

"Gotcha."

Grace looked at him for a moment. "I thought a lot of what you said was really interesting, right on the mark."

"Thank you."

"Sorry you got put on the spot like that."

"Not a problem."

"Though there's one critical thing that you're quite wrong about, you know."

"I'm sorry?"

"Matt Ryan couldn't hit a house from the front steps."

He lit up. "You're a Falcons fan?"

"I follow them. My company has box seats, so we do a lot of business at the games. Now, maybe if their offense would get their act together, I'd be more of a fan." She grinned teasingly.

The waiter stepped up to the table, holding two small plates with smoking, foaming, scented food. "Are we ready for the next course?"

"Very much so," Grace said, her eyes on Dylan.

"Yes," Dylan said, meeting her eyes. "Very much so."

With perfect alacrity, the waiter began to serve.

An hour later

As they finished the fine old wine from the last course, Dylan watched Grace closely, fascinated by how she held the thin stem of the huge Bordeaux glass in her slender hand, swirling the last of the claret, putting her nose in the bowl, and taking in the scent. She brought the glass to her lips, her head back, and slowly poured the last sip into her mouth. As he watched her drink, there were a million things Dylan wanted to know about her. Why had she picked him to come to dinner tonight? Had someone else canceled first? What was she thinking? Or more important, what did she want with his farm?

But she beat him to the punch. "So I have a question for you," Grace asked, feeling a touch of the alcohol in her head now, and enjoying it.

276

"Uh-oh," he said playfully. Then he leaned forward on the table, closer, attentive.

"The other night, do you remember the last thing you said to me, before you hung up?"

Trying to recall, he said, " 'Don't ever call me again, crazy woman'?"

She laughed. "You said, 'And I think you're going to be okay, too.' "

He nodded, as though remembering.

"What did you mean by that?" she asked.

He took a deep breath, for the pause — in truth, Dylan didn't need to remember. He knew exactly what he had meant. But about this, he wanted to make sure he got his words right.

"Some people are big talkers, Grace. But I've always been partial to listening. Partly because I think you can tell a lot about a person just by keeping your mouth shut. Even over the phone, you can get to know a person."

Grace moved her head slightly in a gesture of acknowledgment.

He saw her understanding and went on. "Well, you spoke and I listened and what I heard was someone who claimed to be doing something for business, but actually had something very personal wrapped up in her reasoning."

Grace remembered the specifics of the conversation and the negotiation and how uncharacteristically vulnerable she had been.

"You had a very different tone with that man who just came to the table, and I know that's just business, but I'm guessing that you spend much of your day tucking a part of yourself away. Maybe that's just how it is, how it has to be. I don't know much about that. But I listened, and I've watched — and you asked — and what I hear and see is a woman with a secret side, and for some reason, when we spoke, something about that apple, or wanting that apple, made you whole. I listened and I heard a whole person, the business part, and the personal part — the exposed part that sounded like she wanted to be, or maybe even needed to be, somewhere besides where she was. And listening to you, listening to how you talk about the apple, you strike me as someone who will get where she needs to be." He went silent, hoping that he hadn't said too much.

"Thank you for answering," she said sincerely.

"Can I tell you one more thing, albeit unsolicited?"

She took a deep breath, nodding.

And he slid forward even more in his seat, his large hands but a finger's length from hers. "I enjoyed meeting that person on the phone. That whole person." He looked wide-eyed at her. "I enjoyed meeting her very much."

She held his gaze, lost in what he was revealing about his feelings for her. What exactly was he saying? Was it the wine talking? The buzz from the food? Her head was spinning, and as she was struggling to find the right words to express her emotions, the waiter stepped up.

"Are we ready for what's next?" he asked intently.

That question at that very moment somehow sounded like it was about more than the next course, and — their eyes still fixed on each other — neither responded or dared blink.

As the moment grew long and charged, finally, they both looked up at the waiter to see him holding two strange decorative serving pieces — black marble pedestals with long thin wires protruding — and speared atop each wire were perfect little cubes of food.

Something about the little cubes bobbling before them like novelty toys, and the waiter's solemn tone, suddenly struck Dylan and Grace as hilarious — and they both started cracking up laughing.

"Sorry, sorry," said Grace, hand over her mouth.

"Yes, we're ready," said Dylan, trying to hold it together.

Looking like a couple who had known each other for years, they felt more connected to each other by their shared laughter than by words that might have been spoken.

Ignoring them, the waiter began to serve.

An hour later

Approaching the end of the meal, Dylan and Grace sat with their final tiny sips of the twenty-seventh wine. Grace picked up the glass by its stem, careful not to touch the bowl, and swirled around the old Rhône.

"So I started my day cooking eggs on a farm," said Grace, "and you ended yours eating foamed goat cheese marshmallows." She chuckled and raised her deep-bellied glass into the air.

Dylan laughed, too. "Life's full of surprises." He returned her toast with his glass.

"Yes, it is." Lifting one of her hands off the table, she ran her fingers through her hair, comfortably moving it off her slightly damp forehead, untwining her usually perfect hair a little.

Both of them settled back into their seats, adjusting to the twenty-seven courses in their stomachs. This evening, and really meeting each other, certainly had been a most delightful, exhilarating surprise — that couldn't be refuted. But not all of life's surprises had been so kind to Dylan and Grace. In this moment of reflection, assisted by the fluttering of wine-fueled abandon, their reverie was bittersweet.

Grace, sensing Dylan's change in mood, wanted him to stay here, with her. She looked at him, in his jacket and tie, and blurted out, "I mean, Johnston and Murphy I saw coming, but a pinch-buckle moccasin man. Very nice. Who would've known?"

Realizing she was talking about his shoes, he tried to remember what he had put on. He ducked under the big high table for a moment, seeing his shoes exactly as she had described them.

While he looked, Grace simply sat there, seemingly alone, fingers interlaced and hands resting on the tabletop. She was really enjoying this.

Coming back up, Dylan straightened his jacket and stared at her, taken aback. "That's amazing, how you can do that. I haven't worn these in quite a while."

"They look good on you, Dylan," she said,

not minding if she was saying too much, because she wanted him to know.

Dylan thought about his grandfather, and what he said about shoes. He would've liked Grace. They would have had a lot to talk about.

"Have you always had an affinity for fine footwear?" he asked with a wry look.

Wiggling her toes freely in her fabulous Jimmy Choo pumps, Grace sighed with contentment, realizing she could — and should — open up to this near-stranger. "When I was a kid," she said, "I made myself some promises about how my life would be when I was older." Grace chuckled a bit, hardly believing she was digging this up. "You know how on the first day of school, all the kids look around to see who's who, and most of them have the thirty-two box of crayons, but the really cool kids, they whip out the sixty-four box?"

"Yes, I remember! The one with the built-in sharpener in the back," Dylan replied.

"I had dreams about that built-in sharpener," she said with a wistful smile.

"Well, don't feel bad," he said. "I was never able to convince my parents to upgrade me to the sixty-four either. I was always a thirty-two, and a couple years even a sixteen."

Grace took in a deep breath and leaned close, as if to whisper a secret. Then, rather playfully, motioned for him to follow as she ducked under the table.

He looked around and then ducked under there, too.

Head to head, nearly nose to nose, Johnston & Murphys to Jimmy Choos, under the big black lacquered table in the finest restaurant in town, sated on food and wine and shared laughter, she whispered, "I was the kid with the eight-box."

"The eight-box?" he said.

She nodded and then fired them off. "Black, blue, brown, green, orange, violet, yellow, red. Every single year, same eight colors."

Under the table, she smiled, and then he smiled. And although it was all in play, Dylan sensed something being revealed here, something important, something more than just crayon colors.

They both resurfaced, put their hands nonchalantly on the table, stifling little laughs, and they turned to see the waiter standing there, holding the famed huckleberry sorbet.

"Are we ready for the final course?" he asked, entirely serious, and apparently immune to guests cavorting sub-table.

Grace and Dylan nodded, chastised, while diminutive porcelain bowls with perfect little scoops of purple sorbet were placed in front of them, along with a long-handled silver spoon. Sauternes glasses were exactingly filled with one and a half ounces of the 1967 d'Yquem, and placed in their proper position.

Abiding Herb's instruction to decode the sorbet, Grace leaned over the sorbet, first focusing on its visual elements: color, tone, brightness, hue. Then she put her face even closer to the bowl, drawing in the scent, slowly first, in small inhalations, and then with bigger breaths, closing her eyes. She picked up the spoon and brought it into the sorbet, studying its texture and physical composition. Finally, a scoop of the sorbet on the spoon, she brought it to her mouth, turned the spoon over, and placed a small sample directly in the center of her tongue. She rolled it around, getting a sense of the mouthfeel, the construct of the substance, and how the flavors were picked up on her taste buds. Most important, she slowly exhaled warm breath, now filled with the natural chemicals and flavor molecules in the sorbet, through her nose, allowing the receptors deep inside to take in the scent and, thus, develop a comprehensive sense of its flavor.

Drawing on all her senses, she closed her eyes, putting the profile together, and when she opened them, she saw Dylan just watching her, fascinated.

"What do you think?" he asked.

"I think we have to get ahold of this recipe."

Dinner over, most of the patrons paying and grabbing coats and filing out of the restaurant, Grace and Dylan stood patiently by the kitchen entrance. They were quiet, listening to one particularly animated couple talking about Chef Thomas in hushed tones, about what a genius he was and how he had utterly humiliated his opponent last week on *Iron Chef.*

After a moment, the waiter motioned for Dylan and Grace to come in.

The kitchen was intensely bright and stark, especially in comparison to the warmth of the dining room. Cooks and their staff went about the grueling task of cleaning the high-tech kitchen, which, along with all the state-of-the-art commercial appliances and cookware, had several pieces of equipment that looked like they were right out of Monic's lab.

Cole Thomas, in a clean white culinary uniform, turned from one of the many stainless steel prep counters to greet them.

"Hi, Chef," said Grace. "We just wanted to thank you so much for an amazing meal."

Dylan stepped up. "Yes. Thank you for one of the best meals of my life."

Cole Thomas was surprisingly young, late twenties maybe, and despite his youth and baby face, he looked gaunt and exhausted, like a tennis pro after a match.

"Good, I'm glad you liked it," he said, his voice a bit hoarse. "How was the Kobe?" he asked with an almost concerned sincerity.

"Phenomenal," Grace answered.

"Good," said Cole. "I was worried it was a bit too cold."

"No, perfect," said Grace. "As was the sorbet. I'm thinking there's some wintergreen in there."

He looked at her circumspectly, and she could see that he was impressed. *I must be right,* she thought.

"Something like that," Cole said with a guarded smile.

"I think I even saw some tiny flakes of green in there. You used fresh leaves, not flavoring oil. Pretty neat."

He was on to her. "Who are you with?"

She knew he was too sharp and too impatient for nonsense. "Southern Compounds, up in Marietta." She reached into her bag and retrieved a card, which she gave him.

He reviewed the card for a moment, and Grace could tell from his expression that she had better come up with something fast. She knew she wasn't the first one to approach him.

"But I'm not here to talk about the sorbet," she said.

"Really? You're not here to make me an offer?" He wasn't buying it.

"No, actually, I'm here for you to make us an offer." She reached into her bag and retrieved the apple, the ribbon still around it, holding it before her. Dylan watched her, completely unaware of her motives, but nonetheless swept up in the momentum.

"Have you ever heard of Cully apples?" Grace shot Dylan a conspiratorial look.

"Can't say I have," said Cole.

"We're a small family-owned organic orchard up in Ellijay," said Dylan, clearing his throat.

"Given what I know about your work," said Grace. "And what's important to you, I thought this was something you should know about." Grace offered him the apple. "This is truly the greatest apple I've tasted."

Behind Cole, a harried-looking member

of the kitchen staff was walking quickly toward him — one of his sous, it looked like. The guy called out, "Chef! What do you want to do with the truffle shavings?"

Cole took the apple from Grace. He had to go, and this conversation was over. "Thank you for your nice words about my meal." And tossing the apple in his hands, he turned and walked away.

Grace exchanged a look of disappointment with Dylan. That was the end of that. They continued to stand there, but there was really nothing left to do. So, finally, they turned, and just as they got to the kitchen doors —

"Wait!" a loud voice called out.

Grace and Dylan stopped and turned to see Cole, an amused look on his face.

In the chef's hand was the apple, with a large bite taken out of it. "Have you harvested yet?" Cole asked.

"Any day now," said Dylan.

The chef nodded. Fruit was still on the tree. This was good. "How much of your year is spoken for?"

"We're still considering offers," said Dylan rather cagily. "Whole Foods has been by."

Grace sneaked a look at Dylan, wondering if this was true. And Dylan nodded to her. It *was* true. They hadn't exactly *com-*

mitted, and they were just sniffing around, but they had been by.

"I'd need at least a few hundred barrels for it to make sense," said Cole, being drawn in.

"That's a lot for us. We're a family farm. I have to be up front with you — I'd try my best, but it's always been about quality . . . but I could work on the quantity," Dylan said, continuing the negotiation. It was immediately clear that this was the right thing to say to Cole Thomas.

Grace was breathless.

"I'll tell you what," Cole said, grasping the apple, studying it, smelling it the same way Grace first had. "Guarantee me three hundred bushels of fruit of this quality and composition, and as soon as I take delivery, I'll give you the sorbet recipe."

"I believe she'd like access to the suppliers," said Dylan.

"I'll put you in touch," he said to Grace, sniffing the apple again. Then he turned to Dylan and said, "I'll pay you ten percent over your season wholesale rate."

Taking another bite of the apple, Cole extended the ribbon to Grace.

Dylan sat next to Grace on one of the long leather upholstered benches in the back of the limousine. The oversized vehicle swayed while navigating the streets of Buckhead, the brandy in the crystal decanter rippling like a bottled little sea. His leg touched hers ever so slightly, and neither moved away.

"Thank you again for doing this, Dylan. I had a great time."

"You were amazing back there," he said. Not only was Dylan impressed with her negotiation, but he was also thrilled that more than 10 percent of his harvest was already accounted for, not to mention this new and potentially valuable future market.

"*We* were amazing," said Grace.

He gazed at her as the lights of the city rushed by in the dark glass behind her. "So all those promises you made to yourself when you were a kid . . . Did you fulfill them?"

She smiled, stretching out her slender legs, someone who was very comfortable in the back of a limousine. "Yes, in fact, I pretty much have."

"That's quite something. How do you think you managed to do it?"

She thought for a moment, and then answered as honestly as she could. "Those surprises in life? I did what I could to keep them to a minimum."

He understood. The limo came to a stop,

idling, and as it was about to turn onto Peachtree, they both got a magnificent view of the downtown skyline, both focusing on the most prominent building in sight, the tall cylindrical Peachtree Plaza Hotel. And inside it, the memory of a red scarf and a seductive perfume — and Dylan's one love.

Neither spoke about it, and what it meant, but it was there, and the silence was great.

Finally, Dylan had to speak. "Never felt that you were missing anything?" he asked her.

And perhaps it was because the end of the night was near, or perhaps because she just felt so comfortable sitting here right next to him, Grace decided to stop dancing around the heart of the matter. "How did you know when you were in love?" she asked.

She saw him swallow and pause — heard his deep inhale as if to gather both air and strength. "It's like that moment when you wake," he said. "Right before you open your eyes, it's still dark, but you know exactly where you are."

"My alarm wakes me up," she said with a rueful smile. "Every morning. Eyes wide open."

The limo came to a stop in front of Grace's building, and Dylan immediately opened the door and hopped out. He extended his hand to her and she took it and he helped her out, her high heels stepping over the curb onto the sidewalk as she stood up next to him. Still holding her hand, he took a step toward her, lowered his face to hers, and lips parted and moist, he kissed her lightly on her cheek.

He pulled back and looked her in the eyes. "You should try sleeping in sometime," he said.

Something about that idea, and the sensation of his tender mouth on her, made the blood rush to her cheeks.

"I'll see you tomorrow," he said, releasing her hand. Then he slid into the limousine, smiled up at her, and shut the door.

Gripping her handbag, Grace stood on the sidewalk, watching him ride off down Peachtree Street and into the night.

Just over twenty-four hours ago, she'd felt that everything was as it was supposed to be, that her life was just as she wanted it. But now, standing there on the sidewalk, her luxury condo building towering and sparkling over here, she felt dizzy and disoriented, like she had just been kissed for the first time.

GHOSTS

Dylan rolled down the window of the limo, watching the lights of the city fly past him in a blur and letting the air hit his cheeks and rush through his hair. He felt as though he had been in a deep dream, and though part of that was possibly due to the food and the wine, he knew there was much more to it. He knew the real intoxicant was Grace, lovely Grace Lyndon. As the wind came at him, it carried her face as it had been for so many hours across the table, her exquisite features, enchanting smile, eyes fixed on his. She had gotten into him so deeply that even the cool air on his face and in his hair did nothing to release him of her.

Her intertwined fingers, an ear exposed by tossed hair, the skin at the curve where her neck met her chest, her cheek that he had kissed — it all flashed over and over until he was left with a sensation so vivid and arresting, it was almost as if Grace were still in the limo with him.

He closed his eyes slightly, ushering in the feeling of his lips on her soft skin, his nose grazing her cheekbone beneath her eye, and the scent of her skin there. He held tenuously to the image of her, the effect of it coursing through him.

Thinking of her this way quickened his breath and pulse, and he did nothing to calm himself, turning the glimpses and sensations over in his mind. And the long drive home in the moonlight flew by, as though she were indeed still with him.

Grace's open laptop perched on the granite countertop of her kitchen bar, the cursor blinking silently on the screen.

In her dimly lit condominium on the twelfth floor of the high-rise building, the patio door open and the breeze fluttering the curtains, Grace Lyndon lay on the floor in the clothes she'd been wearing for many hours, in the middle of her essentially barren living room, shoes kicked off on the carpet, hair spread out all around her like a halo, her hand, the one that had just held his, softly upon her face.

The ribbon that had been on the apple lay strewn across her torso as she stared up and off, thinking about the day, and the night, and him.

She closed her eyes, lost somewhere between dream and conscious thought, memory and sensation, and a gust of wind blew into the room, tossing the ribbon off her. Unfazed, she did not move.

Dylan stepped out of the limo, shut the door, and the long black vehicle drove back up the orchard driveway. He stood in the night air, assessing the temperature, wind, and dew. It was cold, and that concerned him somewhat. On instinct, he walked over to the closest apple tree, kneeled, and put his hand gingerly on the soil, feeling the heat rising from the ground. Then he slipped his hand into the dirt, a good two or three inches down, just to make sure the earth was still warm. It was. Just barely, but enough for him to rest easy. Then he rose, slapped the soil from his palm, and inspected the tree before him, feeling the moisture of the leaves, checking for insects, appraising the weight of the fruit and the stress on the boughs. Finally, he grasped a sample apple, broke it off the stem with a twist, and headed for the house.

As he reached the front porch steps, he saw Pablo, in a bulky flannel jacket, in a rocking chair, head back and to the side, asleep. Dylan strode up the steps, and when one of them creaked loudly, Pablo opened his eyes.

"*Buenas noches,* Mr. Dylan," Pablo said, righting his head and yawning.

"Pablo, go home." Dylan walked up to him and put a hand on the heavyset man's thick shoulder.

"We threw the shade tarpaulins over the west ridge trees. The ground is still warm, but the breeze is very cold on the ridge tonight."

"I don't deserve your labor, my friend. Thank you."

Pablo rose, looking concerned. "Some of the men left this morning on the bee truck for Florida. The others are leaving for California soon."

"A few more days. It's almost time." Seeing Pablo's unease, Dylan found an easygoing smile. "The trees will tell us when they are ready."

Pablo appreciated Dylan's efforts and laughed a little. "Please tell the trees to hurry," Pablo said. "They are raising the pressure of my blood."

"I will be sure to let them know. Thank you for your help. Go home."

Pablo thumped down the creaking porch

steps. "Good night, Mr. Dylan."

"Good night, my friend."

Then, just as he reached the ground, Pablo remembered something. He stopped, turned, and pointed back up at the porch. "Oh, I found those in the henhouse," he said with a strange expression.

Turning to where Pablo was pointing, next to the front door, Dylan saw Grace's mud-encrusted black high heel shoes, the ones he'd given her in the barn. She must've been in a rush to get out of the henhouse and forgotten them there.

"Thank you, Pablo."

Pablo just raised his eyebrows. Then the man turned, and Dylan watched him lumber across the gravel to his pickup, get in, and drive off. Then Dylan picked up the shoes and went into his house, the apple still in his hand.

Opening the front door slowly, trying to control the squeak in the hinges, which like so much around the house was in need of attention, he stepped into his dark foyer. He slipped out of his dress shoes and tapped them, knocking off the soil from the orchard. The wind blew a few dry brown and gold leaves into the house as he closed the door. Mist-softened moonlight, greenish and glowing, streamed in from the windows, mixing with the faint light cast by the single fluorescent tube over the desk in the nearby kitchen. He carefully closed the door behind him, and stepping by his muddy work boots near the door, he set his dress shoes on the stairs to bring up later. Then he picked up the local paper on the foyer table and placed Grace's shoes in the hall closet on top of the paper.

Stopping in his stocking feet, Dylan observed the sight of his big heavy boots standing right next to his daughter's small shoes, both similarly dirty. Although Carter was out for the night, the foyer right here smelled of her and her things. He picked up her backpack and her sweater, the special one he'd bought for her in Atlanta that she must have left because it really didn't fit her and she didn't want to wear it around a friend. Hanging it up with the backpack, then looking at their shoes standing diligently and silently together in the hall, he was overcome with the sense that something was missing. For so long, there were three pairs of shoes, lined up as *she* had liked them, Carter's growing from those tiny toy-like baby shoes into these of a girl on the cusp of young adulthood. Shoes that he had noticed were already too small for her. It went by so damn fast, he thought. Everyone with kids muttered it like a mantra, but it was true. Trying to hold on to a child was like trying to hold on to sand.

So was this how it was to be now? he thought, two pairs left, and then finally one? He thought about Grace's shoes and wondered what they would look like in this hall. He liked her so much — truth be told, more than that, actually. But could another pair of shoes ever fit here?

Physically and emotionally drained, Dylan slid into the kitchen, took off his jacket, and hung it on the back of a chair at the kitchen table. He set the apple down on the table, walked over to the desk area, and hit the Return key on the family computer, bringing it to life.

An English-to-French translation page came up. It featured a scenic picture of the Avenue des Champs-Élysées, the Eiffel Tower in the background. Dylan smiled, thinking about his daughter sitting here, reading up on France because she'd just met someone who had been there. Carter was amazing, so curious about the world around her, and smart. Her understanding of the computer was so intuitive, Dylan had recently asked her for help a few times. Despite her poor grades in math, which simply bored her, when there was something that intrigued her, she would quickly become expert in the area. She had realized that the computer was a window to the world, which for her was surrounded primarily by apples trees and pasture.

In the address bar, he typed in the first few letters of the National Oceanic and Atmospheric Administration's weather service, a site he frequented very often this time of year, and he immediately pulled up the national maps.

The skies over the southeastern region were clear. There was a moderate northern front blowing through, but he was not quite as concerned about it as Pablo was. A bit of chill could be beneficial to the fruit this time of year. Some farmers even felt that a little frost could give an apple depth of flavor, but most didn't risk keeping their fruit on the tree long enough to find out, because an extended hard freeze could be catastrophic. And this time of year, a cold snap was always a possibility.

However, a hard freeze was often preceded by some warning, but what truly struck fear into a farmer's soul, what kept many awake on short fall nights, was fear of a sudden storm. An arctic front might keep the air chilled in the North Georgia mountains, but peak hurricane season in the tropics ran well into November, and a rapidly moving low in from the Gulf of Mexico could easily pass over Georgia, collide with a cold northern air mass, and cause a powerful hail-filled late-season storm. Even fruit that had succumbed to a hard freeze could be sold for juice or cheap commercial-grade flavoring. But fruit that had been hit by hail was done.

Dylan saw that on the latest NOAA map, way out in the lower western Gulf, a small *L* had been placed inside several concentric irregular circles. A low had formed, and with his fruit still on the trees, he would certainly have to watch it vigilantly. For more than just apples hung in the balance, of course, and more than just his year's work and investment — pretty much everything was at risk. There was very little room for a bad crop in farming, and virtually no cushion for no crop. And with a small family-run operation like his — one that couldn't afford crop insurance, had one single crop, no other meaningful source of income, and quite literally lived season to season — a single bad harvest would be the end of the farm. So every year, Dylan Jackson found himself playing chicken with the universe. This time of year, days and nights like this, Dylan often felt he could hear the kitchen clock ticking louder and louder throughout the farm. Indeed, these next few days and hours where he was trying to balance the perfect time to pick with the risks and hazards of whatever the heavens might throw his way were filled with a sense of breathlessness.

He could only shake his head, laughing to himself. *What a time to think about falling in love!* What was he doing? And why? If there was, indeed, some kind of reason for things, some kind of plan, it sure was fraught with risk.

Dylan looked around his softly lit home, set in the middle of the burdened orchard, and he thought he could almost feel the strain rising and swirling and pressing upon his house. There was a part of him that wanted to call the men right now and get that fruit in, but damn it, he wasn't going to be pushed around. The apples were almost there. If the heavens could just give him a little more time, he'd be good.

Thinking about his fruit, Dylan went back to the table and retrieved the apple. He walked to the sink, turned on the water, and gave the apple a quick rinse and a shake. Then he turned off the water, put the apple on the table, grabbed a wood cutting board and a well-worn paring knife, and brought those to the table as well.

After pulling out a chair at the table, Dylan sat down, picked up the apple, and plopped it down on the cutting board, and he sliced the crisp fruit in half vertically, from the stalk all the way through to the calyx sepals at the bottom. The two halves fell away from each other simultaneously, wobbled on the board, and then lay still. Using the knife tip on one of the halves, Dylan popped a few seeds out of the soft sac inside, carefully studying how the fruit was developing.

He was always fascinated by how each apple had the same general biology, but each one was different in its own way, depending on where in the orchard it grew, how much sun it received, how much care.

He palmed one of the apple halves, considering its shape and size and scent, the curves and folds where the fleshy mesocarp met the inner core. Each one was perfectly imperfect. Only nature could do that. Only nature could create something as original and beautiful as an apple. The same force that created a woman. As well as tropical lows and lightning.

He put his nose right up to the halved apple, deeply drawing in its fragrance. Then he took a few short sniffs, intentionally holding the scent of the fruit in his nostrils. All that came to mind was his wife's hair, the way it lay across the pillow around her head.

Dylan held a half to his mouth and took a bite, snapping through the skin, savoring the sugar content, rolling the meaty flesh around on his tongue to ascertain the consistency. They were so close. He swallowed. Man, were they close. Just about at peak juice and firmness. A few more days, maybe. Then off to market. How nice to have a real shot at selling to Cole Thomas, and perhaps Whole Foods this year. Their regional buyer had been through last week and sure seemed interested. This really could be the year that finally put them in the black. Dylan knew he could pull his fruit in the morning and most likely get five times a bushel what his conventional-farming neighbors got. And maybe seven times the day after tomorrow if the Brix levels held or rose.

The demand for what he had was great — organic apples from Georgia, a region virtually devoid of such produce in any notable quantity. The trick, of course, was actually growing it successfully all season, and getting a healthy crop all the way to harvest. You really had to go up into North Carolina to find a serious organic apple operation. This wasn't Washington State, with its cool dry breezes and limited natural pests. This was Georgia, which meant humidity and rain, and the critters that flourished in such environs. Some of his neighbors had toyed with organics, with mixed results. But that was exclusively with vegetables. Growing organic broccoli and strawberries, particularly on a small scale, was one thing. A vigilant combination of traps and potassium saltwater sprays could provide reasonable control. It was still expensive and labor intensive, but it could be done.

But *apples* — favorite food of the codling moth, the infamous worm in the apple core — and on a commercial scale! Not to mention that you had to provide picking crews with special gloves and jumpsuits. You really would have to be driven by something that very few people had in them.

What so many people took for granted as a commonplace grocery store item, he so often thought, something to toss in the lunch-box with a dash out the door, he knew was a mature ovary from what nine months ago had been a budding flower blossom — the result of earth and water transported through living breathing roots and transformed into nutritious compounds and simple sugars by the sun.

His chin began to fall slowly to his chest, and he involuntarily nodded a few times, so tired, so utterly and wholly exhausted. He was asleep in the chair now, his head lolling back and forth as his eyelids fluttered, welcoming sleep and dreams.

He saw a woman who stood near the stove, pulling her long hair away from her smallish ears with a fine-boned hand. In the shadows of the kitchen, Dylan could make out only glimpses of her. A smooth high cheek. A long neck, fluid and graceful. Around the lower part of her neck was a red scarf.

"Dylan, could you get up and set the table, please?" she asked with a big broad smile on her face as she heated some butter in a cast iron skillet.

She turned to him, and he could now see her clearly.

"Let me just watch you for a minute," he said from the kitchen table, unable to take his eyes off her.

"What? You've never seen a woman cook eggs before?" she said while cracking an egg on the edge of the sizzling hot pan and then opening it perfectly over the pan.

"How do you do that? It's always amazed me, the way you do that."

"What?" she said, looking at him and cracking another egg. "This?"

"Yes, how do you do it without looking?"

"I know what I'm doing."

"So do I, but I don't think I could do that."

"C'mon, Dylan," she said, "sometimes you just have to have a little faith."

He leaned forward, reaching out to her, but she turned away. "Becca?" he asked. "Becca?"

And suddenly he was in the elevator again, alone, and it was flying upward. His face pressed to the glass, he looked out, scanning the lobby and the people scurrying across it, all growing smaller as he was rapidly pulled up and away, and then he saw her — hands down and open, in her long fitted coat, she stood alone in the center of the lobby, looking up, watching the elevator, looking directly at him. And he stood alone in the elevator, looking directly down at her, the scarf dangling from his hand. He reached up to the glass, reaching out to her, and just when he was about to connect with her — the elevator shot through the roof of the atrium, disappearing into darkness.

"Becca!" he called out, the scarf in his hand.

And he woke with a start; in his hand was half an apple.

Getting his bearings, Dylan rose, tossed the apple in the compost bag, turned off the light in the kitchen, and headed upstairs, thinking about the night.

Would Rebecca Jane have wanted him to find love again? Rebuild a life? Find another mother for Carter? He'd thought about these scenarios before — but only as the musings of a man walking the orchard rows alone late at night. They'd never been real possibilities before, only hypothetical questions. But tonight, with the memory of Grace Lyndon still fresh in mind, tonight was different.

Walking through the foyer to the base of the stairs, he found himself thinking about Carter's words, that it was okay for him to fall in love again, okay with *her.* Was that true? Was that what she would want? And if so, why did it feel so much like *she* was still here?

Rebecca Jane really *would* have liked Grace Lyndon, he thought, stepping up the wide old staircase. He was even more certain of that now. She would have enjoyed her passion for food and cooking, the way she ran around so joyfully and carefree out in the barn with those pop-top chains wrapped around her neck. Dylan smiled at the recollection. Yes, Rebecca Jane would've liked her and her presence in this house. Then why did he feel so conflicted?

How strange all this was, he thought as he stood at the top of the landing, looking down at the foyer. That the woman he finally felt something for may hold the key to finding his lost wife. Oh, it was crazy to even think that! And he knew it. Still, Dylan had seen her in that elevator, or seen someone, and if there was any way to meet her or see that person again, he had to pursue it. Maybe it wasn't rational, but maybe there really was a plan at play here — an order to things — that involved an apple and Grace Lyndon and a woman with a scarf in an elevator.

In the upstairs hallway, Dylan walked to the open door of his dark bedroom, *his* bedroom alone now. Standing there, his mind drifting, he remembered his thoughts about Grace when he first saw her in the barn, looking up at him, her thick golden brown hair a mess, and how naturally beautiful and fit she was, and the way her hip had felt through her thin skirt when his hand was on her, his body so near hers. For a moment, his tired tossing mind wondered how nice it would be to have her beside him right now, at this late hour, with him. He didn't know what to do with his thoughts and the feelings they inspired. To feel this way even for a brief involuntary moment, was it a betrayal? Even if it was about someone his wife would have liked so much? Wasn't this exactly what Rebecca Jane would have wanted for him, someone like Grace Lyndon? He had no idea. And even if she did send someone for him — the truth of the matter, the real hard truth that appears to a man only in the darkest hours of night, was that he did not know if he would ever be able to love another woman, even if he wanted to, even if it was wanted for him.

There was one thing, though, that he knew with certainty and clarity, with all senses as well as his mind. He was looking forward to tomorrow, when he would see Grace Lyndon once again. And despite the questions, there was something rather wonderful about that.

A PLACE FOR ALL THINGS

The next day
Hands relaxed on the wheel, looking bright and rather chipper, Grace drove along, talking into her Bluetooth.

The sun had just begun to peek up over the Appalachians, and in the hazy aurous light along Route 52, she could finally see the orchards. They lined both sides of the rolling road up here in Apple Alley, though unlike Culpepper Farms, many were already in various stages of harvest. Most areas of the orchards had been picked; a few of the late harvest sections, with the last of their Yates and Pink Lady and Granny Smith, were crawling with workers and their equipment. Several open-bed apple trucks, on their way to market in urban and industrial centers, passed her as she headed north. It was a spectacular drive and a gorgeous day, and thankfully Grace didn't bother with the navigation system. Today, she knew where she was going.

Herb Weiss's booming voice filled the car as it came in over the speaker. "I understand you received the new HFCS data."

"Yes," said Grace coolly. "I sent Jonah some preliminary thoughts on recommended formulations a couple hours ago."

"Well, you were up early."

She reached for the Venti-sized coffee in the cup holder and took a big satisfying sip. "Nothing is more important to me than your beverage line, Herb."

"Care to give me the headlines?"

"Here's the deal." She took a deep breath, composing herself and finding her most professional tone, as she had promised both Bill and herself that she would. "If this is the way we're going to go, HFCS 55, which is approximately fifty-five percent fructose and forty-two percent glucose, is our best choice. Despite a fairly high water ratio, about twenty-five percent, the sugar profile, at least on paper, is comparable to sucrose, cane and beet, though as you know, it's obviously a lot more cost effective, particularly on the scale we're talking about."

"I'm quite familiar with HFCS 55," he barked. "We've been using it since the earth was cooling under the bottling plants. What I *don't* know are your thoughts on how it will affect your flavor."

Her thoughts? Her thoughts were that it would taint all her hard work. Her thoughts were that to put a highly processed product widely linked to a variety of medical problems in a consumer beverage marketed as wholesome and healthful was not a way to build brand truth. But he knew her thoughts, and that's not what he wanted to hear. She knew exactly what he wanted to hear.

"I can make it work," she said. It was harder to say than she thought it would be, but she did it — rather convincingly, too.

"The focus groups want it sweeter, and they like the HFCS," he said, feeling her out even further.

She wasn't even going to address that rationalization. "I can make it work. It'll be just as good as anything nature could make on her own." *Not entirely,* she thought, *but he knew that, and it'll be so much cheaper, he won't care.*

"Thatta girl," Herb said with relief in his voice. "So how was the dinner last night?"

"The dinner was fabulous. Thank you again. And we have a very good shot at getting that recipe. I should know in a few days."

"Good, good. Did he make the goat

cheese marshmallows?"

"He did, actually."

"I love those things. I have to triple my Lipitor dosage for a week after I eat them, but it's worth it. Well, you have a mighty fine day now." With a click, he disconnected and was gone.

Just after dawn, Grace drove down the winding gravel driveway into the apple orchard. It just ate her up inside to play this game with Herb, to dump high-fructose corn syrup 55 into her beautiful natural drink and, moreover, to do it with a can-do smile. But this was business. What choice did she have?

She parked the car in the wide clearing in front of the Jackson house, grabbed a paper sack from her front seat, hopped out, and headed for the house. Clomping up the front stairs in her pair of borrowed boots, she took in several deep breaths, filling her lungs with the morning-cold mountain air.

Before she could even knock, Dylan opened the door, surprised but pleased to see Grace standing on the front doorstep. Barefoot and in deeply worn jeans, faded gray flannel shirt, and a slightly mischievous grin — he looked even more enticing than Grace remembered.

"Mornin'," said Dylan. "You're up early."

"Isn't that de rigueur on the farm?"

"This is Georgia, ma'am. Best to speak English round these parts."

"Is French *food* acceptable?" she asked, holding up the medium-sized brown sack in her hands.

"Pretty much any kind of food is acceptable. C'mon in," he said warmly, stepping back from the doorway so Grace could walk by him and enter.

"Thank you kindly."

Grace stepped into the foyer, and Dylan shut the door behind them, noting that she had worn a fleece zip-up over a soft fitted shirt, comfortable but well-cut corduroys, and the boots. She saw him noticing her attire.

"I know, I look like I stepped from the pages of a Woolrich catalog."

"You look great," he said quietly.

Carter came running into the foyer. She was dressed for school, safety patrol belt and all. "*Bonjour,* Grace!"

"*Bonjour,* Carter!" Grace looked truly surprised, which Carter saw and loved.

"Carter has discovered the talking Google Translate page," said Dylan with a singsongy tone that indicated he'd had quite a lot of French that morning.

"*Très impressionnant,* Carter!"

"I have no idea what you said, but thank you!" Carter beamed.

"I said you are amazingly impressive, and your father should be very proud of you." Grace smiled at Dylan, then turned back to Carter. "Would you like some fresh *croissants?*"

Grace held up the paper sack, opening it, and the aroma of the flaky, buttery, crescent-shaped breads filled the foyer.

"Okay, now *that* is a word I know," said Dylan. "And the answer is yes!"

They started to walk into the kitchen, the three of them — Carter in her striped woolen socks, Dylan barefoot, and Grace in the boots that used to belong to Rebecca Jane.

The morning sun was already soaring in the pastel sky, cottony high clouds wisping across it, as Grace and Dylan trekked into the orchard.

Grace carried a heavy tool kit in her hand and a knapsack on her back. Dylan carried a large duffel bag filled with Southern Compounds lab equipment as he led the way between the trees.

The leaves and fruit were covered in clay from the recent spraying, and soon they were both streaked with it.

316

"So rain forests in Gabon, jungles in Madagascar, the streets of Shanghai — Georgia must seem pretty tame after working in those places."

"I like tame."

"Really? That why you went to an all-girls college?"

Grace looked confused, unable to recall mentioning anything to him about that.

"Carter told me."

"Right. Yeah, much more tame I'm sure than UGA. Which Carter told me as well."

Dylan stopped and grabbed a large branch before them, holding it back and out of the way so Grace could pass.

She just smiled, meeting his eyes as she passed by close to him, appreciating the gesture.

Directly in front of them, they came upon a tree with glossy green leaves and bright clean fruit, which very much stood out against the matte beige sea of kaolin-covered trees.

"Looks like you missed a tree, Dylan."

He walked up to it, examining the leaves and the fruit carefully. "No, this one belongs to the moths. We left it for them."

He held out a branch, and looking very closely, she now saw that on many of the leaves sat numerous little codling moths, grayish white with tiny copper stripes on their tight wings. They looked harmless enough, but on closer inspection, judging from the holes in the leaves and the fruit, she became aware of the danger to the orchard.

Now that she knew what she was looking for, Grace stepped back and took in the entire tree and immediately realized that it was covered with moths, and they were feeding on the tree. It was alarming.

"Don't you want to spray down the tree or do something immediately?"

Dylan smiled, touching one of the small moths gently. "They're smart little creatures, the codling. You spray down every tree in the orchard, and they have nowhere to go to lay their eggs. So they just fly about, circling and waiting. They know. And as soon as the good hard rain comes, and it always does, and washes off the clay, they're everywhere on all the trees and all the fruit before you can do anything, and your year is done. So every acre I tend, the moths get a tree. It's costly, but a small price to pay for the alternative." Dylan looked at the moths all over this one tree, considering how they were leaving all the others alone. "My grandfather used to say that there is a place in the orchard for all living things."

"I like that," Grace said.

"Yeah. Me, too."

Grace heard in his voice and saw in the way he was sharing this place the depth of what the orchard meant to him. It was more than somewhere to grow fruit. It was a way of life. And even more than that, it was a world, *his* world, that he cared for. This was not a man who would build bridges or construct skyscrapers or have monuments like the one she saw in the Ellijay city square named for him, but he had put his heart and his soul and his sweat into this place, tending to this orchard, and that would be his legacy.

She watched him motion for her to follow, and they continued on, making their way through the thick fruit-weighted branches, their boots leaving two pairs of tracks intertwined in the soft fertile earth. Dylan stopped a few times to examine the apples, feeling them, smelling them, analyzing how some were riper than others, depending on sun exposure and soil quality.

Each time he moved to examine a branch, the lines near his eyes grew deeper. Grace saw not only his love of this place, but also his concern over when to pick. You could feel the tension, she thought, as though the orchard were pregnant.

They came to a clearing where several especially large trees were planted with full exposure to the sun. Their limbs were thick and full with leaves, which filtered the sunlight on the warm ground below.

Grace dropped her tool kit and approached one of the trees. Dylan dropped his bag and helped Grace remove her knapsack.

Dylan stepped back as she began unpacking and setting up, nothing short of fascinated at her expertise with all this scientific equipment. He definitely had work to attend to today — for starters, he needed to find out the latest on that low and the associated front coming in off the Gulf — but he couldn't pull himself away just yet. "I have to say, this is pretty amazing."

Slipping into her attentive business mode, Grace focused very intently as she snapped a small battery into the back of a minicomputer that was about the size of a deck of cards. She reached for her toolbox while holding a wire in place. "Could you hand me the little Phillips?"

Dylan jumped up and retrieved it and handed it to her, watching as she expertly and rapidly tightened the screws on the back of the device, which she then carefully hung securely from a branch with black Velcro straps. She then attached a flexible clear plastic tube to the bottom of the device, and wrapped it around a limb right up next to a perfect ripe apple.

"What *is* that?" Dylan wanted to know, pointing to the device.

"It's a little computer we developed at Southern. Other firms have their own versions of the technology. Think of it as a hundred human noses with a memory chip."

From her knapsack, Grace removed a crystal-clear Plexiglas globe, similar to the glass ones in Monic's lab, and carefully placed it around the apple she'd picked out. Putting the available end of the clear plastic tube into an opening in the globe, she then carefully covered the rest of the opening around it with thick, sticky waxed paper, creating a seal.

While she was working, she explained this so-called headspace technology to him. "The apple's aroma changes throughout the day–night cycle, so using a software algorithm to determine when the fruit is at its olfactive peak, the device will draw the scent through a series of microfilters, capturing all its subtle components, soil, air, nearby fauna.

"Each scent molecule is identified and digitized, creating a perfect snapshot of the apple's aroma, which can then be re-created in the lab, using a variety of analysis techniques — gas chromatography, mass spectrometry, a lot of really neat stuff."

Dylan shook his head. Listening to Grace speak about capturing the scent of apples, watching her with rapt attention, he realized just how impassioned she truly was about her work, how much it was a part of her. He had heard it in her voice when she called him on the phone that very first time. He had been wary about it at first, but now he could see quite clearly that her interest in this orchard was in so many ways just like his. She, too, had a love for the apples, a scientific kind, but nonetheless real.

Dylan watched as Grace threw several wires up into one of the high branches. Watching this attractive and intelligent, agile and fit woman at work was far more compelling than pruning or spraying or anything *he* had to do today. He could not tear himself away from her movements in and about the tree — as if she were dancing with the boughs.

Grace looked up from her work, screwdriver in hand, wires hanging from her arm, and realized how intently Dylan was watching her. "Now, I know you have work to do, Farmer Jackson, so don't let me hold you up!" she yelled to him teasingly.

He laughed. "So, you're good?" he asked, rising slowly.

"I'm good." She smiled broadly at him.

"Okay, just holler if you need anything."

"Will holler away," she replied.

Dylan trekked out of the clearing and back into the trees as Grace pulled some long wiring out of her bag and began affixing it to a branch, feeling very at ease in this lush, tranquil place.

Several hours later

Ducking her head, Grace monitored a meter reading on one of the minicomputers under a thickly leaved limb. Hanging by inconspicuous dark Velcro straps, the device swayed gently in the southwestern breeze.

Stepping out and standing up fully, getting a feel of the moist dew point and warm temperature, Grace was astonished at the additional ripeness the fruit had acquired in just the last twenty-four hours. She took in the scent of the bursting orchard, honeyed and vinaceous, a woozy luscious fragrance that permeated not just the rich air but everything out here.

She heard a rustling and looked toward it.

"Are you hungry?" Dylan called out as he

approached from the trees with a picnic basket.

"Ravenous!" she replied happily, stepping away from the minicomputers in the trees and coming to greet him.

"Yeah, working in the mountain air will do that to you." Brushing some leaves and twigs from his hair, Dylan marched out of the orchard and into the clearing.

"So will eating nothing but croissants for breakfast."

Looking around, Dylan immediately saw that during the four or five hours he was gone, she'd hung several more pieces of equipment from his trees. Apples were enclosed in various clear casings; some had long needles inserted into them, their wires running into another small metered device about the size of a bread box.

Dylan approached, walked right to Grace, and with one quick motion of his arm unfurled and threw down a blanket, the same one that Carter had had with her in the apple tree.

"Yeah, well, hopefully this will reciprocate your treat this morning. And dinner last night. And for breakfast yesterday. Come to think of it, I've been eating very well since meeting you."

Grace laughed as he placed the big basket

down on the blanket, curiously leaning over it. He noticed her trying to peer into it, and he shooed her away. She did like to eat. A simple thing, but one Dylan always regarded, farmer that he was, as an important trait in a person.

"Okay, I have to admit, you're an intimidating individual to prepare a meal for."

"Please. You had me at the first scent." She leaned over the basket again, taking in the mouthwatering aromas wafting out of it. "Fried chicken? Oh, I'm thinking buttermilk fried chicken?"

Dylan was once again amazed. "How do you do that?"

"I like food."

"You don't say."

"And I love Southern fried chicken." She tried to open the basket, and he tapped her hand jokingly.

"Sit," he said.

And she did, crossing her legs and plopping down on the blanket.

Opening the basket and playing waiter, Dylan began removing flatware and plates and red-checkered napkins, and then wrapped food. "For lunch today in Chez Orchard de Pomme, we have some lovely cheese, made from the milk of my buddy Mike's goat Shelia." He removed the plastic wrap, which covered a small log of fresh white cheese on a small plate, and handed it to her.

Grace put her nose to the cheese. It was heavenly. "Oh, Shelia is my new best friend."

"It's good stuff. And we have some fresh chili corn bread. The corn, I think, is from Peter Lindsey's new crop, just cut out of the maze, which is right down this hill." He motioned with his head toward the field, and then he handed her a big loaf of the fresh corn bread wrapped loosely in wax paper.

"It's still warm!" Delighted, she held it to her cheek.

Then he pulled out a large oval Tupperware container. "And, yes, we have Dolly's buttermilk fried chicken."

Grace peeled open the top and smelled. "Fabulous."

"It is!"

He also pulled out a mason jar of sourwood honey, a sack of pecans, and a couple very cold bottles of a local mountainbrewed beer. He picked up a bottle opener, popped the top off a beer, and offered it to Grace, which she gratefully took. Then he opened one for himself, and they started giddily plating their meals.

"Dolly runs the Apple General Store

down on 52. Dolly and the quilting ladies have made a full-fledged avocation out of looking out for me. Truth is, I don't fight it as much as I claim to, and mainly because of Dolly's chicken," he said with a grin, leaning over the food. "I dream about this stuff."

Grace imagined there were plenty of women who would love to care for this man. "Well, it looks to me like you're being very well tended to," she kidded, looking at the lovely food.

"I have to tolerate a good bit of lecturing from the quilting ladies, but I think it's a small price to pay."

"How you should be running your life?" she said knowingly.

"You sound like you know those lectures."

"I know those lectures, though I get no food for my tolerance of them." Thinking about Monic's speeches, she ripped into a big drumstick. "Oh, wow, that's good." And it was, crisp savory skin, rich moist meat, just the right tang from the buttermilk.

"Of course, lately I've been getting the lectures at home, too." He bit into some chicken, too. Fantastic.

"Girls can be very opinionated. You just wait."

"Great. It seems like every person in the

world has an opinion on how I should be running pretty much every aspect of my life."

"We must be living in a parallel universe." Grace thought about all the people telling her what she should and shouldn't be doing lately.

"Yeah, well, I seriously doubt you're the social recluse that I am."

"Oh, really?"

He just looked at her, this lovely, charming, successful woman, and gave her a very wary gaze.

"Okay. You want to hear what a disaster I am? I had a date the other night when I called you. A blind date that I finally agreed to from one of those lectures. That's what I was doing in the Four Seasons." Feeling a sort of freedom, Grace let the words pour out. "I drove all the way to Midtown, valeted my car, and walked on in. I even saw the guy."

"And?"

"And I called you instead."

"Well, I'm flattered." Which, among other things, he was.

"And after the call, I never spoke to him. Let him walk right by me without ever saying a word. And there was nothing wrong with him! It was me. And I . . ." Her sense of catharsis was suddenly supplanted by the realization that she was revealing a lot about herself. "I can't believe I'm telling you all this."

"You're making me feel better."

"Really?"

Dylan found himself surprised by honestly how much he was enjoying getting to knew her. "People tell me that I focus too much on the apples," he said.

"People tell me I'm obsessive about my work."

"Are you?"

"I don't know. I'm too busy working to think about it."

They laughed hard, both of them, juggling plates of juicy fried chicken and the cold beer. Dylan threw a napkin at her, and she swiped it up, dapping at her mouth.

"Well, I dunno, Grace, if you're such a social disaster, what do you call this?"

"Well, this . . . this is work, isn't it?"

"Indeed, it is."

"Well, here's to work." She held up her beer bottle.

"Hear, hear!" He held up his bottle.

They clinked the necks of their bottles together and took deep pulls of the golden wheat beer.

After a moment, Grace looked around.

"This is a good spot," she said. "Must be nice, to have a place like this."

Though it was a statement, there was longing in her voice. Others would have missed it. Dylan did not. Nor did he miss that she was talking about more than just the beauty of the orchard.

He just nodded, and smiled a little at her.

Several hours later

In the kitchen, Dylan paced about in the fading sunlight pouring into the windows from the west. He spoke intensely on the phone to Pablo while at the same time viewing the NOAA Web site at the desk.

Grace worked on a meter-covered device that she had set on the kitchen table, a MiniVOS.

"The storm is tracking to the north," Dylan said into the phone.

Grace looked up from her work as Dylan spoke.

"I know, and it may very well do so, but we still have time to see. Another two, maybe three days would be ideal. I know. I know, Pablo. Let's talk in the morning. You, too. *Buenas noches,* my friend." Dylan hung up.

"He seems like he cares about you," said Grace.

"He's a good man."

"You really think you have two or three days?"

"Pablo doesn't," said Dylan with a smile that did not entirely mask his anxiety.

Dylan walked over to the table and took a look at what she was doing.

"Would you like to smell the essence of your apples, Dylan?"

"Sure."

"C'mere." She scooted her chair over, pulled another chair right next to hers, up against hers, and he sat down in it. "This is only a preliminary sampling from a few of the filters. I'll need a full twenty-four hours to thoroughly capture the entire spectrum and balance, but this is close."

Fine-tuning a few of the meters and dials, Grace hit a switch, and there was a very low but constant hum and hiss. Then she raised the supple plastic nose cup to his face.

Grace held it out in front of him, but Dylan looked unsure, not really knowing what to make of all this.

"Lean back," she said. Then she put her hand on his chest and gave him a gentle push, and he acquiesced, leaning back in the chair. She held the nose cup to his face and held it there. "Breathe in," she said, close to him, watching his face intently.

As Dylan inhaled a strong concentrate of the fragrance of his apples, his eyes went wide. Grace knew how powerful this kind of experience could be, and she was happy to be able to share it with him. Just as she felt when she had offered the blotters with her work to Herb Weiss's team, this was precisely what she loved most about her work, sharing the pleasure of fragrance and flavor.

"It's quite a thing to capture nature," Grace said.

Dylan continued to inhale, a multitude of images and related feelings sweeping over him, and Grace could see each one as though she were experiencing it with him.

"Take small interspersed breaths," she said. "You'll see that the aroma has a complexity that changes as you take the gases through different receptors."

Dylan followed her direction, and he saw his wife working in the orchards as she so often did, he sensed her, but there was more, the concentrate of the scent took him back to the day he first brought her to the farm to meet his grandfather, and his wedding day in the orchard, and the day Carter came home from the hospital, and the scent of apple on the wind the day they buried his grandfather, the cycle of the soil and the rain and the sun — it was all there in the scent.

He pulled away from the nose cup. "I don't even know how to begin describing that. I'd forgotten all the things that smell reminds me of."

"Smell is our strongest and really most unappreciated sense. It's hardwired to everything we experience throughout our lives, and it stays in our brains, like a record locator. A good fragrance is really a powerful cocktail of memories and emotion."

He couldn't quite pin it down. "Yeah. It smells like my life," he said whimsically.

She smiled at him, and then she held the nose cup to her face and inhaled, closing her eyes as she did when she bit into the first Cully apple. There was something about the scent of apple, she thought, that was truly unique to just that fruit — it really did touch on so many childhood memories. Probably because it was among the first baby foods so many ate.

"This is going to be very popular," she said thoughtfully. "I might tone down some of the earth notes, maybe bring up some of the brightness."

Dylan observed as she made some exacting adjustments to the dials while simultaneously watching their correlating meters.

Grace took a few quick sniffs, smiled, and then held the nose cup to his face again. He put his hand on hers and drew the cup even closer.

"I think this balance would make a lovely cider or a blend to an organic cinnamon and apple oatmeal," she said.

"Yes," said Dylan, nodding. "Hot from the pan on a cold autumn morning. I can absolutely smell that."

"Let's bring up a spice note, warm up the composition a bit." Watching his face, her left hand still with his, her right hand reaching out to the dials, Grace adjusted the machine, and she could see from his face when she was hitting just the right notes.

Dylan started laughing.

"What?" she asked happily.

"I smell my mother's apple pie." He pressed his warm hand to hers on the cup as he inhaled. "That's amazing!" Then he grabbed her hand and moved the cup toward her. "Here, you have to try this."

Their hands still together, she inhaled. "Oh, this *is* amazing. Yum." Grace reached for a dial and adjusted it. "I think I can bring up a butter note in here." A blissful expression came over her face as she sniffed the computer's new modulation. "Try this," she said, moving the cup toward Dylan.

Eagerly, he leaned in to her, his head nearly against hers, their hair touching as she held the nose cup out for him. He took in a whiff. "How about just a little more butter?"

She adjusted a dial and leaned in even closer, so that they were both taking in the scent from the one nose cup.

Grace turned to him and they locked eyes, their faces together, their hands together on the nose cup before them, which eased forth the intoxicating aroma of hot apple pie.

Never in her entire life did Grace Lyndon want to be kissed as she did at this moment.

Dylan stared at her lips, then moved up and looked into her eyes, and a million questions were asked and every single one of them answered in the breadth of a few blinks.

In the stillness of the room, the only sound the low humming and hissing, Grace was suddenly deeply aware of the scent of his skin, mixing with the aroma of apple, and it made her heart beat even faster as he seemed to be moving even closer to her. Or was she moving closer to him?

"Dad! I'm home!"

As Carter slammed the front door behind her, Grace and Dylan quickly moved away from each other and dropped their hands and the nose cup, which hit the table with a bounce and a hiss.

Dylan jumped up as his daughter ran into the kitchen and threw down her backpack and a sack of fresh corn. "You're early," he said, snapping out of the spell.

"The fog's coming in off the river, and an apple truck overturned right next to it," she said excitedly. "The road into town is closed." Catching her breath, she took in the sight of another person in the kitchen. "Grace!"

"Hi, Carter."

Dylan gave his daughter a hug and at the same time looked out the kitchen window, where he saw an SUV pulling away. He waved and the driver saw him and honked. It was entirely dark out now.

"Excuse me a moment," said Dylan as he picked up the phone and dialed Sarah's mother's cell.

"You have something in your hair, honey," said Grace as she pulled a long corn husk off Carter.

"How was the corn maze, honey?" Dylan asked, phone to his ear.

"Awesome!" Carter exclaimed. "Have you ever been to a corn maze, Grace?"

Tucking some stray hair behind Carter's ear, Grace smiled. "No, I can't say that I have." Grace exchanged a look with Dylan as each wondered what the other was thinking.

"Hi," said Dylan into the cell, breaking the moment with Grace. "Thank you for having her today. Yeah, I heard."

"Grace, are you going to stay for dinner?" Carter wanted to know.

"No, honey. I have to get back."

Grace and Carter watched Dylan get the news about the road closure. "Okay, thanks," said Dylan, and then he hung up. "It's going to be a few hours until they open 52," Dylan explained. "Unless you want to drive up and around the mountain in fog, I think you should stay for dinner."

"Yes, Grace! Stay!" Carter liked this idea.

"You sure? I've been here since sunrise, and I don't want to be an imposition."

"We'd love to have you. Can't you tell?" He pointed to his exuberant daughter.

Of course, Grace was wondering how *he* felt, but Dylan did seem to be genuine in the offer. "You sure you have enough?" she asked, waffling.

"Absolutely." Dylan sounded very definitive about this, and she liked that.

"What are we having tonight, Dad?"

Dylan realized he still hadn't had a chance to go shopping. And with access to town cut off, he wasn't going to do any tonight.

"Turkey," he said. "How 'bout turkey?"

"Great!" said Carter.

"I'd be happy to help make dinner. In fact, I'd love to," Grace offered.

Carter clapped her hands together. "Sounds like a plan!"

"Is it in the refrigerator?" Grace wondered, ready to get started.

Carter cracked up laughing.

"No," Dylan said, sharing a look with Carter.

"It needs to be defrosted?"

Dylan shook his head and reached for a large butcher's knife, the blade twanging as he pulled it from a big block on the counter. "I'll go get it."

Understanding, and not interested in fighting him for that task, Grace just nodded.

"What is all this?" Carter asked, pointing to the MiniVOS and equipment.

"Carter, how would you like to taste your grandmother's apple pie?" Grace asked.

Never having met her grandmother, Carter looked confused.

Dylan smiled happily at Grace as he headed out the back door with the butcher knife, and Grace reached for the nose cup.

■ ■ ■ ■

After several hours of preparing, cooking, eating, and laughing together, the kitchen was now lit by the glow of candlelight, and the entire house filled with the glorious aroma of freshly roasted heritage turkey. While Dylan had readied the bird with a few sprigs of chopped rosemary, ground black peppercorn, and a splash of maple syrup, Grace and Carter gathered fall beans and bush squash and a few little sugar pie pumpkins, and cooked the vegetables along with the sweet corn that Carter had brought home.

The house hadn't smelled this way or sounded this way or felt this way in a very long time. Sipping a cup of after-dinner tea, Grace helped Carter with her homework while Dylan cleaned.

" 'How can a bill that is passed by the Congress not become a law?' " Grace read from a practice test.

"Uhm . . . The Congress changes its mind."

Grace shot her a look. "Try again."

"The president vetos it," she said with a bored tone.

"Good," said Grace encouragingly. " 'Why

339

is democracy referred to as self-government?' "

"Because people participate in the decisions that affect them," Carter rattled off.

"Good! You totally know this stuff." Grace put the paper in Carter's notebook and closed it.

"Time for bed, Carter," Dylan called out from the sink area.

"Dad!"

"It's time. It's past time."

"This house is a dictatorship!" she said with a smirk.

"That is not true," he declared, wiping down the counters.

"Okay. Then I vote to stay up as long as I want tonight."

"We have a fair and democratic system of representative government here," he said. "And I am all parts of it. Now, bedtime."

Chuckling, Grace was amused with the repartee between them.

"Can Grace put me to bed tonight?"

Dylan looked at Grace, who nodded. "Sure. But make it fast. Grace isn't falling for any shenanigans."

Carter ran to her father.

Holding his soapy wet hands away from her, he gave her a kiss on the head. "Good night, honey."

"*Bonne nuit,* Papa."

With a tooth-baring smile, Carter ran off and joined Grace, and the two of them began walking out of the kitchen.

"What are shenanigans, anyway?" Carter whispered to Grace.

Grace smiled and put her arm around the girl. "Carter, I think you know exactly what they are."

Standing alone in the kitchen now, wet sponge in hand, Dylan turned and stood there, watching them walk out together.

Sitting on Carter's bed, in the light of the small lamp on the bedside, Grace tucked Carter in.

"I'm glad you were here tonight," Carter said, yawning. "It was fun."

"Yes, it was." Grace chose her words thoughtfully. "And I'm glad I was here, too."

"Grace, do you still talk to your mom?"

"Of course I do," Grace said gently. "Of course, I do, Carter. She's my mother, and no matter what, she'll always be my mother."

Carter never took her eyes off Grace's, as though searching to make sure the truth was there, which it was. "You smell good," said Carter.

"Thank you."

"Is it a fancy perfume?"

Adoringly, Grace leaned in closer. "Wanna know a secret?"

"Yes." Carter's eyes widened.

"It's vanilla."

"Vanilla? Like the kind you cook with?"

"Yes, an extract like that, from sweet beans near a little village in Madagascar that I like. But really, it's just plain old vanilla." Grace didn't bother explaining that it was a pure naturally extracted oil.

"Well, that explains why you smell like cookies."

Grace leaned over Carter, placing her lips gently on the girl's forehead, and Carter lifted up her head a tiny bit, breathing in the milky warm scent of Grace's neck.

"You've got a good nose, my dear," said Grace. "And now you'll definitely have sweet dreams." Grace tucked the soft covers around the girl's shoulders, turned off the light on the nightstand, and headed out of the dark room.

"Good night, Grace," whispered Carter, already half-asleep.

"Good night, Carter," Grace replied in a hushed voice, closing the solid wood door behind her. "Good night."

In the clean kitchen, still lit mainly by the

flickering candles, the dishwasher humming peacefully, Dylan stood at the computer, checking the weather. He looked concerned.

"She's terrific, that kid," Grace said, walking up to him.

He agreed with the comment. "She is." Then he turned to Grace, a worried expression on his face. "Listen. There's a Heavy Fog Advisory up until four A.M. You don't want to be on the mountain roads with no visibility. It's very dangerous."

"I have to get back, Dylan. I have work in the morning."

"I think you should stay the night."

Grace didn't respond.

"You can stay downstairs in the guest room," he said, anticipating her reluctance. "And leave in the early morning."

"I don't know." Entirely unprepared for this, in virtually all ways, Grace was really unsure how to respond.

He stood before her, looked her in the eyes, and she could hear in his tone that this was serious. "You need to stay."

She looked up at him and found herself nodding.

THE SPACE BETWEEN

Standing in the steamy bathroom, Grace looked in the mirror and slowly combed out her hair, a thick terry cloth towel wrapped around her, tucked into itself under her arms, over her breasts, draping down her torso to the tops of her thighs. It had been so long since she'd just sat in a hot tub and soaked, took time like that for herself.

With its original little white porcelain hex tiles, Craftsman-era fixtures, antique mirror, Grace loved this bathroom. This was not a reproduction in some obnoxious spec house. This was real, and that imparted something to her.

Grace unwrapped the towel and hung it on the decorative steel hook on the back of the bathroom door, which she then opened.

The cool air in the guest room felt nice, refreshing, on her warm damp skin. Her bare feet touched the smooth oak planks, and then the big braided country rug, as she walked over to the bed. On the hand-made quilt on the high queen-sized bed, next to an extra set of towels, Grace reached for a large loosely folded clean shirt.

Allowing it to drop open, she held up the long shirt before her, certainly one of Dylan's downy lightweight chamois button-downs, made even softer and lighter from extensive wear.

Instinctively, she held the material to her cheek. She smiled to herself: Even with her eyes closed, she knew this was his shirt, he was in the fabric.

She slipped it on, the cuffs hanging a good six inches below the ends of her fingertips. Holding up her arms, she let the sleeves fall back and open, freeing her fingers, which she then used to fasten a few of the bottom buttons at the front of the shirt.

Such an intimate thing, she thought, standing there in his shirt, to put this on. At least that's the way it seemed to her. Did he know that? Was that the point? Did he want her to feel close to him this way?

Or was she simply imagining this, wanting it to be true? Perhaps this was nothing more than a simple expression of hospitality. After all, what else in this house could he offer her to wear?

Grasping the collar between her fingers

and palm, she pulled it to her face. Did he want her to want him? In this room, on this bed, her body warm and damp and seeking him just beneath his soft worn shirt.

Grace heard footsteps, far off. His. And they were coming this way, toward the guest room.

She froze, listening, and the steps grew louder. They were slow but purposeful as he made his way down the hall.

Was he coming to her? Where else would he be going? She ran the geography of the hall over in her mind. There was no other room down the hall, and except the exterior back door at the far end, no other door at all this way.

Easing her feet silently along the rug and then the wood floor, she moved toward the door, the long sleeves brushing against the sides of her legs. She just stood there, listening, the steps coming closer.

Staring at the door, Grace looked at the old brass Victorian-style sliding bolt, which she had not slid out on the back of the door and locked through the strike plate on the jamb. The door could easily be opened in one quick move, a single turn of the hand, by either of them.

The steps kept coming, and with each one, the her heart rate jumped and her smooth breathing shortened into stifled gasps. As she stood there, thinking about what was to happen, urges at once strange and natural swept through her.

The footsteps approached the door.

And in another few seconds, without hesitation, they kept going — his footsteps moving past the door and continuing down the hall.

An immediate moment of relief was followed by a plunging of her heart.

Grace saw a light outside the guest room window go out. He had come down the hall not to see her, but simply to turn off the back porch light.

Continuing to stand there, hearing his steps coming back, she felt foolish for letting herself get swept up in this — until he stopped, right outside her door.

The guest room was lit softly with two shaded lamps and the crystal-covered fixture in the bathroom, and she knew light was pouring out from under the guest room door, filling the dark hallway with the telltale sign that she was unmistakably still awake. She imagined him standing there, the light all around him.

Breathless again, leaning forward toward the door, watching the handle, listening, Grace wondered what he was doing, what he would do.

As she leaned even closer to the door, a tiny trickle of water from her wet hair dripped over the nape of her neck and into the open collar of the shirt, onto her back between her shoulder blades, running down her spine, tracing the length of her curvature there, slowing to a stop between the two dimples at the small of her back, and was quickly absorbed into a spot on the back side of the shirt, where it met her skin. The sensation gave her a shiver.

She had had enough of this, and just as she was about to call out his name — he moved on.

If she did not know before that she had wanted him to come in, she knew it now. And despite the hint of sadness and longing that came with this unfulfilled wanting, there was also a certain ease afforded to her simply by knowing.

Grace walked back on the wood floor and turned off the light in the bathroom, and then the two in the room, and pulled back the nice quilt and climbed up into the bed, the sheets smooth and cool against her lower thighs and calves and feet, the scent of Dylan still vaguely present on the soft shirt around her.

The strange dull glow of the nearly full

moon swathed in heavy fog crept into the dark room. Head relaxed on the deep pillow, Grace lay there, top sheet and quilt upon her, eyes open. Usually she was asleep within seconds, partly the result of intense daily exercise, and partly because for Grace Lyndon, sleep was a means to an end. Several hours of rest so that she could get up and get right back at it. But tonight, she was very much awake.

Scent carried all manner of information about people, like a secret primal code. Grace had studied this, the chemicals of attraction, how the scent of a woman's breath and skin revealed when she was ovulating, how the scent of a man's clean sweat on his shirt could keep a woman's body stirred, no matter how tired her mind.

She could take off the shirt, she knew, and probably get in a few hours of insensate rest. But she did not.

Several hours later, the fog blown mostly clear of the mountainside, Grace quietly slipped down the guest room hallway, through the kitchen, and into the foyer. In stocking feet, in yesterday's clothes, hair tied back, carrying her shoulder bag, she strode softly on the planks in the foyer, partly sliding, trying her best to be silent.

As she slid along, seeing the moon now shining through the open windows in this house, she thought about that first conversation with Dylan and how he had been in this very spot, very much as she had pictured, looking out at the moon, speaking into her ear.

Near the door, she bent down and retrieved the boots she'd been wearing, which were right between Dylan's and Carter's. As quietly as she could, she put them on.

Above her on the landing of the open hallway, in the shadows, Dylan stood, watching her.

Standing there above her, in jeans and untucked flannel shirt, barefoot, watching her tie the laces of the boots, he thought about whispering to her, coming down the stairs. But he felt it best just to let her slip out. If he came to her and she looked in his face, surely she would see that he had been up all night thinking about her. Surely she would know how close he had been to knocking on the guest room door and telling her how he felt. And kissing her. And it would not stop there. He didn't think he could stop it there. Not tonight. The attraction he felt for her was too intense and too powerful, and so before he changed the course of their lives, he had forced himself away from her door and sent himself back down the hall, walking away while he could. Because he had to get this right.

Above the foyer, Dylan took a few more steps forward, his face just out of the shadows, his toes approaching the railing on the ledge, looking down at beautiful, smart Grace Lyndon in faint light cast only by the stars and planets and moons outside. This lovely kindred soul who had shown him how to taste huckleberry sorbet, to open his senses further than he'd ever considered. He felt that he was on a ledge, on the brink of a sheer drop from which there could be no turning back. And where he went, his daughter went, too. So he had to get this right. There was no room not to get this right.

Boots laced up, Grace stood and moved to the foyer mirror, where she paused, considering herself. It was the most private of moments, but Dylan watched without reservation as she ran her fingers through her tousled hair, straightening it, neatening herself to present herself to the world. He'd seen her toss her head back a few times, moving her hair with that purposeful motion. He saw it in the restaurant when Carl Fisher had approached. But this was different. This was an honest appraisal of how

351

she saw herself. It was the real Grace Lyndon, vulnerable and profoundly determined.

And it was then, at that exact moment, that he knew he could fall in love again. As he watched her alone like that, the feeling rose and overtook him with such an urgency that he could not deny it. He couldn't quite explain it, but he knew it.

He wanted so badly to go to her right now, reach out to her, hold her angel face in his hands and kiss her eyelids closed, and place his cheek to hers. To have her near in his arms.

Grace slowly opened the door, and as it always did, it creaked. He saw her recoil at the sound, but she eased it open as quietly as she could and slipped out, and then she shut the door behind her. He could see her clearly in the bright moonlight — walking across the front porch, down the steps, and toward her car — and he heard the engine start and the distant crunching gravel as she drove up and away.

He did not know where these feelings would lead, or even if they would ever go anywhere. But after pacing these halls for hours, sitting on the top of the staircase and watching the resolute wind blow the fog from the orchard, and now watching her leave, bag on her shoulder, slipping out the door in the dark before dawn, he knew these feeling were real. They filled him with an odd vertiginous swirl that seemed to begin in his gut and go to his head and then spread out like a tonic dispersing in his blood.

After a few moments in the starlit darkness, Dylan took a deep breath and carefully moved across the landing and then down the steps he knew so well. First turning in the foyer, he walked into the kitchen and tapped the computer to life.

A browser window with the weather came up immediately. The fog had indeed cleared, which gave him some relief about Grace and her journey back into town.

But he saw the storm, a tropical low that was slowly coming in over Mississippi, heading for Alabama and, inevitably, Georgia. There were still questions about timing and severity, and they were broken down and addressed by meteorologists up at this time of day just like him.

It was coming. He knew how these storms tracked and he knew what a low did and he could do the math and see that this one was coming. The question now was when. Precisely when.

After closing the browser window, he went

back into the foyer and put on his boots. Then he headed out to check on the apples.

Under a Sanguine Moon

That afternoon

The twenty small clear beakers were lined up along the steel counter in the development lab, notations made on them with black grease pencil, each one filled with a different colored liquid measuring exactly twenty-five centiliters, about a cup. Alone in the lab, Grace paced along the length of the long counter, pensive, carefully studying the different liquids, leaning over and smelling some, lifting others and swirling them, studying the colors and textures and even the occasional light effervescence. A few of the liquids she tasted.

They were fine, she thought. Fine. The high-fructose corn syrup 55 percent formulation was indeed the best option. For *her* palate, the various test flavors were now too sweet, the lower and mid notes too syrupy, the top notes cloying, and most of the flavors were now redolent of green corn husk. But how many people would really notice this? How many people had palates — or cared about their palates, what they smelled and tasted and experienced — like Grace Lyndon? In the end, she thought, the HFCS-enhanced test flavors were fine.

Half the beverage products on the world market had similar notes and aromatics, and Bill was right: That didn't seem to impede their success.

Leaning over a beaker, she took a few sniffs. Holding up another, she swirled the liquid and then took a sip. It made her crazy to see and smell and taste her work this way, to have her labor and creative vision turned into this, but she had to let it go. Because after all, this wasn't about *her* palate. She sold her work for money. That was the deal.

She was well aware that someone whose regular lunch was five perfect cherry tomatoes next to five little broccoli florets next to five baby carrots and five cucumber slices and five slices of green bell pepper could be fairly called a bit obsessive. How many people knew — or cared about in the slightest — the difference between a Syrah glass and a Bordeaux glass? She understood that she could be what some would call fanatical about her work — okay, and perhaps about other things, too. Most people weren't wired this way. She got that. Things simply were not so important to them, at least these kinds of things. For most, a beverage like this, those on the counter before her, was something to slurp down with a turkey sandwich and SunChips during lunch break.

So, Grace told herself to just get with the program and get on board with it like everyone else. Like many other things had been in her life, this was simply a means to an end. She had to let her work go. No matter how much it was eating her up inside.

Holding up a purple-colored liquid, hibiscus flavor, one of her regular favorites, she took a sniff, considered it, and then put the beaker down, uninterested in having this particular liquid in her mouth.

Clipping along the tiled hall in her designer shoes, Grace noticed that her feet were really hurting today. It was impossible to spend so much time in this kind of footwear and not have occasional pains, but she was more aware of it today than usual. Which seemed odd to her, as she had spent a lot of time recently in those very comfortable boots she'd been given at the farm.

Turning a corner and approaching the executive suites in Development, she found herself wondering: Perhaps having spent so much time with her feet so comfortable had made her more attuned to their optimal state.

So much on her mind — Dylan Jackson, high-fructose corn syrup, her aching arches in her gorgeous pumps — and now Grace saw her assistant watching her attentively up ahead, looking gleeful.

"Good afternoon, Ms. Lyndon," said Emma, even more cheery than usual.

"Hello, Emma," replied Grace when she reached her assistant's desk.

"The new calibration data is in. The file's on your credenza, and I made sure Jonah got his settings right — poor Jonah, bless his heart." Emma grinned sympathetically, thinking about Herb Weiss's overwhelmed assistant. "Oh, and Accounting released the funds I requisitioned for Cully. The check is on your desk."

"Thank you, Emma," said Grace, and headed for her office. "Oh, when you have a moment, would you see if you can dig up any information about a little restaurant in Cozumel that specializes in fish tacos. Jimmy's, or something like that."

"Sure thing, Ms. Lyndon!" Emma was already on it.

As Grace turned, her eye came across the picture of Emma's brother, the handsome young man in uniform. And Grace looked back at Emma, this optimistic, dedicated, nice person, whom Grace had thought little about before now. Caught up in her own life, her own struggles at work, Grace had been so self-involved, she felt she had neglected to appreciate the depth of a terrific person sitting right outside her door. Something had happened to Grace, which she wasn't particularly proud of.

"And Emma, one more thing."

"Yes, Ms. Lyndon?"

"From now on, call me Grace."

Emma broke out into a huge smile. "Okay. Grace."

Sunset

The streetlights above her beginning to buzz on, Grace strode along the sidewalk on Peachtree in front of her building. Her hands thrust deep in the long pockets of her tailored coat, evening traffic still hurrying along in the street beside her, Grace saw the seemingly massive ruddy gold full moon peek out ahead of her, from under the city skyline, right next to the Peachtree Plaza. Low in the sky, and even among the lights of downtown Atlanta, it was dazzlingly bright.

A few days ago, she bit into an apple, and

now her entire life seemed to be in a state of upheaval. No matter how fast and how hard she walked the concrete on this brisk night, the yearning for Dylan had not left. No, as she looked at that rising orange orb, it was clear to her that something was growing in her that had not been there before. Grace was both giddy and anxious; butterflies had escaped her stomach and flown into her soul.

Her phone rang, startling her, and after a moment, she retrieved it from her pocket and checked the caller ID.

It was him.

"Hi," she said, not caring to disguise the fact that she was happy he'd called.

"Your red lights are on," he said.

"Is this a prank call?" she said.

"On your gear, in the orchard." Dylan sat outside on his front porch steps, watching the sunset over the orchard, phone to his ear.

"The minicomputers!" Realizing he was talking about the data lights on her equipment, she stopped walking and leaned against the side of a building on Peachtree Street, holding the phone tight to her ear. "Oh, wow, that was fast. That means the runs are complete."

"That *was* fast," he said, surprised, looking up at the big moon, too, and wondering what this meant for them.

"I think it's all the extra days of light you're giving your crop. The aromatics were really high."

In fact, they were much higher than Grace had expected, and he could hear the amazement in her voice, along with a bit of something else — a tinge of sadness, perhaps, that her work at the farm was nearly done?

"Wonder if all this moonlight is helping the fruit, too," he said kiddingly.

"Could be," she kidded back.

"Have you seen it tonight?"

"I'm looking at it right now. Yes, bright as day. Pretty amazing."

"This is going to help the harvest. It's a good omen."

"A harvest moon," she said, looking up at its luster.

"Well, a sanguine moon. Technically speaking, the harvest moon was last month. The Cherokee were big fans of this one, as they did most of their winter prep late, too."

"This sounds like a subject you know a lot about, Mr. Jackson."

"The moon and I, we go way back."

They both looked out at the moon from their locations, the city street and the farm, which were so different, and yet they both felt like they were together.

"Sounds quiet where you are," she said.

"Sounds busy where you are."

And they thought about that first night on the phone, when they'd first heard and sensed and felt a common view of things.

"So, I guess I'll be picking up my equipment tomorrow."

"That really was fast." Now he was the one who had a hint of sadness in his tone.

"Blame it on the moon," she said wistfully.

Grace standing, Dylan sitting, they both knew that if they were to continue to be together, it would have to be by choice and action. Fate and fortuitousness provided but a chance, so if they were to continue whatever this was, after tomorrow, one of them would have to take the next step.

Finally, Dylan broke the moment. "Well, I look forward to seeing you tomorrow, Grace Lyndon from the Southern Comp Corp."

She smiled. "Good night, Mr. Jackson."

"Good night," he whispered in her ear, and then hung up.

Dylan continued sitting on his porch, looking up, and spotting the first dark clouds coming in. He felt the balmy tropical southwestern wind, saw it whipping up the branches and tossing the apples. Several fell to the ground.

Dylan stood, looking out toward the west, and then he headed inside. There was very little time left indeed.

Just before sunrise
No alarm, the first predawn light sneaking into the darkness of her condo from under the curtains — right before she opened her eyes — Grace Lyndon awoke. She lay there in the bed, her eyes remaining closed, allowing herself to wake and simply be where she was, and a strange smile broke out across her face: She knew. What Dylan had meant when he described this moment, she knew — all of it.

Then she opened her eyes, realizing that she'd neglected to set her alarm and that for the first time she could remember, she'd slept in.

Grace sat up and stretched, feeling like the world had a certain glow around it. Yes, life felt wonderful. She hopped out of bed, joyful, thrilled to greet the new day.

The alarm was distinctively piercing in Dylan Jackson's bedroom. He ran from the closet where he was getting dressed and knew immediately that it was not the alarm clock.

By the time he'd jogged over to his dresser, where the NOAA Weather Alert Radio was plugged in, and slammed off the alarm button, the computerized voice was already speaking: "The National Weather Service in Peachtree City has issued a Severe Weather Advisory for the following counties, Pickens, Cobb, Gilmer —" He snapped the MUTE button, and the voice stopped but the small red ADVISORY light remained on.

Dressed for her chores, Carter opened the door and shuffled in. "What's going on?"

He turned to her. "It's time."

Then they heard the doorbell ring repeatedly and loud knocking, and they immediately stepped out onto the open hallway, where through the foyer windows they could see Pablo on the front porch.

Behind him, trucks were pulling down the gravel driveway. The men were coming.

Dressed for the day, moving happily about her apartment as she got ready to leave, Grace approached the breakfast bar adjacent to her small kitchen and tapped the computer out of sleep mode. She immediately noted an e-mail from Monic titled "Connection Made!"

At once, Grace's stomach dropped. She realized that this was about the woman in the elevator.

Taking a deep breath, she opened the e-mail.

All her attention focused on the computer, Grace anxiously, devoured the e-mail — which she saw was actually part of another one that had been forwarded to her. At the top, Monic had written: "CC corporate says '08, Batch 702, went to Neiman Marcus, who says went to Southern Region. For kicks, put an ad in Atlanta Missed Connections. Just got this!"

Grace read the forwarded part of the message: "Well, you sure took long enough, man in the glass elevator. I would love to see you. aprilday27@google.com And oh . . . Burberry."

At first, Grace thought this must be a joke, Monic teasing her, but, heart pounding, she immediately navigated to the Craigslist "Missed Connections" page and read the ad Monic had written, describing Dylan's experience exactly as Grace had explained it, and providing specific details about the perfume and the scarf — although just to be sure, she asked respondents to name the maker of the scarf. Monic was definitely the person to go to with this, Grace told herself, now with oddly mixed feelings.

So this was it, thought Grace. The elevator woman had been found, this Clive Christian Burberry-wearing woman of exceptional taste who was obviously so beautiful and compelling and bewitching that the most remarkable man Grace had ever met in her life spent the last year and a half thinking about her and searching for her. *Well, aprilday27, you are one lucky girl.*

For an instant, Grace allowed herself to consider the possibility that Dylan might meet this woman and decide that she was not what he wanted. But then Grace stopped herself. She had spent too many years and too much of her life working to protect herself from just this kind of thing. She'd let her guard down and she'd allowed herself to fall, and there was now no doubt in her mind that it had been a mistake. Her heart sank.

Ghost or flesh and blood woman, destiny or simple heated attraction, it was clear — Dylan would desperately want to meet her, and aprilday27 felt the same way about him. And now it was going to happen. Only an idiot would stick around and keep her hopes up, and Grace Lyndon was not going to play that role.

She reached for the keyboard, about to print the e-mail and contact information, and for another brief moment hesitated. And in that tiny slice of time and space, Grace ran all sorts of possibilities over and over through her mind. But finally, she did what she knew she had to do.

She hit PRINT.

THE DAY

As soon as Grace drove over the rise in the orchard road, she could see it and hear it — the army of workers and trucks and crates that had descended upon Culpepper Farms.

Driving down the gravel road, hit with the amazing sight of this hectic, bustling, joyful activity, she could hear music, upbeat country music, blasting on the portable radios of the workers throughout various parts of the orchard. Despite the pressure of the day and all the hard work, the atmosphere was festive and celebratory.

Pulling her car around several tractors that were hauling large carts of apples, slowing around some of the busy workers who waved and tipped their hats to her, she drove up to the clearing in front of the house and turned off the car.

Stepping out, she was hit with the music and the laughter and the men shouting directions and exchanging information in

Spanish and broken English. She just stood there for a moment, right in the middle of it all, looking around as strong black-haired men with dark complexions walked right by carrying apples in large sacks on their hunched backs, others with equipment and tarpaulins and tools and ladders. A small tractor hauling a large cart of apples honked at her. She jumped out of the way, and headed for the house, ducking and bobbing and weaving through this cacophonous chaos. A few yards from the front porch, squatting to avoid being hit by a ladder on the back of a man next to her, Grace bolted up and suddenly saw *him* — standing there on the front porch. Swept up in all the excitement around her, Grace just stood still and, wide-eyed, took in the sight of Dylan.

Like a general on the front lines, Dylan stood perched at the top of the steps, a phone to his ear, coordinating teams of workers who were coming and going all around him, pointing up into the orchards, simultaneously talking on the phone and directing those approaching and shouting to men on tractors, when he turned and saw her.

He locked eyes with her from the distance and smiled broadly. And despite all the activity around him, all that he was running and doing and directing and leading, the look he gave her, the connection he made with her across the distance between them, truly made her feel like she was smack-dab at the center of the universe.

Despite all that she had just told herself over the last couple of hours driving up here, Dylan Jackson had the remarkable ability to melt her worries with a look.

She trotted up the steps, joining several heavyset men, most of them in muddy frayed hats, bottles of water in their back pockets, dirt and small twigs already stuck to their sweaty hands and faces. They stood listening to Dylan give directions in English and Spanish.

A small tractor with a forklift sped up and halted in the clearing in front of the house, and before the driver could even speak, Dylan pointed at him, hollering out direction. "Acres five and seven on the ridge are starting to come in. Get the empty bins still up there over to number eight, pronto!"

"You got it, Mr. Dylan!" And the tractor driver was off, heading out into the orchard.

Dylan saw a man carrying ladders up into the orchard. "Juan, they need help up in . . . *en la zona norte.*"

"*En el camino ahora,* Mr. Dylan!" the man said enthusiastically, changed his direction to the north, and headed quickly up into the field with the heavy ladders.

Dylan saw two men trying to lift a heavy container full of apples and pour it into a bin on a parked tractor forklift. They struggled with the three-hundred-pound wood-slat container.

Dylan was about to call out for some help; then on impulse, he simply bounded down the steps and grabbed the container, and the three of them carefully lifted it and poured the fruit into the bin on top of the layers of apples already in the bin, careful not to bruise them.

"*Gracias,* Mr. Dylan," said one of the men.

Dylan patted the man on the back, smacked some dirt from his hands, and turned to see Grace. "Hi," he said to her.

She just smiled at him. The sun behind her, on her hair, she was radiant. He looked at her, with her hair back, face fresh and clean, in her pretty fall jacket, sweater, and cords: a stunning sight on his front porch steps.

"Busy day," she said.

"I'm glad you're here."

"Me, too."

"I told the men to be careful around your equipment."

"I'll go get it in a minute."

There was an awkward moment when they simply looked at each other, so much running through both their minds, so much to say. They both opened their mouths and began to speak at the same time, and then they stopped and laughed.

"You go first," said Grace, in no rush to tell him her news.

"I have something for you," he said, motioning for her to follow him up the steps. "Walk with me."

They dodged a man carrying a telescoping fruit picker — a long pole with a small wire basket atop — and then another lugging a big five-peck field basket overflowing with just-picked apples.

Grace continued following as Dylan marched across the porch and to his jacket, where he retrieved a small wrapped gift. He stood before her and, holding the gift in his hands, presented it to her.

"What is this?" she asked, more than a little surprised as she slowly took the gift from him.

"Open it," he said, beaming.

Grace looked at the gift in her hands, then up at him. What was he up to? Then she tore into the present, ripping off the paper, unable to hide how delighted she was. The wrapping paper torn off, she looked at the object in her hands: a box of crayons, the big sixty-four pack.

"Dylan." She laughed a little as she looked up at him again, as touched as if the gift were a great diamond.

He smiled affectionately at her. "It has the sharpener in the back."

She turned it around and saw that above the crayon sharpener, he had taped a small folded note. After removing the note from the box, she opened it and read his careful handwriting: *Here's to life's many colors.*

"Thank you," she said.

"Hey," he said, "it's never too late to have periwinkle in your life."

"Excuse me!" Pablo yelled up at Dylan. "The bins are set in tract eight. I think we should move on to the eastern side next. The rain is coming — later tonight, maybe."

"Okay, I'll be right there," Dylan replied, nodding. Then he looked up, assessing the wind speed and cloud velocity. "This is a slow system. We're gonna get it all in. Thank you, my friend."

Looking out from under the porch, Grace noticed that the thickening clouds in the skies cast a strange and beautiful reddish hue on the morning. It was the kind of light that set sailors and farmers into a state of immediate action. A eerily warm breeze blew in from the southwest, much too temperate to be from nearby.

Pablo took off, and Dylan turned back to Grace. "I have to go," he said.

"I know."

"Can you stay? After you get your equipment?"

She found herself nodding. "I'd love to."

Leaning against the porch railing, the box of crayons in hand, Grace watched him go and sighed.

Hiking through the orchard to the clearing where she'd hung her equipment, Grace took in the sights and sounds of the harvest. The men worked at a remarkable pace, and despite all the various tasks and dynamics at play, there was a sense of order to it.

Most of the men wore Cordura picking sacks with padded straps over their shoulders as they moved through the trees, their hands in fingerless cotton harvesting gloves, twisting the apples from the thickly leaved limbs, taking care to keep the stems intact on the fruit whenever possible. In their hands were the sickle-shaped harvesting knives, with fruit clippers worn in the leather sheaves on their belts.

Tarps were tossed and spread out beneath trees where the men worked to catch falling fruit. Ladders of various sizes were set beneath and around the trees and laid up against the trunks and low boughs so the workers could reach the crowns and high branches.

When their picking sacks were full, looking like big barrels strapped on their bodies, the men streamed down the ladders from the trees, waddling over to the massive nine-hundred-pound wooden harvest bins built onto pallets that were stationed every fifty feet or so by the forklift tractors through parts of the orchard that were being actively worked.

Squatting down over the bins with the heavy bags, each one laden with sixty-five pounds of apples when full, the men very carefully poured the fruit, slowing raising the bottom of the bag while simultaneously sweeping it over and across the mounds of fruit already in the huge bins, trying hard not to bruise or crush the apples. It was laborious, exacting work, and the men did it with a grace that was nothing short of remarkable.

When the bins were full, nearly overflowing, the tractors would appear, slipping their forks under the pallet on which the bins sat, lifting them and moving them quickly out of the field toward the barn for inventory and storage and delivery prep. And as soon as a full bin was loaded and hauled, a new empty one was brought in and set almost simultaneously.

As she walked through the activity, it seemed to Grace like a great ballet that they all seemed to have rehearsed. Grace had seen this kind of activity during the grape harvests in Burgundy, and being here now reminded her of just how much she had loved that. The fragrance of fresh ripe fruit — as strong as it had been in the orchard before — was now nearly overwhelming. Working in the orchard on harvest day was like swimming in the middle of an apple-scented ocean.

With a dreamy smile, Grace entered the clearing in the orchard, walking through the picnic spot, and went to her equipment hanging and swaying in the trees. Yes, the red data lights on the instrumentation panels were on. She had what she had come for, the complete Cully apple formula. But as she began to take down and pack up the equipment, she was overcome with a sense of bittersweetness that she had not expected when she first bit into that apple.

By midday, the thick southwesterly breeze kicking up a bit, nearly a third of the fruit had been picked. The mass of workers continued to move through the orchard, acre by acre, lot by lot, tree by tree. Nearly all these men of various ages knew Pablo well, worked with him regularly, and had picked for Cully for years. Some of the older men had worked here with Ros Culpepper and remembered him fondly. Stories were swapped among the workers while they were in the field.

Labor was one of the most costly line-item expenses of running an orchard, and every year it went up. There were, of course, many ways to pick an apple today, and Dylan knew about them — the tree-shaking tractors, and the suction cup machines, and the high pressure robots that used algorithmic measures to determine what to pick — and they were all essentially useless, destroying branches and bruising good fruit. One of the things that Dylan loved so much about growing apples, particularly their harvesting, was that the process was still what it always had been. There would never be an adequate replacement for a man's hand picking an apple. In a world where so much changed so very quickly, there would never be a replacement for this magical day. He loved it, and his favorite place to be on this day was at the center of it, in the barn.

While the men were picking, ceaselessly filling their sacks and tarps out in the field, the bins came in, bottlenecking at the barn.

The lift-tractors loaded with fruit lined up outside the open east-facing doors of the big red multigabled apple barn. As soon as the traffic cleared and there was room inside, Dylan waved in a loaded tractor.

On his instructions, they drove around inside, unloading bins and placing them in various demarcated areas. After depositing their loads, the tractors turned and moved out the west door. Marking and numbering the full wooden bins as they were brought in, a trip ticket book in hand, Dylan also made inventory notations to keep up with what was coming in from various sections and areas of the field and where it was being stored in the barn. Occasionally he would pull out his long slender produce knife — the ivory-handled one his grandfather had given him when he was a boy — and examine an apple from each lot, testing Brix and salinity, texture and overall integrity.

Finished loading her equipment, Grace stood at the eastern entrance of the barn, the light still behind her, where Dylan had stood when she first saw him. And she watched all the activity, an entire year of fruit brought into this one building over the course of these hours; she watched Dylan jogging from bin to bin, jumping on crates, making notations, directing the tractors and the men and the entire operation.

Dylan looked up and saw Grace observing him from afar, and he lit up and waved to her with a broad sweep of his arm, and she waved back — and once again, despite all the commotion around them and the distance between them, they were connected.

"Grace!" a voice hollered over the din of the tractors.

And she turned to see Carter approach from behind her, a picking sack over the girl's shoulder, another one in hand.

"C'mon! No standing around today!" said Carter, and she threw the sack to Grace, who caught it.

While Grace tossed the strap over her shoulder, Carter waited nearby, when Peter, Pablo's boy, ran up to Carter and tossed a big pile of hay at her. Carter screamed and ran after Peter, throwing hay at him. While the boy and girl chased each other around the barn, throwing hay and small apples at each other, Grace adjusted the picking sack strap and watched them. As did Dylan, looking over his shoulder with decidedly mixed feelings at his daughter enjoying the attention of this handsome boy.

Grace caught Dylan's eye from a distance, and they exchanged a look that amused Grace and made Dylan maybe a tad more comfortable.

By late afternoon, the sun was already throwing long shadows across the trees. Most had been picked now, and their branches and boughs lifted upward, noticeably lightened by the removal of their long and heavy loads. Beneath them and among them was a thick new carpet of fallen leaves and stalk pieces and twigs.

The last hours of light closing in, the men picked up the pace in the field, and the labor in and around the barn increased, as it did throughout the farm. All this work and the orchestration of it required a great deal of effort from a variety of different places, and now with the pressure increasing, it all seemed like a collage of seamless moments and tasks running together to keep the apples coming in.

After spending hours with the picking teams, and with several of Carter's friends who left school early to help out, Grace jumped in with other various tasks, helping out wherever she could.

Everywhere she turned, she seemed to see Dylan. They waved at each other from distances, exchanged glances and smiles, but in the hectic pace were never really able to spend any time together.

Grace rolled up her sleeves and joined the group in the kitchen, where Gladys, Pablo's wife, had worked all day directing many other women who kept food pouring out the front and side door, onto a long series of folding tables, all covered in checkered paper tablecloths. While some of the women prepped and cooked, others did nothing but bring food out and set it on the table — Southern food with a Mexican twist, and rivers of it: fried chicken, chicken and dumplings, chicken mole, shrimp and grits, turnip greens, field peas, fried apples, fried calabaza, bread pudding, corn pudding, fried hush puppies, fried burritos, fried okra, buttermilk biscuits, black-eyed peas, butter bean succotash, pecan pie, corn bread, and, of course, apple pie, hot and fresh with sloppy big scoops of local hand-churned ice creams.

As the dinner hours approached, Carter grabbed Grace out of the kitchen, and they both joined Sarah, Carter's friend, helping Sarah's father throw up a half-steel-kettle barbecue drum on the side of the house.

Mesquite and pecan hardwoods were quickly set ablaze, and Dolly and the quilting ladies descended on the barbecue with a hurricane of food that went right onto the grill, whole chickens and fresh catfish and still-kicking mountain trout alongside local old-style grass-fed burgers all slathered with homemade spicy barbecue sauce. And the Lindseys, the elderly couple who owned the fields adjoining the orchard, pulled up in their pickup and started unloading ears of corn that had recently been cut. The corn was thrown on the kettle drum, too, and in minutes massive plumes of roasting savory-sweet smoke filled the air around the house. It wafted into the orchards, toward the workers who soon began pouring out toward the house.

Standing behind one of the long tables, passing out thick paper plates filled over with food to the men coming through the line, swaying happily to the great country song on the radio blasting behind her, Grace found herself simultaneously greeting lines of women to her sides and behind her — Sarah's mother, Mrs. Lindsey, Dolly and company, several of the neighbors, teachers, moms from school.

Dylan marched by several times, hard at work but smiling at her, almost teasingly, and she returned his playful looks.

While she was serving and helping to unload pails of incoming coleslaw, it became quickly apparent to Grace that these were more than friendly greetings from the neighbors. She felt herself being distinctly observed. Clearly, people had heard a thing or two about her and used the harvest meal to check her out. Understanding the way news spreads in a small Southern town — news like a good-looking widower being picked up in a long black limousine sent by some woman — Grace was tickled and even flattered.

Dolly, a boisterous older woman, nudged up next to Grace with a plate overflowing with mounds of food. "Okay, sugar, you're a woman, not a bird. And a woman's got to eat. Now, go! And that's an order!" Dolly shoved the plate into Grace's hands and scooted her off with it. Smiling broadly, and pretty much starving, Grace offered no resistance.

Big and fat like nearly all the fruit in the entire harvest, four to five inches across, larger than a man's palm, the last apple was pulled off the tree in the gold green light around midnight. Dylan was right, the storm had slowed and they were able to get the entire harvest in. Once again, his instincts had been correct, and in this game of chicken he played with the natural world, he had won. Judging the quality of this season's luscious and bountiful crop, perhaps the best ever, he had most definitely won. There were handshakes and pats on the back all around, but still, even at this late hour, there was much work to be done.

After paying all the workers, Dylan began the task of final inventory on the fruit in the barn. With help from Pablo and a couple other men, each and every bin and lot were accounted for, marked, and properly prepared. Tarps were pulled over some for long-term storage, others were moved by tractor to the west side for delivery over coming days, and still others, in need of a little more ripeness, were moved to the eastern doors, where they would receive further sun.

In addition, the tractors had to be loaded up or stored, and all the farm's equipment and tools had to be accounted for, assessed, and then repaired or stored.

This work would go on until at least sunrise, and Dylan remained on top of it all.

After putting Carter and Sarah to bed in Carter's room, and helping Gladys and the ladies clean the kitchen — a Herculean task — Grace sat outside on the front porch for quite a while, watching the tractors being loaded and driving off, the last of the workers grabbing bottles of water and heading out, and seeing the bright light pouring out of the barn as though all the fruit now inside were generating its own sunshine.

The music had long stopped and the din of the work subsided, and she could once again hear the crickets and cicadas and creek frogs, and every few minutes she could hear Dylan, from the barn, and occasionally see him standing there in the bright light, joyous and glowing, as he finished the task of bringing in his fruit.

With Gladys in the guest room watching over the house, and with the promise of light in the eastern sky, Grace rose and walked into the orchard, so much on her mind and in her heart. She felt lost in it all.

Moments after she stepped off the porch, Dylan looked up for her, but Grace was gone.

Dawn

The dark ruddy glow permeating the orchard this time of morning felt eerie and portentous. Normally this would alarm Dylan, but with his crop in, and still buzzing with the thrill of such a successful harvest, he barely noticed. No, as he made his way through the orchard, now airy and thinned, the only thing on his mind was Grace.

Her car was still here and he'd seen her only minutes before, on the porch, but now she was nowhere to be found. He'd enjoyed having her at the farm so much today, loved sharing this day, this community, all that it meant, with her. And even though they'd exchanged just passing glances, he felt that she loved being here, too.

He'd waited all day to talk with her, be with her, and he had an idea about where she might be.

As charged and weighted as the orchard

had been when expectant, there was something equally remarkable about the peacefulness that swept through it now.

Dylan approached the clearing in the orchard, near where she'd hung her equipment, the spot where they'd had their picnic. He walked into and through the clearing, saddened to see that she wasn't there.

Dylan admitted to himself that he had truly hoped to find her here. And he'd thought about sitting, too — next to her — and perhaps telling her how he felt. And then he'd kiss her. After the last hours, seeing her but not being able to be with her, putting his hand to her face and drawing her near and kissing her were things he simply could not go one more day without doing.

Standing there on the western ridge of the orchard, he realized that with the fruit and so many leaves and twigs gone, he could now see through the trees and down the hillside, where off in the distance near the field at the bottom of the hill, he thought he saw some movement.

After stepping forward through the trees and pushing aside some low branches, he stood on the top of the slope and looked down into the field where the corn maze had been planted, and he saw Grace nearing it.

Growing all season on nearly fifteen acres, the corn was extremely high. The maze had just closed to the tourists, and it would be cut down any day now. From the hill, Dylan could make out the twisting, winding paths that had been cut into the maze, and he saw Grace approaching the entrance to it.

He thought about going after her, took some steps forward toward the same path she'd taken down the slope, but then changed his mind as he watched her enter the corn maze and disappear into it. What was she doing down there?

He looked up at the sky, then back at the maze, and with thoughts of her growing even stronger, he made a decision.

Although she was only a few hundred feet into the maze, Grace already felt like she had left the world. Lost in her thoughts, she walked down a narrow path that had been cut into the cornfield. The stalks rose well over fifteen feet in height, in some places as high as twenty feet, nearly two stories. It was very much like walking through a maze with solid walls that were much too high to see over; only everything around her was alive, moving and rustling in the temperate breeze. There was nothing out here but rippling waves of browned green leaves and high shifting stalks and pale gold silk and ears and ears of yellow dent corn towering over her in the almost surreal light, purple and faded as old burgundy.

A warm gust on the back of her neck sent a tingle down her spine, and suddenly she was aware of how entirely alone she was out here in the middle of this maze in the middle of a field.

Grace turned and began retracing her steps. After several paces, she took a left into an opening onto a path that she had walked earlier. Though after several more steps, she started to wonder if this really was the direction from which she had come.

Looking around, trying to remember exactly where she had walked, she realized that she had no idea. Everywhere she turned, everywhere she looked, it was all the same. High shifting corn. Walls of it. She had no idea how far into this she had gotten and no idea how to get out.

She took a deep breath, trying to control a rising and building sense of being out of control. Beads of perspiration ran down her neck, and small flecks of corn silk stuck to her. She removed her jacket, tied it around her waist, and tugged on the top of her sweater to let the air hit her skin.

In the middle of the corn, in the middle of that puzzle, wiping sweat from her brow and fighting a panic, Grace slowly turned, trying to decide which way to go, when she heard a rustling in the corn.

She moved toward the noise and then froze still, listening while the rustling grew louder and her heart pounded faster. It was clear now that something was there and it was coming toward her, directly at her, and just as she was about to run or shout — Dylan parted the corn and stepped out from it, right before her.

She opened her mouth and just stared at him.

Covered in corn silk and dried green husks, he stared back. "I was looking for you," he said.

"How did you find me?"

"Intuition. Luck. I don't know exactly." He took another step, toe to toe with her, his face just inches from hers. "But I found you," he said with quiet resolve.

Grace continued to simply stand there, speechless, her breathing still fast, her heart still pounding.

And he reached for her; just as he had dreamed of doing, Dylan reached out to her, putting his fingers to her temple, gently touching the fine hair above her ear, and putting his palm to her cheek. Their eyes exchanged a thousand million words.

He pulled her close and pressed his lips to hers.

He had thought about this moment and envisioned it, and for a portion of second, it was as he'd imagined, and then it turned into something else, unanticipated, and in her widening eyes, he saw this unbound thing rise up in her, too.

Feeling herself dangling, Grace pulled her head back. "Dylan —"

But he cut her off. "We're supposed to be here, Grace. Right now. That's why you bit into the apple. Grace," he said as he held her face and looked into her eyes. "I see you. All of you."

Grace turned her head to his hand, bringing up her shoulder, feeling the warmth on her cheek. She felt open and exposed, and at the same time safe, but certain that any moment it could end. She was afraid to move in any way.

Dylan dropped his eyes to her lips, considering them with a newfound longing, then met her eyes again. The sky darkened above them, but they didn't notice. The wind ripped into the corn, rustling the stalks and shaking the walls around them. But they didn't hear it. Nothing else existed but them.

Dylan moved her face toward his, slowly and carefully now, and he put his lips on hers once more.

He heard the pace of her breathing increase and he pulled her closer.

She wrapped her hands around him, across his wide back, wanting to feel him nearer, and she brought her body lightly to his, and this made him tremble.

"I want you, Grace." He whispered it in her ear, and the heat in his breath and the ache in his words made her want him, too — here and now, right now — even more than she had with his shirt around her, even more than she ever thought possible.

She began to kiss him back, slowly and fully, openmouthed, his fingers loosely in her hair, moist kisses along his neck and exposed chest where she took in the scent of him, and with that, as though a switch had been thrown in some secret place, she softly gasped.

Sliding his fingers deep into her hair to the back of her head, he brought her closer toward him, kissing her deeply now, running his hands over her shoulders and down her back to the sides of her hips, where he pulled her near and held her there, and she saw in his eyes now the depth of his want for her, heard it, felt it throughout her.

She wanted him with such an urgency and immediacy that she thought she would cry or scream out. She hated her clothes and his clothes in a way that she had never even considered, hated this fabric between them, and she began pulling and tugging at it all, hands running down his chest to his waist, searching for his skin, seeking it out, the scent of him close like this driving her mad. She lifted up his shirt and slipped her hands under it, needing to feel him, needing to feel his skin and his body before her mind stepped in and made her act otherwise.

A massive crack of thunder boomed overhead, but neither Grace nor Dylan paid it any mind.

Dylan took off his coat and threw it on the ground, grabbed the jacket at her waist and tossed it on top of his, and her hands moving all over him at once, he swept her up in his arms, and laid her down on the jackets in the corn.

A humid mist began to fall in the corn maze, spattering on the husks and building quickly as they faced each other, on their knees, kissing and touching. Hands grasping her arms, her wet sweater clinging to her skin, and now he ran his lips behind her ear, under her dripping hair, moving down along her neck, her face agape at the oncoming rain.

Lost in their need for each other, Dylan and Grace pulled at their clothing, tugging it off as fast as they could, their hands sliding along each other's warm wet skin.

They came together, embracing, the rain falling harder, her breasts against his chest as they rolled to the ground on top of their clothing, removing the rest of it along with their boots. Dylan laid her down again and, with a deep breath in, his body shaking, moved to her side, pressed up against the outside of her thigh there, and leaning on an elbow, simply took in the sight of her as though he wanted to make sure she was here and real.

Grace lay there with him against her, his leg partly across hers, looking up at his perfect face, chiseled as it was the first time she saw it dusted with clay.

Dylan reached his quivering hand to her sopping forehead and slowly ran it down her cheek and jaw and throat, tenderly following the curve over her breast, down her belly, his fingertips moving lightly across her lower abdomen, palm and open hand sliding down her thighs, all in one motion on her wet skin, never taking his eyes from hers, listening to her sounds as he touched her until he just could not bear it any longer, and he moved over her, and in one movement they were one.

All her life, Grace Lyndon had been running, fueled by a passion that got her impossible jobs and sent her into jungles and drove her up trees and brought her to this place to this man to this moment, and looking into his eyes right now, she knew what had been missing from her life.

After so many years of thinking about the senses, Grace now gave herself over to them fully and completely, without any of the control that governed most of her life. She released herself, gave herself to the joy, and to him: kissing him, running her tongue across his neck and tasting his skin, burying her nose into him while he moved over her faster now, giving in entirely to where he was taking her. He grasped her hand tightly. Both were crying out loudly and fully in the wind and the rain, and they went there together.

A crackle of cloud-to-ground lightning lit up the sky and shook the earth, and the wind screamed through the corn. They lay together, entirely drenched and muddy, corn silk stuck to their glistening skin. The couple slowly sat up and faced the deluge around them, finally noticing the danger of the storm.

"We have to go!" Dylan said loudly.

Grace nodded as another boom of thunder roared overhead. They both grabbed at their soaking clothes, throwing them on as best they could, laughing at the craziness of this, being out here like this.

Grace put on her pants as fast as she could, but didn't notice the piece of paper that flew out of one pocket. Dylan saw it fly up in the corn and blow open, and he caught it. After turning it over, he could make out the opening lines of text. He stood paralyzed in the pouring rain, read all of it.

Grace looked over, and in the light of a nearby flash of lightning, she saw him reading. "Dylan!" she yelled out over the storm.

"What is this?" He held up the paper, which fluttered in the wind.

At first she didn't speak as he stood there unsteadily in the gusts, pieces of wet husks smacking against his face while he read it again. She saw the expression on his face, the disbelief. "I was going to show you!" she finally yelled over the howling wind. "I brought it here to show it to you!"

The thunder and lightning near and all around, he stared at her, the paper waving from his hand. All she could do was stand there, too, her heart sinking.

There was another loud *boom* of thunder, and he grabbed her by the wrist. "Come on!"

And they started to run into the wildly whipping corn.

They emerged from the maze into a clearing, hair and clothing soaked, covered in husks and stalk pieces and corn silk. On a rise, they found Dylan's truck. They ran to the truck, the water rushing toward them in fast-flowing rivulets. Sprinting and splashing through the ankle-high mud, they closed the distance. Grace threw open the passenger door and jumped in and slammed the door, after which Dylan ran around the driver's side, jumping in, slamming that door.

In the relative calm of the dry cab, the rain pounding on the metal roof and pouring over the windshield in sheets, Dylan turned to her. His voice was calm and even pained now. "I don't understand."

"I was going to tell you."

"Why didn't you?" He was so quiet, his voice almost a whisper.

"I was going to tell you yesterday morning, and then this morning and . . ." She trailed off; the words she was about to offer just sounded so thin and stupid. "Dylan, I'm sorry." It was all she could say.

He simply stared at her, perplexed. Her hair was wet and matted; mud had splattered all across her face and neck and arms. Running his hands through his own dirty wet hair, he didn't know what to think.

He looked at the wet paper, and all he thought of was Rebecca Jane. And Grace could see on his face the pain she'd caused with her weakness, not telling him sooner, and she hated herself for it.

Before him was a beautiful, brilliant, captivating woman with whom he really thought he could . . . with whom he really thought he *was* falling in love. In his hands was the name of someone he saw in an elevator a year and a half ago who he had thought might somehow have some connection to his wife.

Much had changed in the last year, and even more had shifted over recent days. Looking at Grace sitting before him on the sopping vinyl seats of his old truck — her lovely, open, caring face focused entirely on him — he was overcome with the urge to roll down the window and throw the note away and start his life anew . . . but after standing at the altar and having a child and spending many years both challenging and bountiful, *after love true and real was lost in an instant,* he knew that he could not live his life, with Grace or with any woman, until he saw where this note led.

And Grace could see all this anguish in his eyes. "My mother was like yours, Dylan," she said. "My mother was a great cook. When I was a little girl, I would stand on this little wooden stool in the kitchen and watch her make miracles from the simplest things. Eggs, flour, milk, a little sugar, some fresh blueberries, and she'd create these pancakes that weren't just food, they were . . . to me at the time, they were like magic. I'd watch her in her apron standing there, she was so young and beautiful, and I'd think, that's what I want to do. I want to make that kind of magic. I want to be like that. And I dedicated my life to that."

Grace paused now, feeling tears pressing, but looked away and willed them to stop. Then she took a breath and turned back to him.

"I never went to college. I took the bus to Decatur just to get away for a day, and I walked around Agnes Scott, dreaming of escaping, and inside a building there, I saw a painting of a woman from long ago, successful and confident like she didn't need anybody. Grace Lyndon, the plaque said.

400

And that's who I became. I left behind an aunt and a trailer and Adlen Walker, that dreamy-eyed little girl I used to be, and I got everything I thought I ever wanted, until an apple brought me to you."

He held up the paper. "I have to know," he said.

She nodded. "I know you do."

"Why didn't you just tell me?" he asked her again.

"Don't you see? Because I'm falling in love with you."

And he said nothing.

The tears forming in low pools in Grace's eyes went running down the front of her cheeks in straight lines. And *she* had nothing left to say.

There was a startling flash, and then — *boom!* — a bolt of lightning struck the ground nearby, shaking the truck.

And something immediately ran through Dylan's mind. "Carter!" An alarmed look on his face, he found the keys and jammed them in the ignition. Dylan started the truck and threw it into gear. He hit the accelerator, and the tires revved in the mud, but when he turned the wheel, they found traction and the truck lurched and took off. "Carter's petrified of lightning."

Torrents of rain pounded on the windshield, and the wipers couldn't sweep the glass clear even at full speed. Ragged quarter-sized hail, the kind that could destroy an entire crop in minutes, battered against the roof of the old truck like falling nails. But none of this deterred Dylan. Leaning forward in his seat, wet hands gripped to the wheel, he sped the truck through the mud and slippery gravel, driving partly on his recollection of the road. He was driving too fast to see it fully.

They hit a deep pothole and the old truck fell and lurched and Grace bumped up and down in the squeaking wet seat. Work orders and newspapers on the floorboard flew up into her lap along with mud from their boots and she grasped the handle on the door to steady herself.

Coming over the rise and driving down to the house, Grace saw Dylan look away from the road and out his window, over toward the tree — *the Tree* — and saw the memory of what had happened right here in this spot overtake him. And it was as if he were disappearing right before her eyes.

Boom! Another flash of lightning struck nearby.

Dylan flew down the hill, and they hit another bump and they both bounced around on the old bench seat, the rusty springs creaking as he whipped the truck into the clearing in front of the house, threw it into park, turned off the ignition, opened the door, and jumped out. Dylan slammed the door behind him and sprinted across the clearing, then bolted up the porch steps just as Gladys and Pablo appeared at the front door.

Grace ran from the truck, too, and from the expressions on the front porch knew that Carter was gone. She saw panic hit Dylan.

He paced a few times on the front porch, then jumped over the porch steps and ran as fast as he could through the pouring rain to the barn.

Grace followed him, running past the front porch, past the henhouse, into the east door, which was now open only a few feet. Hit with the overwhelming aroma of ripe apples, the sound of the rain pelting the high-gabled roof and causing a strange reverberation inside the barn, she looked around. Running her hands over her hair to knock some of the water from it, she raised her head, turning it until she finally saw, in the far corner of the barn, next to the barrel that held the pull tab chains, Dylan holding his daughter.

Carter cried in his arms, frightened by the power of what had taken her mother from her.

Dylan looked up and saw Grace, held her eyes, and then turned back to his daughter.

Grace set her jaw and threw her head back, sending water flying, swallowed hard, and walked out. This was not her family, not her place.

A little while later, the thunderclouds moving on and leaving a light but still steady rain, Dylan emerged from the barn with his arm around Carter.

The two of them walked toward the house, then up the front steps. And there, near the door, was a pair of boots — the boots Grace had been wearing. On top of the boots was an envelope.

Dylan picked up the envelope, opened it, and pulled out a check for twenty-five thousand dollars, made out to *Dylan Jackson of Culpepper Farms.*

They stood in silence on the porch, the boots beside them, the check in Dylan's hard, the rain pattering against the porch roof.

A Fork in the Road

Evidence of the storm was everywhere. Winding down Highway 52 out of the mountain in her sports sedan, Grace saw downed trees, large branches in the road, local creeks that had easily overflowed their banks and ran now onto the road beside her. Driving by a fallen WELCOME TO APPLE ALLEY billboard, she slowed around an emergency crew, lights flashing on their work trucks, that had cordoned off part of the roadway where a huge mud slide had occurred.

Soaked, shivering, feeling that her entire life had been put in a washer and then hung out to dry, where did she go? She thought about work, her nice clean office with files of data to be read about high-fructose corn syrup. She thought about her apartment, barren and lonely.

She pulled up to a stop sign where two roads came together, a fork. The one to the left led south, back to her life, and the one to the right led west, to where she did not know. Wipers intermittently knocking the mist from her windshield, she looked at the two choices and thought long and hard about them, finding the one to the west most appealing. That was her impulse: to run.

Monic opened the front door of her nice suburban Atlanta home, and her mouth slowly fell open. "Well, I have now seen everything," she said.

And there on the front steps, next to the big clay pots with the still blooming hydrangeas, her hair dried into a tangled mess, clothes still damp, caked mud all over her, Grace stood barefoot.

"*What* happened?" Monic asked, hardly able to believe this sight.

"I was going to call," said Grace. "But I just drove by, and I saw your car."

Looking Grace up and down, and up and down, Monic was speechless.

"Can I come in?" Grace asked.

"Yes, yes, of course, come in." Monic stepped aside. "We have strict rules and covenants in this community, and if the neighbors see you, the homeowners' association will probably fine me."

Grace stepped into the spacious foyer, her feet tracking a little mud on the high-gloss oak floors.

"Sweetheart, what happened?" Monic asked, reaching up in fascination and pulling some husk from Grace's filthy hair. "You smell like a corn dog."

Grace did not laugh, and for the first time, Monic could see how troubled her friend really was. "This is about the apple man, isn't it?"

"I didn't know where else to go."

"Oh, honey." Monic smiled at her. "Come on, let's go sit down in the kitchen. Try to walk softly because the baby just went down for a nap. Which is a good thing — because you'd frighten her."

"Stop it." With a little work, Monic could at least make Grace smile, even now.

They tiptoed into the kitchen — a spacious room with the requisite granite countertops and midlevel black appliances, which opened to a den pretty much like all the other tract homes in the area. On the refrigerator were pictures and photos and notes and cards, a collage of a happy family. A baby monitor sat on the counter, turned on.

They quietly pulled out chairs and sat at the kitchen table.

"I tried," Grace said. "I finally found the guy and I opened up, and it's over before it really ever got started."

"You gave him the e-mail?"

"After."

"Ah, so there was a *during*."

"I don't know what I was thinking."

"How *was* the during?"

"Actually, I do know exactly what I was thinking."

Monic sighed. "I'd love a during."

"Are we having a conversation here?"

Monic looked hard at her friend. "So you didn't tell him until you were good and ready, and now he's gonna go see her, which he was gonna do anyway, and now you know what it's like to be with him, which judging from that expression on your face and the stuff all over you, looks like it was better than warm Irish soda bread."

"Is there a point here?"

"Yes, there's a point here. For the first time in your life, you jumped off the high dive and you hit the water and you're flopping around, and so what? What did you expect? Pat yourself on the back and get back in line and go up there again."

Grace still wasn't sure what her friend was getting at.

Monic leaned over the table, closer to her.

"Grace, love is work. It has its moments — oh boy, does it have its moments — but it's work. Believe me, I'd love to roll around in a field in the rain, but truth be told, most days I'm happy if he just loads the dishwasher."

They laughed together rather loudly, and the distinctive sound of a baby waking started on the monitor.

Monic closed her eyes in dread. "She didn't sleep long enough," Monic said, fearing the battle before her — as well as the hell that would be the rest of her day if that child did not get in a decent nap.

Then they heard something else on the monitor as Simon, Monic's husband, opened the door to the child's room and went to the crib. Monic turned up the volume and they continued to listen over the monitor while he picked her up and comforted her.

"It's okay," Simon's voice said. "It's okay, you just had a bad dream. Do you want me to rock you?"

The women exchanged a smile as he started to sing.

"Night, night, Emily. Night, night, little Emily. Night, night, little Emily. Daddy is right here."

Satisfied that her spouse was properly tending to matters, Monic turned down the volume. Then she faced back to Grace. "It's not always glamorous, but if it's real, it will come to you."

"I just don't see how that's gonna happen." Grace shook her head and looked up as though there were some answer on the ceiling.

"Don't give up on it. Don't run. Do the work."

"I don't know. I think maybe the universe has made a mistake."

Monic put her hand on Grace's mud-streaked forearm. "You're gonna be okay, Grace. I can't tell you how this is gonna go, but when I look at you, I know it in my heart. You're gonna be okay."

It was the second time someone had said that to her recently: that she was going to be okay. The first time, she believed it. This time, she wasn't so sure.

A light mist continued to fall on the orchard. There was something cleansing about it. Dylan looked out at all the fallen limbs and leaves and counted himself lucky for getting in his crops just hours before the storm. Still, sitting here on the front steps of the porch, he couldn't stop seeing her face, hearing her words, the sense of the feel of her body still so present in his mind.

And now there was this note, this woman, April Day. Who was she? For whom exactly had he just upended the promise of something that seemed so right, so destined?

He heard the squeak of the screen door and turned a little as Carter walked out and joined him. "Dad, why did Grace leave like that without saying good-bye?"

Dylan took a deep breath, knowing this was going to be hard. "Carter, sit down for a second."

Already not liking the sound of that, she sat next to him on the front steps.

"I don't think we're going to be seeing Grace for a while."

She turned to him, immediately upset. "What happened?"

"Nothing happened."

She looked even closer at him, this terrible liar. "What did you do?"

"Carter —"

"Did you say something to her? What did you say?"

"Carter, I know this is a lot for you to understand, but —"

"Don't talk to me like I'm stupid. I'm not!"

"I'm not talking to you like you're stupid. I'm trying to explain something very complicated, that I barely understand."

Carter pursed her lips together and stared at him, waiting to hear what was so complicated.

He spoke very slowly, as if trying to explain it to himself as well. "Grace and I . . . we may be looking for different things."

"Right," Carter said pointedly. "She's looking for us, and you're looking for Mom."

"Carter —"

Again she just stared — *yes?* — waiting for an explanation, but there wasn't one, because the kid had pretty much nailed it.

"Mom brought her to us," she said. "She brought her to me. Don't you get that?"

"Carter, it doesn't work like that." He tried to be gentle but ended up exasperated.

"Mom's gone! She's gone and she's never coming back. When are you going to get that through your head? How will I ever have another mother if you don't get that through your head!" Carter jumped up and ran across the porch and into the house, the screen door slamming hard behind her.

Grace opened the sliding glass door of her apartment to let in the evening air. The storm had cooled the city down quite considerably, but she was still warm from the hot shower. It felt good to get the mud off her, the remnants of the farm — at least, that's what she tried to tell herself. Her bare feet on the nice Berber carpet, the fine silk robe against her skin, she was back in her world once again. How strange the juxtaposition, the silk and the mud, the solitude and Dylan Jackson with her in the field. Thinking about it now in the stark clean condo, it truly seemed surreal, except for a throbbing inside, a longing for something that had been so real and then suddenly vanished in the wind. It was him, and Carter, and the farm, and the community, the entire world, all of it, and the feeling associated with it: a sense of belonging.

Hungry, she walked into the open kitchen, looking for something to eat. She moved to her Sub-Zero and opened the big heavy stainless steel door. In the bright light, she scanned the massive and virtually empty refrigerator. There were some high-end condiment jars, and a few shriveled onions and desiccated carrots in the vegetable drawer, a couple to-go containers with food long past edible. It was a sad sight, particularly after the harvest feast. She closed the door, not even interested in tossing the old food.

She looked over her counters, and again

there was nothing. Just a single bottle of wine on the bottom of a small rack. She pulled it out, looked at it, the 1978 DRC La Tâche — perhaps the most exquisite wine she knew — a gift from the owner of the vineyard where she worked, a time that now seemed so very long ago.

She put the bottle back and saw the message light blinking on her answering machine, which she hit.

Herb's booming voice filled the solitude. "Grace! I just want you to know we need to kick up the HFCS percentage a hair. We're thinking we can squeeze another half a point in there. Jonah will send you the specs."

Grace shook her head. How had she ended up here? Was this what she had imagined when she started at Givaudan? Was this what she loved so much about the vineyards that had gotten her on this track in the first place? She couldn't help feeling that somewhere along the way, she'd gotten lost.

Grace went back to the bottle of La Tâche, pulled it out, considering it and remembering the smell of those vineyards. So much love had gone into that bottle. Thinking about that, and the recent days, she made a decision.

■ ■ ■ ■

With Carter finally asleep on what now seemed like the longest day of his life, Dylan walked around slowly, trancelike, in the master bathroom of his house. Deep in thought, he went into the long walk-in closet and turned on the light.

In the far back part, Becca's clothes were still there. He'd neatened them and straightened them, meticulously removing dry cleaner plastics and papers and every single unused hanger and taking care that all the hangers in use faced the same way. He'd cleared away and packed up many of her things throughout the house. He'd let her juice glass sit for a week on the counter, exactly where she had left it, a little bit remaining in the bottom, which he figured she'd finish when she got back from her run. Of course, she didn't come back and didn't finish that juice, and eventually — for Carter, mainly — he started cleaning up her things down there, including the last glass she had ever used.

But the bedroom was hard. That's where most of her cherished belongings were. The little things and the personal things that were so dear to her. Letters from friends and old broken watches and all manner of odd little boxes. He couldn't bear to pack them up, these things of hers. What to write on the crates? And he couldn't bear to pack her clothes. A silly blue cotton cape Becca wore around the house to keep warm in the winter, which now seemed like some rarefied object. Her ripped jeans. So they hung as if in a museum of sorts, in this closet. His private collection of the things that were hers.

He ran his hand along the tops of the hangers from which her garments and accessories hung neatly in rows, and then he walked out and into the bathroom, where they had spent so much time just talking.

He opened a drawer, passing over a few pink razors, the kind that Carter thought she wanted now. He picked up an ivory-handled hair brush, a prized antique that she had loved. He put it back and opened the drawer farther, and from the far back, he picked up a plastic hairbrush, inexpensive, but one that she had regularly used. She was always buying these kinds. He held it closer and saw that it was filled with her hair. He pulled out a few strands, and then a few more, bringing them to his face, the scent of her still present.

Very quickly he put it all back.

Carter was right, of course. There was no way that he — or they — could move on if he didn't let her go. Carter was convinced she was gone. But he wasn't.

Turning off the lights, Dylan walked out of the bathroom and out of the bedroom and headed downstairs for the computer.

My Heart Is in the Work

A couple of days later

At one of the long stainless steel counters in one of the Southern Compound Corporation test kitchens, Grace sat, two large and beautifully curved Riedel burgundy glasses before her, and next to them, the bottle of La Tâche, which had been opened. The glasses were empty, nothing yet poured, yet the room was filled with the exquisite and otherworldly fragrance of the fine old wine.

But there was another scent in the room, too, and it was growing. Something warming in the small industrial toaster oven over on another counter.

The door opened and Bill came in. "Grace! Good to see you!" He walked right up to the table, taking a seat across from her. "The board is working on your package now, I hear."

She did not speak, letting him absorb the sight of the table and the wine.

"So what are we toasting?"

"My resignation."

"Oh, Grace, tell me you're joking," he groaned.

As she stood and began pouring the wine, he saw in her face that she was not.

"I did what you said, Bill, and I asked myself what was missing from my life, and it wasn't the money — I thought it was, but it wasn't it — and whatever I had to prove was only to myself, which I did, ten times over. What was really missing from my life was something that started with a love that I first found in the vineyards, and then somehow lost again along the way. *That* I can get back. I know how to get that back, and I can't do it working for Herb Weiss."

"I'm going to talk you out of this."

"You can't."

"We'll figure something out."

"I already have." Grace retrieved two folders from the nearby counter and slid them over to Bill. "I've accepted a consultancy for Carl Fisher."

"Grace! You haven't thought this through."

"Oh yes, I have." She swirled the wine in her glass, considering it, and then took a sip. It was stunning. She continued. "They're looking for a new vanilla source, and they're sending me to Madagascar to do some fieldwork."

"I'll double whatever he's offering you — just please don't walk away from the Weiss account."

She sighed. The poor man didn't get it. "I've been working very closely with Emma — she's very talented and smart and knows everything, and when I get back from my first trip, I'll spend some time training her and anyone else you want to put on this. I'll make sure you're in good hands, but I can't work on that account."

Finally, he realized the degree of her resolve and sighed.

Pointing to one of the folders, she went on. "Everything Herb wants to know about Cole Thomas's huckleberry formulations is in that folder."

Now, that perked him up. "How did you get that?"

"With some help. But I got it." Cole had e-mailed it to her last night, right after Dylan apparently delivered his apples. "But there's something I want in return. I want the apple. All rights to the Cully apple for the huckleberry. I think that's a reasonable exchange."

Bill nodded. Of course he could do that. "And the other folder?" Bill asked.

"That's my resignation letter, which

includes some information about me that you may or may not care about, but I wanted to be forthright, so there it is."

He was curious, but as he was reaching for the second folder, something else just grabbed his attention. "What is that smell?" he asked.

"You know it, don't you?" She couldn't restrain her smile.

He focused on the scent, raising his head, sniffing, turning toward the oven from where the aroma originated, and an expression of disbelief came over his face. "That couldn't be."

Grace walked over to the oven and pulled out two warm plates of fish tacos, and she brought them to the table. "It turns out that Jimmy has done very well for himself. He has several taco stands now throughout Cozumel and is opening one soon in Cancún. It's all there on his new Web site, along with his phone number. And for the right price, he's also happy to overnight on dry ice."

Bill leaned over the tacos, reveling in the aroma; then he looked up at her with amazement. "You're really something," he said admiringly.

"Sometimes," she said, "when you're chasing a taco, if you look in the right places, you really can find it."

"Well, whatever it is that *you're* looking for, Grace, I hope with all my heart that you find it." He raised his glass. "It's been a pleasure."

She clinked her glass to his, and then they both took sips. After putting the glasses down, they began eating their fish tacos, which paired perfectly with the 1978 La Tâche.

APRIL IN NOVEMBER

A week later

The attractive young woman stood and smiled when she saw Dylan approach. It was him, just as she remembered. "Hi, I'm April," she said with her sugared Southern drawl.

Clinking flatware on plates, the din of laughter and conversation all around in the trendy restaurant bustling with people — but Dylan did not hear or see any of it. Every part of him was focused on this woman standing before him. "Dylan," he said, shaking her hand. Without ever taking his eyes from her, he took a seat across from her at the table.

In very tight low-rise jeans, a blouse with a plunging neckline, a good bit of gold, she looked like she was probably quite well known at the Saks up the street at Phipps Plaza.

"I was excited to see your ad," she said. "I

have to admit, I've never done anything like this before."

Searching her face intensely, as though trying to peer deep into her for some kind of unseen clue, Dylan did not respond to her cheerful attempt at conversation.

She tried again. "You?"

"Me?"

"Have you ever done anything like this before?"

"Oh. No. No, I haven't."

There was a long awkward moment, and it was apparent that something was wrong with Dylan. He sighed and looked away.

After another long moment, he turned back to her and began to speak. "I hope you don't mind, but I just have to ask, after eighteen months, you were still looking for me?"

"No," she said with a deep laugh. "My sorority sisters like to read that column. And I am the only person they know who wears that scent. Daddy gave me Clive for my birthday last year."

"I see," he said quietly.

She leaned in, now studying *his* face closely. "Are you okay? You seem . . . disappointed. And excuse me for being so frank, but, well, I'm used to a lot of reactions from men, but that's a new one."

"I'm sorry," he said. "I thought you were someone else."

She kept looking at him for a few more seconds and summed him up. He seemed like a sweet guy, she thought. And she found herself feeling sad for him. "I've had that happen before, too," she said. "I once followed a guy off a subway, up the MARTA escalator, and into a Chili's because I could've sworn he was my college boyfriend. He was not. And his wife, who he was meeting, didn't take real kindly to me."

Dylan smiled a little.

"Look, if it makes you feel any better," she said compassionately, "you're not what I was expecting either."

"What were you expecting?"

"A guy in a different pair of shoes."

Dylan looked at his boots, then looked back at her, and understood what she meant.

"No offense," she added.

"None taken."

Despite all the makeup and gold jewelry, she was a very beautiful young woman, obviously from money, Dylan thought. "Can I be frank with *you?*" he asked.

"Why, of course you can." She leaned forward across the table, closer to him.

"You strike me as someone who . . ."

"Yes?"

"Why are you meeting with a man you saw in an elevator?"

"Why, Dylan, I'm looking everywhere for my man. And I will keep looking everywhere until I find him."

"I see," he said, nodding slowly. And it was really hitting him now — how far this woman was from his wife, and how long ago that elevator seemed now, how long ago everything seemed, before Grace.

"My grandmother has a saying: For every pot, there's a lid. I want my lid, Dylan. And I will keep searching until I find him."

He nodded silently.

She leaned even closer to him, examining his eyes very carefully, continuing. "I know a thing or two about sweethearts, and looking at you, I think you've found yours and lost her, haven't you?"

"Yes. Yes, I have. What do I do?"

"Why, go find her, of course."

"I don't know that she'll still have me."

"Well, sugar, my grandmother has another saying." She reached across the table and took his hands. "Bless your heart." And she smiled at him, warmly and ruefully.

A STEP FORWARD

Dylan held the last box closed with his left arm and pulled the packing tape dispenser across it, sealing the top of the box. He tossed the dispenser to the carpeted closet floor, retrieved the black Sharpie, and wrote in bold letters across the top in the designated lines: RJ'S SHOES.

He stood up, taking a look at the entirely cleared-out closet. A few miscellaneous hangers hung from one of the racks, and the carpet definitely needed a good vacuuming, but it felt right. It was time.

Squatting and lifting the box using his leg muscles, he then hoisted it up on a shoulder and carried it to the hallway and down the stairs, and then down to the basement with many of the other boxes.

Sitting on the front step, Dylan guzzled a glass of cold cider. It was more work than he had imagined, boxing and moving all those items, but it was done and he felt a lightness that was new to him. It was a good feeling, an acceptance of the forward motion of life.

Waiting as he always did at this time of day, he saw the school bus approach at the top of the drive, heard the crunching gravel, and watched as the bus stopped.

In a moment, Carter appeared, and with the bus pulling back up the drive behind her, she came bounding at him. But the heaviness that had been in her step lately was still there.

He stood and hugged her, as he always did. Today he had something to talk to her about. "Carter, there're a couple thawed peaches on the kitchen counter. Could you get them and bring them to me, please?"

She shrugged, started heading in.

He called out over his shoulder at her, "And don't slam the —"

Bang! It had already slammed behind her.

Dylan took a deep breath, shook his head a bit, and smiled to himself. Then he looked up. Perhaps it was the way he was feeling from clearing out Rebecca Jane's things. He wasn't sure, but he felt better about this than he'd thought he was going to. He felt like such a grown-up today, and he was okay with that.

Carter returned with the peaches.

"Sit down, honey."

She did, sitting next to him on the porch, wondering what was going on. "What's up, Dad?"

"My father taught me how to shave. I was a little bit older than you are now, and I know it's not exactly the same, but from what I understand about it, it's pretty close. I lived with a woman the better part of my adult life, and I think I understand this." He reached into his shirt pocket and removed a couple of his wife's unused pink razors.

Carter's eyes widened and lit up as he handed her one.

Then he took one of the peaches from her and held the razor to it. "You want to remove the fine hair, not the skin." Dragging the razor, he began to shave the peach, showing her how to do it.

"Like this?" she asked, doing the same movements with her razor and peach.

"Yes, that's good. The idea is to go with the grain, and very lightly against it. But never to the side. And never apply pressure."

They leaned against each other, shoulder to shoulder, and he continued watching her and instructing her.

430

"Very good, Carter. You want to drag the razor lightly. That's right." Satisfied that she knew what she was doing, he stopped and looked directly at her. "And you want to start by soaking your legs in warm water."

He remembered how his wife would do that, nights that seemed so very long ago now.

Then he reached in his pocket again and pulled out a few more of the razors and held them out to her. "Why don't you use the guestroom bath. There's more room in there than in yours upstairs."

Carter was overjoyed. She grabbed the razors and then threw her arms around his neck and kissed him. "Thank you, Daddy!" And then she ran off to the guest bathroom.

He knew that she was going to cut herself, as he had done, but there was nothing he could do about it. She would learn, and he had to let her.

Dylan continued to sit there, looking up and off, thinking now about the one thing he needed in his life: Grace. He had been thinking about calling her and knew that eventually he would do so. He didn't know what the response would be, of course. Nor did he know what to say. He'd also thought about going to see her, but that didn't seem right. He'd been chewing on this, waiting for the answers, but they just hadn't come. More time, that's what it needed. He'd just give it more time.

He was looking out at the orchard, wondering which tree had produced the apple that brought Grace Lyndon into his life, which tree had started all of this, and wishing there was some sign that the universe could give him now about what to say or how to say it — *something.*

He jumped a bit as the screen door slammed again, and he looked up as Carter came out, a long shirt in her hands. "Dad, is it okay if I go upstairs and get your shaving cream?"

"I don't think that stuff is what you want. Why don't you stick with soap for now until we figure out what's best for you?"

"Okay," she said. "I found your shirt hanging on the back of the door in the guest bathroom. Thought you might want it."

It was the shirt he'd given Grace to sleep in. He reached for it, taking it from his daughter. "Thank you, Carter."

She ran back in, screen door slamming, and Dylan considered the shirt, holding it before him, longing for Grace Lyndon. He held it to his face, breathing in her scent, and his insides turned over as though a thousand butterflies had been set loose within him. *That's it.* He had to call her. He had to hear her voice or see her, had to connect with her once again and tell her how he felt. A strong and powerful clarity suddenly grasped hold of him: He *had* to call her. Now. Right this second.

He stood up, the shirt still in hand, and walked across the porch. Dylan pulled the screen door open, then let it slam loudly behind him.

He found the phone and dialed her cell, readying himself — but she did not pick up. He knew she had caller ID, so it worried him that maybe she was screening her calls and didn't want to talk to him.

Finding her business card on the desk, he dialed the number.

"Grace Lyndon's office," Emma said into the phone.

"Hi, Dylan Jackson for Grace."

"Oh, I'm sorry, Mr. Jackson. She can't be reached right now."

"What do you mean?"

"She's leaving for Asia later today."

"Asia?"

"Yes."

"For how long?"

"I don't think she'd mind me telling you, she's taken another position, and she'll be moving there permanently soon."

Dylan looked like a load of bricks had just been dropped on him. "When is she leaving?"

"The flight is early tonight. But I'm taking over a lot of responsibility here. Is there something I can help you with?"

"Just tell her I called. Will you do that?"

"The next time I talk to her, sure."

He hung up and put down the phone, the shirt still in his hands, and he did the math. There was still time.

Hit with an idea, he threw open the closet door, reached down, and grasped Grace's high heels. Holding them up, he carefully read something on the inside of one of them. Then he tossed the shoes back in the closet and shut the door.

A New Pair of Shoes

The big leather hanging bag was laid out on the floor in her living room as Grace carefully packed for the trip. In typical fashion, everything was neatly arranged and the bag was full, but she had several pairs of footwear before her and she had to make some difficult choices about what to pack and what to leave behind.

The phone rang and she checked the caller ID, seeing that it was Dylan again. Of all the times for him to be calling. She'd finally made a decision and gotten all her plans together and set her life on these tracks, and she knew that he was the one thing that could derail her. His voice could melt her, his glance — like the one he gave her on the day of the harvest when she first arrived — could make her lose all reason.

She'd call him later. Maybe. Or maybe not. But she knew that to speak to him now was just to risk too much. She'd snapped a part of herself shut, just as she needed to do to this luggage right now, and it was too late. Timing was key to so many things in life, and it was simply too late for whatever that call was going to be right now.

The old red pickup pulled up to the curb in front of Grace's building on Peachtree Street. In his jeans and flannel shirt, work boots, Dylan hopped out and very quickly started heading in when he was met by the doorman.

"You can't park there, pal," the doorman said.

"Just a minute, please. I need to see some-one."

"I'm sorry. It's a loading zone."

Dylan saw that the guy was serious. It was getting late, maybe too late. He had to do something. "Listen, would you call up to Grace Lyndon, and just tell her that Dylan is here."

The doorman smiled a little now, remembering him from the limo. "Sure, buddy, I can do that."

Pacing anxiously on the sidewalk, Dylan watched as the doorman called up, saw him talking to Grace on the phone, nodding, and then putting the phone down.

"I'm sorry. She can't talk to you right now."

"Did she say why?" The stress in his voice was noticeable.

"I'm sorry." The doorman took pity on Dylan, and what he seemed to understand about the situation. The big kind guy had his thoughts, but he kept his mouth closed.

Dylan headed back to his truck, pacing some more. He'd come too far to just drive off like this. Dylan marched back to the doorman. "Could you call her again, and just ask her to look out the balcony? Please?"

The doorman considered him, thinking about the night he'd seen them together, and he found himself reluctantly agreeing. "Yeah, yeah, I'll try."

Dylan went back to the truck, grabbed a box from the cab, and then hopped into the open bed of the truck with it. Bending down, he opened the box and removed some paper lightly wrapped around something inside, right as Grace stepped out onto her balcony.

And from the back of the truck he looked up at her, making eye contact with her, smiling, and even from that distance, there it was, just as she'd thought — just a look from him and she felt herself falling for him all over again.

What was he doing here, in the back of that truck? What did he want?

Cell phone in one hand, Dylan hit DIAL with his thumb. Then he stood up right in the bed of the old truck and held up what he had just removed and unwrapped: two beautiful new boots. Grasping them by their tops with his free hand, he held them up even higher.

Grace gasped a little at the sight, and her phone began to ring. She picked it up and walked to the rail, looking down at him standing there and then looking at his name on the phone. Her thumb, which somehow seemed to have a mind of its own, hit ANSWER.

Nervous about hearing his voice, never taking her eyes from him down there, she brought the phone to her ear.

"I've been sitting in traffic, trying to figure out what to say to you," he said. "I've been sitting in traffic for days, really, trying to figure out what to say."

She just looked down at him, silent, letting him speak as he had let her speak that morning in the rain in the truck.

"And I'm here to say the only thing that makes sense," he continued. "Don't go."

"Don't go?" she asked.

"Don't go. Because you can't go. Because I'd be lost without you, and because you are meant to be with me, and not because an apple brought you to me, but because I want you, Grace, and I've come to get you."

Several bystanders had stopped now to watch this tall handsome man standing in the back of a truck on Peachtree Street, holding up a pair of boots to a woman in the balcony.

He talked with even more purpose: "And what you need, what you've needed all along, is a pair of comfortable shoes, your exact size, that belong to you and you alone. So I got them for you. Because I love you. With all my heart, with all my senses, I love you."

As Dylan stood there, waiting for a response, people all around now watching, the doorman watching, a taxi pulled up behind the truck and honked. The doorman waved to the driver. It was the cab he'd called to take Grace to the airport.

She looked down at Dylan Jackson in his faded jeans and soft flannel shirt, and right behind his old red pickup, a yellow cab was ready to take her away.

Grace looked and thought hard, the breeze rippling her dress and blowing back her hair, a swell building that became apparent on her face as she made a decision. "What size are those shoes?" she asked.

A smile began to grow on Dylan's face.

ACKNOWLEDGMENTS

There are so many people who have contributed in so many ways to the creation of this book. First, I'd like to thank all the readers whom I've met and corresponded with over the last year. Thank you for letting me share my stories with you. Thank you also to the many booksellers and fellow writers I've met. I greatly appreciate all your support and friendship.

Special thanks to my amazing editor, Katie Gilligan, who brings out my best work and who never loses her sense of humor. Thanks to everyone at St. Martin's and Thomas Dunne, great people and great supporters of writers, particularly Sally Richardson, Matthew Shear, Tom Dunne, Pete Wolverton, Matt Baldacci, John Murphy, Joe Rinaldi, Dori Weintraub, Katy Hershberger, Lisa Senz, and Sarah Goldstein. Thanks also to my incredible agent, Daniel Greenberg, as well as to Beth Fisher,

Monika Verma, and the entire team at Levine Greenberg. And many thanks to Jerry Kalajian at IPG.

Thanks to Lora Sommer for the early read, Pam Morton for all the great work, Professor Thierry Léger, and everyone at Kennesaw State and in the Georgia Tourism offices.

Heartfelt appreciation to my parents, family, and friends. I am so blessed to have all your love and support. And as always, my deepest gratitude to my wife, Elizabeth. Thank you for always holding down the fort. I admire you and adore you, and every day since I first knocked on that door to your apartment, I feel like the luckiest man in the world.